D0498790

The MISTRESS OF NOTHING

KATE PULLINGER

A Touchstone Book
Published by Simon & Schuster
New York   London   Toronto   Sydney   New Delhi

Touchstone
A Division of Simon & Schuster, Inc.
1230 Avenue of the Americas
New York, NY 10020

Originally published in UK in 2009 by Serpent's Tail

First Touchstone trade paperback edition August 2011

TOUCHSTONE and colophon are registered trademarks of Simon & Schuster, Inc.

For information about special discounts for bulk purchases, please contact Simon & Schuster Special Sales at 1-866-506-1949 or business@simonandschuster.com.

The Simon & Schuster Speakers Bureau can bring authors to your live event. For more information or to book an event contact the Simon & Schuster Speakers Bureau at 866-248-3049 or visit our website at www.simonspeakers.com.

Designed by Akasha Archer

Manufactured in the United States of America

3   5   7   9   10   8   6   4   2

The Library of Congress has cataloged the hardcover edition as follows:
Pullinger, Kate.
The mistress of nothing / Kate Pullinger.
Originally published London [England] : Serpent's Tail, 2009.
p.   cm.
1. Duff Gordon, Lucie, Lady, 1821–1869—Fiction. 2. Aristocracy (Social class)—Fiction. 3. English—Egypt—Fiction. 4. Lady's maids—Fiction. 5. Tuberculosis—Patients—Fiction. 6. Egypt—History—19th century—Fiction. I. Title
PR9199.3.P775 M57   2009
2009529973

ISBN 978-1-4391-9505-5 (pbk)
ISBN 978-1-4391-9506-2 (ebook)

PART
1

LIFE

1

T HE TRUTH IS THAT, TO HER, I WAS NOT FULLY HUMAN.
I was not a complete person and it was this thought, or
rather, this lack of thought, that compelled her, allowed her, to act
as she did. She loved me, there's no question of that, and I knew it
and had felt secure in it, but it transpired that she loved me like a
favored household pet. I was part of the background, the scenery;
when she entertained, I was a useful stage prop. She treated her
staff well and I was the closest to her; I did everything for her in
those last years. I was chosen to accompany her on her final, long
journey. But I was not a real person to her, not a true soul with
all the potential for grace and failure that implies. My error was to
not recognize this, to not understand this from the very beginning.
When I did wrong, I was dismissed, I was no longer of use to her.
No, worse than that—I was excised, cut out, as though I'd become
part of her dreadful disease, a rotting, malignant supernumerary
limb that needed to be got rid of. So I was amputated. I was sent
out into the world, a useless lump of flesh and bone cast off from
the corporeal body.

But that's too much, that's too dramatic. I'm not given to drama,
though my situation called for it. The truth is that she hated me for
being happy. She hated me for finding love when love had deserted
her. She hated me for creating a family when she had lost hers. She

hated me for living when she herself faced death. And she could not admit to these feelings; how could anyone admit to feeling this way? So it suited her to treat me as though I was not worthy of the empathy, the considered compassion and generosity, the spirit and humor she bestowed upon her fellow man. I was not worthy.

But that is not where my story starts. And, more importantly, that is not where my story ends either; she was not my ending. Once she cast me out, she could no longer control me. No.

My story starts in England, in Esher, in 1862, a long time ago, and very far away from where I dwell today.

2

So. I am a plain-speaking woman, and I'll tell my story plainly. My Lady collapsed at dinner.

All her favorite gentlemen were there—Mr. George Meredith, Mr. Alfred Tennyson, Mr. Arthur Taylor. She looked beautiful, her hair black and glossy, the threads of gray shimmering like silver in the candlelight, one of her Persian shawls draped around her shoulders. But so pale, too pale, I should have known. When I entered her room earlier in the day, she was in the middle of a coughing fit; she turned away from me and made me leave, insisting she was fine. Sir Duff Gordon will be angry that I played along with her deceit, but I knew she was looking forward to the evening; she hasn't been well enough for supper parties of late. She's been spitting blood almost continuously; when I enter her bedroom I can smell the tang of it.

But wait: this is not what she is like, my Lady, not really, not truly. She is not an invalid, translucent and tilting as though she might keel over and die at any moment. My Lady is robust, she is hale, she is learned and argumentative and adventurous and charming and entertaining and large-souled. People notice Lady Duff Gordon. People remember her. When she enters a room, that room is altered, the lamps shine more brightly, the fire snaps and pops and blows out sparks, ladies sit up straighter, men stand more crisply, and someone in the company always says, as though it has to be said, "Here she is! Lucie!" My Lady is much loved, even by those she infuriates, even by those—her mother-in-law, for example—who feel that her hungry mind is too manly, that she can't possibly be a good wife.

And I knew that she wasn't well enough to host a supper party that day. But I kept quiet and stayed close by. When she began to cough halfway through the meal, I stepped into the room, right behind Cathy and her serving tray. My Lady, her eyes watering from the strain of containing the fit, gave me a small wave, a gesture I understood immediately. I helped her away from the table, not that any one of those great gentlemen would have understood she needed helping; my Lady stood, smiled, and said, "Gentlemen, please excuse me for a few minutes," as though she'd been called away to attend to some domestic duty. It was clear she couldn't manage the stairs, so I took her through to the kitchen; it wasn't the first time. I helped my Lady into a chair, Cook handed me a cloth, and I placed a steaming bowl in her lap.

It was terrible. It was one of those times when the coughing was so violent, it was as though her lungs were tearing themselves apart in their attempt to escape her breast. Phlegm and vomit—and thin streaks of bloody tissue with it. She coughed and coughed and then her breath became so ratty and weak I thought she must faint, surely, if only for a moment's relief. She wouldn't let me treat her; instead, my Lady gasped her way through. After a time the fit ended and, with it, the wretched coughing. She sat for a while, shivering cold, her body's heat dissipated through fever. A few minutes and a sip of broth later, she was on her feet, adjusting her shawl. I accompanied her back into the dining room, where the guests had moved on to the sweet. She waved me away as though I'd been pestering her (I didn't mind) and said to Mr. Meredith, "Now, George, what have I been missing?" When he expressed his concern over her health—Mr. Meredith was always observant of my Lady—she said, "It was Rainey. She woke from a bad dream and the girl could not calm her." I could see Mr. Meredith did not believe her, but he kept this to himself, wisely.

Later, when I looked in once again, she was smoking a cigar and arguing her point with such animation that no guest new to the house would have believed my Lady was unwell. Her husband, Sir Alick, gave me a smile and winked, as though to say, "Look at her. She is a marvel, isn't she?"

OUR TRAVELS FIRST STARTED TWO YEARS BEFORE. WE SPENT THAT WINTER, 1860, in the Isle of Wight at the behest of Doctor Izod, who was adamant that the Esher climate was too harsh for my Lady to bear. It was a low time. I often wondered if Doctor Izod had ever been to the Isle of Wight as it was never dry, nor light, nor warm, nor in any way resembled a place that might effect a cure for my Lady. We crept about the corridors of that tawdry hotel—it was not completely sordid, but near enough—while my Lady lay in bed, all of us, my Lady included, feeling as though she was about to die.

The next winter we embarked on our very own odyssey, all the way to the southernmost tip of Africa and back again. Just the two of us this time, a Lady and her lady's maid. There was no money for any kind of entourage. The Duff Gordons are always hard-pressed financially, though since Sir Alick moved from the Treasury to the Inland Revenue in Somerset House, my Lady says things have become a little easier, and I can attest to that. My wages are almost always paid on time these days. And so, an adventure—a brilliant escapade in fact. I loved it on that ship, I loved the port cities and the sights, ever more exotic as we traveled south. I loved it best when we were far out to sea: no sign of land, no trees, no buildings, no people; just water, the ship, my mistress, and me. "Don't you miss the household?" she asked one day. "The other servants. The companionship?"

I smiled, I could tell she was missing her family. "Not one bit," I said. "I don't miss anything about England."

My Lady laughed. "Well then," she said, "you are a peculiar creature, Sally Naldrett, but you're perfect for me."

I laughed too, but the truth was I was relieved to get away from Esher, to get away from the gossip and malice, the too-close proximity of other servants. I liked being on my own; I liked being in sole charge of my Lady; I liked being away from the younger female staff and their demands, the male staff and their unhelpful expectations. "I'd happily stay at sea forever," I said.

But that trip, though immensely satisfying for me, had not suited Lady Duff Gordon's needs. All that sea-travel, all those thousands of miles of water, when what she wants is clear, dry air and hot, dry sunshine. She needs to parch her lungs, to set them out in the sun and warm their very roots, that's what I think, so she can cough out what ails her once and forever.

And so we returned to England, yet again, after a full year aboard ship. For my Lady, the reunion was sweet. There they were on Victoria Dock, the whole of her family: Sir Alick, waving a white handkerchief; her elder daughter, Miss Janet, Mrs. Henry Ross now, heavily pregnant with her own first child; Master Maurice, grown tall, almost thirteen; and Miss Urania—Rainey—now all of three years of age. My Lady rushed off the ship as though she was one of the lions the captain was transporting below deck, freed from its cage. And I thought, oh, look how my Lady has missed her family! Why didn't I see how much she missed her family while we were away? At first it was as though Miss Rainey did not know her mother, this pale woman with the smell of sea-salt in her hair, but in the carriage the little girl stared and stared at her mother, who could not stop talking of Africa, of crocodiles and elephants and lions and all the wonders we had seen, and after a while she climbed down from where she was sitting on her father's knee and climbed up into her mother's lap. And my Lady stopped talking, and smiled very broadly.

That was this June past. My Lady kept smiling at Miss Rainey through all that transpired during the next few, short weeks. But I knew the doctor's verdict before it came: our year abroad had not effected a cure. Our year abroad had not changed anything. The illness has Lady Duff Gordon in its grip; it is shrinking her, it is draining her, and it is robbing us all of her in the process.

I am desperate for a solution. Everyone is desperate for a solution because, in our hearts, we know there is no cure. They are all saying it, saying it more loudly this time: Lady Duff Gordon will not survive another winter in England. Mr. Meredith and Doctor Izod have both told her, and Doctor Quail traveled down from London to instruct my Lady himself: if she is to live, she must leave. She must leave her beloved home yet again, her expansive household with its warm and embracing fug of books, pamphlets, papers, and endless loud and good-humored debate; she must leave her steadfast husband, and her precious children, and travel to a place where it actually is warm and light and dry in the dread, dark months of November, December, January, February, March; even April can be bitterly cold and wet in England. I would never have thought that one could die from the weather, no matter how miserable and gray it might be, but another winter will murder my Lady.

And so she must go. Her course is set. And I am to accompany her on her travels once again. My Lady and I are going to Egypt.

I'll whisper it again, that wonderful word: *Egypt*.

I AM LADY DUFF GORDON'S MAID; I AM THIRTY YEARS OLD, A VERY great age for a single woman. I reckon I became a spinster some years ago although the precise moment it happened passed me by. I have been in the Duff Gordon household for more than a decade, and those dozen years have been good years for me. Before then, penury. My sister Ellen and I were orphaned when we were very young; our parents, Battersea shopkeepers, were killed in a train derailment at Clapham. We were staying with our Aunt Clara in Esher at the time—our parents were on their way to fetch us home—and that is where we remained. But Aunt Clara could not afford, or was not inclined—I never knew which was more true, though I have my suspicions—to keep two extra children, and so we went into service, me that same year, and then Ellen one year later. My first post was scullery maid in a lowly Esher household; I made my bed on the floor of the pantry while Mrs. Hartnell, the housekeeper (she was also the cook), slept on the kitchen table, "Just like the Queen!" she used to proclaim, laughing. Mrs. Hartnell was jolly and kind and knew how to do good work at speed, and I did well in that house; I was quick to learn. And so I moved to another house, up another rung on the sturdy service ladder, and then, when the Duff Gordons came to Esher and took up residence in the house Lady Duff Gordon called "the Gordon Arms," I was able to apply for a position in that much more illustrious household. Applied and was accepted, and here I remain.

I work hard but my Lady is a most rewarding employer; everything I do for her is exactly right, or so she would have me believe. On my day off—one per month, when we're at home, unless my Lady is too unwell for me to leave her—I put on my bonnet and take the train up to London: my Lady always says that a woman my age has a right to travel up to London by herself and I couldn't agree more. The train up to London, a walk through the city—just saying those words makes me smile with pleasure—the noise, the smells, the people. Up the steps of the Museum in Bloomsbury, through the exhibition rooms, the corridors lined with glass cases, past the giraffe whose neck is so long you injure your own neck looking up at it, past the knives and coins and cups and urns in their crowded display cases, until I reach the room that is my destination: the Egyptian Sculpture Gallery. I take a seat and close my eyes before I've seen too much; I don't want to spoil my anticipation by seeing it all too quickly. I've come all this way to look and yet, once I'm there, I can hardly bear to see. I open my eyes and there they are: the Pharaohs, their gods, and the hieroglyphs—the secrets of that ancient land encrypted in stone.

I have my favorite. The first time I saw his shapely long face I thought he was a woman. But no, he's a man, a colossal Pharaoh. Almond eyes, kohl-rimmed like a cat's; I would run my hand along his cheek if I could reach that high, over his lips, down to his great chin, feeling the stone bones beneath the smooth, cool stone skin. I stare at him, and he stares back at me. I laugh at myself: he's the man of my dreams.

I've been coming here for a long time. I don't know why. The other maids ask me—they think it's very odd—why go all the way up to town to sit in the Museum? Most of them have never been, will end their days having never been. I can't think how to reply. I tried once, with Cook; I said, "Because I like the mystery." She looked at me as though I'd forgotten how to speak English. And it's a coincidence, my visits to this room over the years, and the fact that we are now going to Egypt. A wonderful coincidence that has, for once, gone in my favor.

After the Sculpture Gallery, I go to view the mummies in their cases. This room is disturbing, though I am drawn to it. Part of me feels it can't be decent to remove the dead from their tombs and put them on display, but I can't stop myself from looking. I'm as excited and curious as the nearest schoolboy, and there's almost always a crowd of jostling schoolboys. I stand still, like a palm tree in the flooding Nile, while they eddy around me. I peer at the display case labels and try to decipher the information: Thebes, female, aged about twenty-eight. Oh, I think, only a little bit younger than me.

A man once spoke to me in the Mummy Room; he had a face like a cadaver himself and I was so startled by his appearance that I neither heard his words nor was able to make a reply. He must have thought me an imbecile, a foreigner, or both. I'm not accustomed to having men speak to me directly, at least not men I do not know already. Perhaps he himself was foreign—a homesick Egyptian come to gaze upon his fellow countrymen. Perhaps he was after something. I don't know: I walked away.

When I've finished looking in the Egyptian rooms in the Museum—oh, I'll never be done looking—I walk back through Covent Garden to Charing Cross Station and I return to Esher once again. Back to the Gordon Arms. Back to my Lady.

LADY DUFF GORDON. LUCIE. ALTHOUGH, OF COURSE, I DON'T CALL her by her Christian name. But it's a sweet name, Lucie, sweet and grand, the very opposite of my own name: Sally. Bald. Plain. Like a dog's name, I used to say to my sister Ellen when we were little, and she would giggle. A maid's name.

There's a portrait of my Lady. It's a true likeness. Not of her today, now that she is thin and gray, but of how she used to be— the real Lady Duff Gordon. When Mr. Henry Phillips painted it, he was staying with us in the Gordon Arms. He had broken his knee falling downstairs at Waterloo Station and was housebound while he recovered. "Henry's bored," I heard my Lady declare to Sir Alick; he had written her a note to complain (my Lady's friends always wrote to her with their complaints; "You have the confidence of half of London," Sir Alick used to say). "Let's invite him down to stay."

Mr. Phillips rigged up his canvas on pulleys and ropes so he could paint my Lady while he reclined on the sofa, his bound leg elevated; he rang a little bell whenever they needed their tea and cakes replenished, which was frequently. The house resounded with their gossip and laughter and the other maids and I argued over whose turn it was to take in the tray. When the picture was exhibited at the Royal Academy, my Lady and Sir Alick traveled up from Esher to see it and they laughed, my Lady told me later, they both laughed to see her thus immortalized. "But I was shocked as well, Sally," my Lady said at breakfast the next day. "It was as though Mr. Phillips had seen right inside me." She paused.

"You are a masterpiece," Sir Alick said.

"I'm jolly and fat. It was embarrassing to be seen gawping at myself, like staring in a mirror in a public gallery. The vanity of it." But everyone could see she was pleased.

And now it hangs in the drawing room, and we look up at it when we pass by, and from time to time I see my Lady looking at it, and it is as though she is thinking, yes, that's me. The real me. Healthy and young and greedy for life and living.

THIS TIME NO ONE IS PRETENDING THAT THE DEPARTURE FROM HOME will be temporary. My Lady's only son, Maurice, is off to Eton, the baby, Miss Rainey, to my Lady's aunt Charlotte, and Sir Alick to board with Mr. Taylor in London where he will be nearer to his office. With everyone dispersed, the Gordon Arms will no longer be necessary, and they have let the lease go. Departure is an altogether different undertaking when your home will no longer be there to return to. There is much to do with closing the house and packing for the children. My Lady and I are both grateful for the work; it keeps our thoughts away from the goodbyes which draw closer every day.

Mrs. Henry Ross—Miss Janet—I'm not quite used to her new name yet, though "Mrs." suits her very well indeed—my Lady's eldest child, is here, helping. This is an accident of timing; Cook is always grumbling that Miss Janet doesn't approve of my Lady, "Never has and never will," she says. "Ever since she was tiny, daughter has been disappointed by mother—as if my Lady has failed to live up to her expectations. I never saw such a thing!" Cook says, shaking her head and tutting. And it's true, Mrs. Ross would prefer my Lady to be more conventional. For mother and daughter to have as little as possible to do with each other seems sensible to me; they have little enough in common anyway.

My Lady directs traffic from the settee, but she is weakened again, and I try to prevent her from working. Mrs. Ross is very good at throwing things away, and now that we are packing, it has become clear to us that the house is jammed to the rafters with things no one wants. "Why are you harboring such rubbish, Mummy?" Miss Janet asks. Cupboards full of cracked and broken crockery, linen worn so thin it is beyond repairing. And my mistress nods and waves her hand, as though to say, throw it all away. It is a shock to see such a solid household reduced like this; it turns out we spend our days surrounded by junk and detritus, all of which we were somehow convinced we needed. Even the books no longer seem worth keeping, though we parceled up my Lady's own work, the fourteen French and German novels and histories she has made her career translating, and placed the boxes among the possessions to go with Sir Alick; it was typical of my Lady to decide against taking these volumes to Egypt. "New broom," she said to me, "clean sweep."

Mrs. Ross is married to Mr. Henry Ross, a banker, "a man of commerce," as Mrs. Ross herself says, and they live in Egypt, in Alexandria, a great city at the mouth of the Nile, and this has helped my Lady with the decision to go to Egypt herself. However, Alexandria, with its Mediterranean sea air, is not dry enough for my Lady's purposes, so we will not be settling there. "Alexandria is too damp for you," says Mrs. Ross, "too moldering," and I feel sure she is relieved. My sister, Ellen, is Mrs. Ross's maid, and she is here with Mrs. Ross in Esher, working alongside me, emptying the house. "Alex is, well, a *passable* city," Ellen says, "a little like Marseilles except even more filthy. There are other English people there, and other English ladies' maids." She says this to reassure me, but I don't need reassuring. Ellen is summering in England with the Rosses; Mrs. Ross will have her child here in the autumn, so my Lady and I will reach Egypt long before they do. But, even so, I am heartened by the knowledge that there will be two Naldretts in Egypt at the same time, eventually. My sister and I lived together in the Duff Gordon household for several years and, since Miss Janet married, I have missed having her close by.

It is not for me to remark upon my Lady's innermost feelings. But I can see that she is brought very low by this dispersal of her household, her family. The doctors have declared that two years in Egypt—two years!—might see some restoration of her health. Each farewell is as painful as the last, and for my Lady, the pain is physical as well as emotional; it preys on her condition, worsening her cough. "When will I see my babies again?" she sighs, more to herself than to me, as we are making an inventory of the great, teetering stacks of cases and trunks we are getting ready. "How will Rainey know me?" I have no idea of how to reply, so I speak softly, "Don't fret, don't worry." But the words sound hollow, even to me.

There is no one here for me to bid farewell, apart from the rest of the household staff, and we are equally weighed down by our sorrow, so there is no need, nor desire, for leave-taking. They are losing their employer and thus their employment. But not me. I have a secret: for me, this departure is a joyful thing. I'm leaving Esher. I'm leaving the house and the people who live and work in it. It's almost as though I am leaving myself, my old familiar self, behind.

Nothing holds me here. Oh, I am fond of Esher, I am fond of Cook, and Cathy, and Esther, who works in the grand house down the street. As everyone says, England in spring is a sight to behold; and, yes, I will miss my trips into town to visit the Museum. But my travels with my Lady have given me a taste for the world.

My life in the Gordon Arms is very narrow. My main preoccupation is avoiding people; avoiding talk. Not that I'm awkward and shy—far from it. Avoiding people: to be more specific, avoiding men. Men want things, they make demands, they make themselves obvious; like the man in the Mummy Room of the Museum in Bloomsbury, they put themselves in my way. But a lady's maid's loyalty must be to her Lady; ladies' maids do not marry. At least, they do not marry and carry on being ladies' maids. And I have no desire to leave my Lady.

I was working on my Lady's travel trousseau earlier today; I want to have her clothes in perfect order before we leave. She has continued to lose weight over the summer—Cook's efforts in that department have failed—so there is a great deal of taking in and remaking to be done. Laura, a young maid, was helping me. She'd been in the household only a few months but was already the subject of much gossip and speculation, the kind of talk I've spent my life avoiding, the kind of talk I will not miss once I leave. She was a chatty girl and I was barely listening to her.

"Aren't you frightened?"

"Hmm," I said. "Pardon?"

"Aren't you afraid?"

"We've traveled before, my Lady and I."

"But not to live. Not to live in such a foreign place," Laura said.

"I'm not afraid."

"I wouldn't care to go."

"You prefer your adventures," I said, "in the back alley." I meant it lightly, but the girl gave me a shocked look and, much to my shame, burst into tears.

"I didn't know," she said.

"Didn't know what?"

"It was only a bit of fun, I didn't know it would have such . . ."— she struggled to find the right word—"consequences."

I put my arm around her narrow shoulders and we sat down on the bed. It was my Lady's bed, but I knew she wouldn't mind, given the circumstances. I let Laura cry and I patted her on the back. "What has happened?" I asked, but I knew already.

"I'm—oh." She looked at me; her face was very red.

"Will he marry you?" I spared her further humiliation by not asking who he was.

She shook her head. "He's gone."

"Gone? Where?"

"I don't know," she said. "It's too late. And now the house is closing. He won't know where to find me."

I suppressed a shudder as I realized the extent of her predicament. Predicament is too mild a word—disaster. How will she secure a place in another household? And if she finds a place, how will she keep it once the baby comes along? How will she live? I looked at her and saw myself: this is why I am glad to leave Esher; this is why I'm glad to leave England. "Let's go and speak to my Lady," I said.

"Oh no," said the girl, "I couldn't, I—"

"You must tell Lady Duff Gordon everything. She'll help you. She won't leave you to fend for yourself. Come on." I pulled her up off the bed. "Come with me." I gave Laura one of my Lady's clean linen handkerchiefs and took her downstairs.

It's not that I object to men. It's not that I object to marriage. I have had offers, too many to detail. And a few were from men into whose arms I could well imagine falling. "You are lovely," they say, and then they describe my skin, my hair, my figure, as though I've never looked in a mirror. And there have been handsome men of decent means among them: George Dawson the cooper and Robert Smith from the brewery. But I turned them away. I couldn't leave her; she needs me more than they do. I couldn't leave my Lady. And if I married George Dawson and had his sweet babies, would I see the world, as I will with my Lady?

AND SO, ONE BY ONE, IT IS GOODBYE, GOODBYE, GOODBYE. FOR MY Lady, there is her beloved mother, Sarah Austin, and the other Lady Duff Gordon, Sir Alick's mother. Mr. Meredith, Mr. Tennyson, Mr.

Taylor, and all my Lady's good, true friends. Her children. How can she say goodbye to Maurice and Rainey without knowing when she will see them again? As always, she wears her grief lightly. Sir Alick will accompany us on the first leg of our journey, and his will be my Lady's last goodbye, as well as, no doubt, the most difficult.

WE SET OFF FOR EAUX BONNES ON 20 AUGUST. WE HAD HOPED FOR a warm sunny spell in the French Pyrenees, but it was already cool by the time we arrived and, worse, raining. My Lady wrote to her mother: *The "good waters" of Eaux Bonnes are all pouring from the sky.* She fell ill almost immediately; she was weak, and travel served to weaken her further, the wet weather unwelcome, damaging. I did all I could to make her comfortable but the fever, and the blood spitting, returned. I did my best to make sure that my Lady and Sir Duff Gordon had plenty of time on their own, knowing as I did that they would not be together again for a long while, but Sir Alick was restless and anxious, due back at work in London, worried about his wife and the journey that lay ahead for her. My Lady had been ill for a long time, but there was a part of Sir Alick that still expected her to return to her extravagant old self any day. I could see this in him, and I felt it in myself; everyone who knew her felt the same. And when she didn't get better, continued to not get better, Sir Alick reacted with a kind of subdued and baffled horror, a horror he endeavored to keep hidden from his wife but that was nonetheless in plain view to me and anyone else who cared to see.

Finally, my Lady was well enough to move from Eaux Bonnes on to Marseilles, where she and Sir Alick at last made their farewells. At the station I tried not to listen, tried to fold myself into myself, far away from the scene, but there was little for me to overhear:

"Goodbye, Alick," my Lady said.

"Goodbye, my love," Sir Alick replied.

And then he was gone, on to his train, waving, and I watched my Lady pull herself together as she had done so many times before. We moved on to the port of Leghorn in Italy, where the weather was considerably warmer and my Lady was able to stretch her limbs under the sun. We had a few days' wait before the steamer on which we had booked passage to Alexandria, *Byzantine*, was due to leave. By then my Lady was feeling better once again. She is like no other invalid I have ever known; when feeling well she appears full of vigor and youth and I can't believe, no one can believe, that the illness will cut her down, push her into her chair, her bed, once again. But it does, it always does. Yet in Leghorn she was fine and happy, which was a good thing: my Lady and I both knew that the Italians believe, mistakenly, that the complaint from which she suffers is contagious. Sufferers are banned from their spa towns and havens. So she must look well and pretend to be well, even if she is not.

3

THE BUMP, WHEN SHIP NUDGED DOCK, GAVE ME A QUICK SHOCK, a spark of life: at last, Egypt. I turned to my mistress, who was beside me at the rail, looking out at the city smeary with smoke and heat, and said, "We are here."

She smiled. "They say that Alexandria isn't really Egypt at all."

"No, my Lady?" I said, and though I knew this already, I still felt disappointed.

"An in-between place, Mediterranean, African, and European, full of phantom monuments that have long since disappeared."

I looked at my Lady, unsure of what she was saying, the tone of her voice harsher than I was expecting. On the journey she had seemed as excited as me to be traveling to a place of such antiquity. I was reminded once more of all she had left behind. No doubt arriving at our destination had reminded her as well.

"But you are right, Sally," she said, turning towards me and laying her hand on mine, as though to reassure me, "we are here. Egypt."

Our first journey through the city horrified us both; nothing we had seen in the Cape last year had prepared us for this. Filth. Wretched little children begging for money every time the carriage came close to stopping, which was frequently given the terrible congestion in the narrow streets. One child came too close as the carriage moved forward; I saw a man pull him back off the road to the safety of a doorway, where he began to beat him with a slipper he'd removed from his foot for that very purpose. The language ran past our ears, slippery, unmanageable, full of unfamiliar shapes and growls and wheezes. "I'll never learn a single word!" I said, and as the carriage jerked forward yet again, I saw my Lady go pale as though the precious health she'd regained during our sea voyage had left her body and flown out the window, up into the hard blue-white sky.

The Rosses' apartment was cool and quiet. It felt odd to be there on our own—I slept in my sister Ellen's bed every night and my Lady took up residence in her daughter's bedroom—but I was pleased that I wasn't being instructed in my duties by Miss Janet, as I had been back in England, and I suspect my Lady felt the same. However, there was no one there to greet us, no one there to smooth our passage; the Rosses kept no permanent staff in Alexandria. Miss Janet hadn't thought to arrange any help for us, and my Lady hadn't thought to ask. We would muddle along by ourselves. My Lady was able to rest in the roof garden that her son-in-law had planted; up there she could write letters home and read and consult maps as she planned our journey south up the Nile. I knew she had enjoyed the sea crossing and the ship's exotic cast of fellow travelers—an Italian opera troupe, four Levantine ladies, and a charming Spanish consul to entertain her—but now that we had arrived, she grew subdued and melancholy. I could tell she was concerned about what was to become of us here in Egypt, and after a few highly unsuccessful outings into the dirty maelstrom of Alexandria, my Lady gave up and retreated. As well as the roof garden, there was a library that Miss Janet—I mean, Mrs. Ross—had shipped from England, and my Lady took to spending her days there, moving up to the roof garden in the evening. I was pleased to see her retire; it was plain the streets were full of disease and wherever I walked I heard coughs that sounded much like hers.

Alexandria was, as Mrs. Ross had warned us, moldering, the sea air giving the city's buildings a salty frosting. I made my way through the streets lined with grand white European façades, glimpsing Egyptian interiors of orange and red and gold and green. Mr. Ross's roof garden was orderly, English, shaded, verdant, while the courtyard gardens I peered into whenever I could were full of color, unfamiliar trees laden with flowers, their sweet scent cutting through the base smell of the city. There was no real sightseeing to be done, as Alexandria's historical monuments consist of mere rumor and conjecture—phantom monuments, as my Lady said, no more, no less. This *might* have been where Alexander the Great's tomb lay; Pharos Lighthouse, one of the Wonders of the Ancient World, *probably* stood here; but there was nothing to see. Instead there was the wildest mix of cultures imaginable, all attempting to sell something—a slick Italian barber next door to a Syrian baker with a mud oven, a gorgeous French patisserie with a gaggle of peasant women buying and selling oranges right outside its polished glass doors.

On my own, I made forays into the street markets and shops but too often was defeated, returning home empty-handed with a great crowd of unruly children following behind me. In the streets people smiled when they saw me, and I was unable to tell whether they were greeting me or laughing at me. I had never been anywhere as truly foreign as this place.

ONE DAY, AS I WAS GETTING MYSELF READY FOR ANOTHER OF MY raids on the market—perhaps this time I'd actually succeed in buying a potato or two—two friends of Mr. Ross pitched up, unbidden, at our door: Mr. Hekekyan Bey, an Armenian gentleman, educated in England, dressed in an English suit and wearing a red *tarboosh* with a dark blue silk tassel on his head, an extraordinary combination that somehow suited him, and Mr. William Thayer, the American consul general, young and handsome, with an open, kind face. They were greatly amused by my Lady's tales of our failure to adapt and survive, and as I watched my Lady rise up on their amusement, I realized, once again—how could I have forgotten?—that this is what she needs in order to thrive: other people. She's at her best in company; as soon as they arrived it was as though she began to breathe more freely. Someone to talk to, someone to quiz and coax and debate with; someone to make life more interesting. And here was not one but two gentlemen, both of whom were more than willing to entertain and be entertained. When Mr. Thayer asked my Lady what she thought of Alexandria, she said, "Isn't this the city where Cleopatra took her own life?"

Both men laughed. "What you need, Lady Duff Gordon, is a dragoman," Mr. Thayer declared.

"A what?" said my Lady.

"An interpreter, a guide, a factotum," he said, enunciating the last word carefully.

"Oh," said my Lady, "will that make us feel . . ."—she looked at me as I set down the coffee tray— "less desperate?"

"Yes," Mr. Thayer said firmly. "You can't possible travel in this country without an Egyptian at your side. I know the perfect boy."

And before my Lady had time to ask herself if she really did need or, indeed, could afford such a thing, he returned to us later the same day, bringing with him a young Egyptian. "Madam," Mr. Thayer said with a flourish, "Mr. Omar Abu Halaweh. Father of the Sweets."

"I beg your pardon," said my Lady, amused. "Sweets?"

Mr. Omar Abu Halaweh looked mildly perplexed, and I wondered how much he understood of what was taking place. He was watching Mr. Thayer and my mistress intently and I took the opportunity to have a good look at him. He was a bit younger than me, perhaps in his mid-twenties, though it's hard to tell. He was slender: all Egyptian men are slender, except when they are very prosperous and fat. He was neatly dressed, his clothes well cared for and tidy. Like most Egyptians he was clean-shaven and his skin was exceptionally smooth-looking. He reminded me of someone and this feeling nagged at me until I remembered: the man I used to visit in the Museum. My stone Pharaoh. I felt hot suddenly, and my throat tightened, and my heart skipped a beat. I blushed at my foolish whimsy and hoped no one was looking at me.

"Abu Halaweh—Father of the Sweets," repeated Mr. Thayer, his American accent smooth and rounded, "that's how his name translates. He's from a family of pastry cooks in Cairo. And, I'm assured, he himself is a very good cook indeed. I'll say it again: Mr. Omar Abu Halaweh."

At that, Mr. Abu Halaweh took a low, neat bow before straightening up and smiling broadly and, from behind his back, producing an elaborately wrapped box of sweetmeats in honey, something that I had longed—but failed—to buy. I'd been struggling to cook for my Lady since our arrival—we mainly survived on fresh dates from the market and flat bread sprinkled with salt and spices that by some unknown command a small child brought to our door every morning, delicious, if not completely satisfying—and the idea of employing a dragoman who could cook made me almost swoon with the hunger I'd been ignoring these past days, missing meals in order to ensure my Lady had enough to eat, pretending I'd already eaten. But then Mr. Omar Abu Halaweh came to our aid and, after that, everything was much simpler.

Their interview was brief and to the point; my Lady invited Mr. Abu Halaweh to sit with her for a while, and they conversed, Mr. Thayer chipping in regularly to translate when necessary and to sing yet more of the dragoman's praises. I served tea from the Rosses' larder (when they return from England they will have to do a great deal of replenishing of their stocks, I'm afraid). Mr. Abu Halaweh's spoken English turned out to be rather good and Mr. Thayer claimed that he was skilled at bargaining, essential in this land where, I'd discovered, absolutely everything was open to negotiation.

And so he was ours. He moved into the Rosses' flat the next day. And I began my Egyptian education.

"HELLO," HE SAYS, *"ES SALAAM AHLAYKUM."*

We are seated together, on the terrace of Shepheard's Hotel. My Lady has gone upstairs to rest a while before dinner. The evening sun is pink and rosy, full of city dirt and smoke from the open fires. Below us, Cairo is almost quiet.

"*Salaam* means peace. A greeting, a way of saying hello. *Es salaam ahlaykum.* But there is also *ahlen.* And to that, you reply *ahlen wa sahlen.*"

I make an attempt: in my mouth the words feel full of air and full of earth at the same time. I'd heard these greetings in the market many times, but that didn't make pronouncing the words myself any easier.

"My name is Miss Naldrett," Mr. Abu Halaweh says, and I stifle a giggle; he frowns theatrically. "*Ana ismee* Miss Naldrett."

"That's simple," I say, "*Ana ismee.* It's me!'

"*Weh inti?*" he says.

"Excuse me?"

"*Weh inti?* And you? *Inti* for woman, *inta* for man. *Weh inti?*"

I blush, though I know he isn't actually asking my name; he already knows it. "*Ana ismee* Miss Naldrett. Miss Sally Naldrett," I reply carefully.

THE SMALL CRAFT MOVES UP THE NILE. AS WE TRAVEL SOUTH, AWAY from the Mediterranean, away from all things European, into the heat, I fall in love. Both my Lady and I fall in love. Not with any one person. We fall in love with the river and the country it succors and drowns, the Nile and its people.

There are discomforts. Of course there are, this boat life is so unlike that other life, that previous life, the life of the drawing room, the sickroom, the kitchen and garden. The clothes we wear are not suitable, the high-laced shoes, the gloves, the bonnets, the undergarments, the stays. I sit in my small, low cabin and stare at the things folded neatly in my valise; what can I wear that will not make me suffocate? I think of the children—small boys, thin as Nile reeds—I saw playing at the river's edge yesterday and I speak to myself in a low voice: "I should like to run about naked!" and I laugh and smile at the thought. But still, I must dress for the day and eventually I choose. Brown muslin, high-necked, in England this dress was one of the best—sturdiest—I have ever owned: my Lady gave it to me. She wore it only once or twice at a time when she was a larger shape than me; it was not like my Lady to be profligate with clothing but she did not like the dress, did not like the color brown, and said, "I don't know what possessed me," as she handed it over. Though I am taller than my mistress, I cut the dress down so that it fitted me and, with my dark hair and brown eyes, the color suits me. Now I find myself looking at the garment and wondering if perhaps I should slice vents into the stiff cloth in an attempt to accommodate the heat of my body, the awful heat my body generates. It's meant to be autumn here, as in England, but it's not like any autumn I recognize. Mr. Abu Halaweh always looks so cool, I wonder how he does it. It's not as though he is un-derdressed, he's very well turned out; he pays as much attention to his own dress as I do to my Lady's—his tunic, his wide waistband, his draped trousers, his tidy waistcoat—*sudeyree*, he tells me during one of our language exchanges—and even at first light he is neat, entirely presentable, even as the sun goes down behind the white hills at the end of another long, hot day.

Those white hills, I see them when I close my eyes against the darkness of my cabin; that's the desert, I tell myself. The desert. The word itself is frightening. That's where the lush green ends, where the Nile, despite its abundance, cannot reach. Sometimes, as the sun beats down on our boat, *Zint el-Bachreyn* (I roll the words around my mouth again and again), and I look for somewhere to escape to, somewhere I can lie back and rest and not feel as though I am burning, burning—sometimes when I look across the water, across the cultivated land, and see those white hills, I am frightened. The desert, in all its blank enormity; the Egyptian desert, peopled as it is with the dead, with mortuaries, funerary temples, mummies in their tombs, workers in their graves. I have to look away.

But I am safe, for the moment, safe and happy traveling upriver on our *dahabieh, Zint el-Bachreyn,* which Mr. Abu Halaweh hired once we left Alexandria and moved on to Cairo—oh my word, Cairo! What chaos, what light. We needed to hire a boat: Mr. Abu Halaweh secured one for us. We needed supplies: he secured those as well and, what's more, he allowed me to accompany him on his trips to the markets. He took my Lady and me on excursions, out into the streets of the city, away from Shepheard's Hotel—dank, overcrowded, and smelling of cabbage like that hotel in the Isle of Wight—through the narrow lanes overhung by the tiered upper floors of the buildings that block out the sun with their wooden lattice window bays, wind-catchers they're called, built to capture whatever breeze there might be. We saw the great medieval mosque, Ibn Tulun, where we watched our dragoman remove his shoes, wash his feet, and kneel down to pray, and Khan el-Khalili, the enormous bazaar, where my Lady was treated like a visiting dignitary. We took Turkish coffee, sweet and sharp, and my Lady asked many questions, like an overexcited child who wanted to see, hear, taste, and smell everything, and I felt the same. Mr. Abu Halaweh led the way, and in Cairo we caught a glimpse of the true Egypt, the Egypt we had both longed to see, ancient and modern at the same time, cloistered and open-aired, full of noise, heat, growth, and decay. Mr. William Thayer accompanied us on some of our outings and, in his presence, my Lady was truly restored to her good self, vivid and alive. We led her about the place on a hired donkey we called George ("He reminds me of Mr. Meredith," my Lady claimed) and we acquired a donkey boy called Hassan as well. Poor Hassan quickly became yet another victim of our assault on the Arabic language and after only a single day with us had adopted the habit of continually chanting the Arabic word for absolutely everything he could see. "*Maya*," he would say, pointing at my cup of water. "*Nahr*," he would repeat, pointing at the Nile.

In the evenings we retired to the hotel, where my Lady spent her time writing up the events of the day in her letters home to England. She wrote to both Sir Alick and her mother every day, as well as to her friends, not bothering to wait for a reply before starting afresh. "A reply could take weeks to arrive," she'd say. "I can't bear to wait that long before telling them what we have seen." It was as though writing these letters at the end of the day was as important as the day itself had been, if not more so, as though these letters home had become her work, replacing all the other writing she had done in her life.

Mr. Hekekyan Bey invited my Lady to dinner at his Cairo house, a compound just outside the city, surrounded by fields. In the dim and cool salon where antiquities—pieces of carved frieze, small statuary, sculpted stone heads—were stacked up against the walls like old bricks, I watched as Mr. Hekekyan Bey's wife demonstrated to my Lady the Egyptian way of eating, sitting on the floor cross-legged round a large communal tray. She held up her right hand only. "This hand," she said, "no implements," and she proceeded to use the flat bread as a kind of scoop. I could see how this manner of taking a meal—intimate and relaxed, exotic yet practical—would appeal to my Lady; she laughed and said, "How very efficient," and proceeded to eat with great gusto, as though eating itself was a novelty.

She thrived on the company and the adventure but even so, during the carriage ride back to Cairo from Mr. Hekekyan Bey's house, her cough worsened once again. The last few days had grown a little cooler. "We need to travel south," she said, "to Upper Egypt, where the air will be pure and hot and dry."

"Mr. Abu Halaweh will help me prepare," I replied. "We can leave within a few days."

My Lady nodded her consent and closed her eyes.

And so we left Cairo. We had not seen the pyramids at Giza yet; that would have to wait until our return, despite my impatience, though I was compensated by the knowledge of what we would see en route. In Egypt everything is so utterly unfamiliar, even the moon and stars look altered, strange, as though my Lady and I have swapped planets, not countries.

AND FOR NOW—YES—HERE WE ARE ON THE *DAHABIEH*, TRAVELING up the River Nile.

The language the boatmen speak is full of smooth melodies. In the early morning before I am fully awake, I hear the men singing as they pass the door of my cabin—what a sound to wake up to—and the water slapping outside my tiny window. Later, the men call to each other from stern to prow, from one vessel to another, and I listen. My Lady and I both scrabble for words; we are equal in this. We listen hard, we soak it up and attempt to imitate the men. We learn a few new words every day: *shey*—tea; *ahowah*—coffee, which is similar to but slightly different from *aywa*—yes: words breathed in and sent flying from the back of the throat, and we mouth them to each other, correcting each other's accent, emphasis, matching these words eagerly to Mr. Omar Abu Halaweh's English. *Es salaam ahlaykum. Shukran. Insha allah. Alhamdulillah.* When we are sitting together one afternoon, watching the Nile—my domestic duties on the boat have been lightened considerably by the presence of our dragoman and I feel a kind of freedom that is new and startling—I ask him to teach me the alphabet. "Oh, but Miss Naldrett," he says mildly, "I cannot read or write." I try not to show my surprise, reminding myself that many men in similar positions to his at home in England would not be able to read and write either, and that I am lucky to have these skills, passed on to me, like books themselves, by my Lady.

And so we continue together, exchanging words like glances. Life has become one enormous vocabulary lesson. I am pleased and exhausted by it.

I AM NOT ACCUSTOMED TO WORKING SO CLOSELY WITH A MAN. Washing, cooking, cleaning, attending to my Lady: I am not accustomed to a man having skills so close to my own. It should have been a large adjustment, one set of difficulties, how to cope here in Egypt, replaced by another, no longer having my Lady to myself. He pays no heed to any notion of men's work, women's work; for him a task is a task, to be completed. It occurs to me that, if I chose to, I could sit back and have him attend me as well as my Lady, but that is not in my nature. Instead, to my surprise, I find I enjoy the companionship. I instruct Mr. Abu Halaweh in the ways of our household as Mr. Abu Halaweh instructs me in the ways of Eygpt. I will always be my mistress's maid, there will always be things I can do that Mr. Abu Halaweh cannot, but here in Egypt, on a boat on the Nile, we could not get by without him at our side. Our time in Alexandria and Cairo made this clear to us both: without Mr. Abu Halaweh, we would not survive. We would starve to death, or die of loneliness, whichever calamity overtook us first.

It is extraordinary. My idea of our duo, my Lady and me, on an adventure like no other, has expanded quite smoothly to become a trio.

We are in the boat's airless galley; it is kitchen, scullery, storeroom, and workspace all rolled into one. I draw a breath and stand tall. I am almost used to the feeling of sweat trickling down my spine continuously, like a tiny tributary of the Nile.

He looks at the flat bread he is making; he insists on making bread every day, claiming that the ship cook's bread is no good, his infinitely better. He is right. "Please Miss Naldrett, you must sit down. You will be tired in the heat."

"But I might learn something," I say.

When I look, I can see he is smiling.

I study him. I can't help myself, I stare and stare at everything and everyone in this country. He moves across the room and I catch his scent; he always smells very clean. It occurs to me that this might be because, as a Muslim, he does not drink alcohol; unlike Englishmen he is never beery and bleary of a morning. He looks up from his work, the work we share. His eyes are quick, dark but brightly lit, and he has caught me staring, but he gives no impression of having found me out. Instead, he smiles. His face is transformed, as though he smiles with his entire being. And I, unguarded—there's no reason to feel guarded here, in this place, the Esher household and its gossip and malice are thousands of miles away, there is no one here to see me—smile back. The cramped conditions of the *dahabieh*, simultaneously damp and dry-hot, the sand that filters through every crack when the wind blows, the vermin I see clambering along the river bank, sliding hopefully into the water every time we draw near: all that fades away.

The *dahabieh*. I whisper the name to myself yet again: *Zint el-Bachreyn*. Long and narrow, sturdy, with an enormous white cloth sail. Mr. Abu Halaweh and the cabin boy battle to keep it clean; they have some success. There is a crew of eleven men, including the *reis*—captain—and his mate; Mr. Abu Halaweh says the crew are all from Upper Egypt, Aswan. To a man they are sleek and nimble and when my Lady and I embarked for the first time at the port of Boulak in Cairo, they lined up along the shore, immaculate in new white Egyptian cotton trousers, bare-chested, brown. A parade of half-naked men. I looked at them and thought, This is all so peculiar. It was all I could do not to laugh. Everything in Egypt is simultaneously alarming and entertaining.

Before we left the port, my Lady had the *reis* fix an English flag and an American pennant to the mast, as a signal to the consular agents we will meet along the Nile. Every corner of the boat is packed with supplies purchased during forays into the noisy markets of Cairo: not just food and drink but everything we could possibly need. There is a portable bath. Carpets. Six months' supply of candles. Linen. An enormous copper kettle. I made list after list, checking and rechecking, consulting both my Lady and Mr. Abu Halaweh: we must not forget anything. This boat is our home for the time being. Our home. But not like any home I have known before.

WHAT HAPPENS WHEN YOU LEAVE EVERYTHING BEHIND? WHEN YOU leave everything familiar, not just houses and streets and wet windy wintertime, but husbands, children, friends? For me: the train into London on my day off; the arriving back home again. The branch of the oak tree that knocks against the roof of the stable. The postman who comes down the lane. None of these things have followed me to Egypt. Does this mean I am no longer the same person? Does this mean that I too have changed?

THE NILE: GREEN, A THICK, VISCOUS GREEN, LIKE MILK FLOWING from a great green cow; often brown, churned up, swirling; occasionally clear to the bottom, sparkling, glassy; never blue. At night it is black, its depths infinite. It smells—I breathe in deeply—of vegetation, of grasses, even at times, rather oddly, like an English garden pond. Some days the river stinks, but even that is soon washed away. I stare down into the water for long minutes at a time, longing to dip my fingers, to trail my toes as I see men on other boats doing, but I am unable: the craft is too high above the water and besides, I'd have to take off my shoes and pull off my stockings. I'd have to remove my gloves, unpin my bonnet, put down my parasol.

And besides, there are crocodiles. I saw one our first day out; it slithered along the riverbank and into the water after us, as though we were its prey.

Luckily for me, when the boatmen bring *Zint el-Bachreyn* close in to the embankment, there is much else to see, much to take my mind away from the heat.

But the journey is hard on my Lady, truth be told; her health has been deteriorating steadily since the day we left Esher. The sea journey was too long, Alexandria too damp, Cairo too dirty, too busy. Shepheard's Hotel was too expensive—as always, concern about money is at the forefront of my Lady's mind—uncomfortable, and worse, claustrophobic. "That horrid hotel," my Lady said later. "I couldn't wait to get away. Now," she says, she states uncategorically, "I will regain my strength as the boat travels south up the Nile."

"Yes, you will," I reply.

But a few days out of the port at Boulak, she can scarcely breathe, each breath as labored as the last, her blood spitting continual and debilitating, and none of my usual tricks—bed rest, hot drinks, fresh air, swaddling, steam humidity—are working.

It is evening. Mr. Abu Halaweh has arrived to take away my Lady's meal tray, though she has eaten nothing. I am sitting at one end of her chaise rubbing her feet. "They are so cold, Sally," she says, "like ice. As though my blood no longer reaches them."

"Let me treat you," I say.

My Lady groans and shakes her head.

"Miss Naldrett tells me she can make you better, *Sitti*," says our dragoman. He calls her "*Sitti* Duff Gordon"—*Sitti* means Lady—or just "*Sitti*," which my Lady enjoys. "I suggest you let Miss Naldrett treat you."

We both turn and look at Mr. Abu Halaweh. "Is that an order?" asks my Lady.

I'm too startled to say anything.

"I suspect it is," she continues, "the first of many, no doubt, Omar?"

He smiles his broad smile, winning us both over to his point of view.

And so, I treat her. Now that we are on board our temporary home and my Lady can rest in comfort and, even as she lies prone, be entertained by the world as the *dahabieh* glides along, she allows me to treat her.

But the treatment itself is dreadful: cupping. Neither of us relishes it. I was tutored in the cruel method by Doctor Izod in Esher last year, before we traveled to the Cape. He had adapted the procedure himself, adding a deep incision prior to the application of the heated glass. "There may not be a good, reliable doctor where you are headed, my girl," he said. "We are trusting you with Lady Duff Gordon's life," and I quaked—without showing it, of course—because I had never thought of my position in this way before, caretaker of my Lady's very life.

I clean the scalpel purchased in London for this sole purpose, specially designed, pointed and very sharp. Mr. Abu Halaweh is in attendance; he stands away from where my mistress lies, half-turned towards the door to preserve her privacy, but ready to help if he is needed. I have prepared the cup; I have heated it in a kettle of boiling water. It is hot to touch, but not hot enough to burn her skin, I hope. I am going to go in over the right breast, above the lung that, on earlier listening, sounded the more inundated, the more congested. I move quickly, unlacing my Lady's blouse, pulling her undergarments to one side, baring her breast; this is only the second time I have undertaken this procedure unaided, and I want my movements to feel assured, definite—precise. I look up and meet my Lady's gaze and she nods at me calmly; we have agreed she will not speak so as not to provoke more coughing. She took a steep draft of brandy before I began. I lower the scalpel and press down hard, making the incision, one inch long, perhaps an inch in depth. Blood wells up around the blade. My Lady cries out loudly before her head rolls to one side. Mr. Abu Halaweh steps forward but I reassure him, "It's all right, she has fainted. It is a blessing."

Moving swiftly, I unwrap the glass cup and, gripping it with the cloth as it is too hot for my bare hand, place it directly over the incision, pressing down firmly to create the cupping effect. The suction takes hold, the cup begins to cool and as it cools it fills with blood.

"Raise up the candle, please," I say, and Mr. Abu Halaweh obeys. "Look," I say, and he leans over for a better view, and I am pleased to see he does not appear squeamish. "Matter," threads of white floating in the dark blood. "Pus. Sickness. It is being drawn out of her. This is what we want."

Mr. Abu Halaweh says, his voice uncertain, "Are you certain this will make *Sitti* Duff Gordon feel better?" He clearly does not believe such a treatment can possibly work.

I find my hand begins to shake. I am having difficulty keeping the cup in place and am afraid I will lose the suction I have created. At first, I think his question ridiculous, but then I see the truth of it. "No," I reply. "I'm not sure this will make Lady Duff Gordon feel better, Mr. Abu Halaweh. But this is what I've been taught, this is how I've been instructed to treat her by her English physician. And Lady Duff Gordon and I agreed: cupping, Mr. Abu Halaweh, it is what is needed."

To my relief, he nods and I am able to keep my grip secure on the cup until it is full of blood and other bodily matter.

WE TRAVEL SOUTH. THE CREW SWING FROM STERN TO BOW WITH tremendous ease. The river narrows into a steep canyon, bringing with it a kind of night blackness that I have never before experienced, as though the cliffs press together until they meet, high above our heads. Then the valley widens, broadens out again, pastoral. "Biblical," my Lady proclaims from where she reclines on her makeshift daybed, and indeed, I think of Moses in his reed basket, floating along beside us. My Lady likes to be on the deck, under the shade of the canopy the crew have rigged, where she can watch the boatmen and the country, and she is making a good recovery now, the cupping wound healing well. In Cairo, Mr. Abu Halaweh wanted to hire a man to stand over her with a fan for the journey, but she would not agree. "There must be economies," she declared. She lies back in the shade as a small breeze lifts off the water, not enough to cool anyone, but a breeze nonetheless. I move around the boat. I ask my Lady if there is any sewing, even though I know there is not. "Tearing," says my Lady, "we should be tearing these clothes of ours to let in the air." And yet with every mile south her breath grows a little easier and after a few more days she takes up her letters home once again. She is happy when she is writing; happiest when surrounded by her friends and family and making a great occasion of it, it's true, but away from all that, her letters home are her family.

In the middle of the night, I wake. What is it? What is different? Then I realize—I am cool. I do not have to peel my nightdress away from my skin. There is a breeze, a real breeze, and it enters through my tiny window and departs by slipping beneath my cabin door. What month is it now? I ask myself, and I have to think hard before I can remember. November. I wrap a shawl around my shoulders and follow the breeze out onto the deck of the *dahabieh*. I walk forward, step on something, and skid back, alarmed. A half-awake Egyptian oath, followed by what sounds like an apology. There are men sleeping everywhere, the deck is covered with men, rolled up like carpets in a *souk*. The breeze lifts their hair and drops it again. I find a perch and sit down, taking long, slow breaths, and

I marvel at the fact that here I am, awake in the night, surrounded by sleeping men, and it feels perfectly natural to me. The air is sweet, clear, and so pure that I suddenly feel that all my life, up to this point, I have been choking. No wonder my mistress has begun to improve at last. The night is moonlit and soft; the river is wide and the banks are broad. A lone ox moves along beside us. Egypt is sleeping, as it has slept for millennia.

The boat floats quietly on the water, and it takes me a while to realize we are moored. Over the past two years there have been many boat journeys. But this small sailing craft is not like those other boats; this boat is *our* boat, this journey *our* journey. And I realize, at this moment, that despite the uncertainty, despite my Lady's illness and our exile from England, I am happy. Here, on the Nile at night, in the white Egyptian moonlight, I am happy.

4

$\mathbf{A}$ND SO WE JOURNEYED FURTHER SOUTH STILL, INTO UPPER Egypt, then Nubia. We visited all the great monuments—the temples at Abydos and Edfu, Luxor, Karnak, and Dendera; we rounded that famous bend in the river at Abu Simbel and came upon the four huge statues of Ramses II seated against the cliff, sand up to their knees. "Compared to this," my Lady said gravely, "we are so . . . temporary," and then she laughed at herself as we clambered off the *dahabieh*. We traveled all the way south to Wadi Halfa before we turned around and were sluiced back down the Nile. It was as though every day brought a new visit to the Museum in Bloomsbury, except here everything was sunny and sandy and much brighter and more enormous than anything I could have imagined in Great Russell Street. I studied the ruins and tried my best to learn more about the culture and religion of the ancients, but I found myself continually distracted by Egypt, by the country around me that lived and breathed and did not require excavation. I was helped in this by my Lady, who was much more curious about the people—the modern Egyptian people, the *fellahin*, their mothers and sisters, fathers and uncles, where they came from, where they were going—than any number of crumbling antiquities. Even though her Arabic was still rudimentary, she did not hesitate to engage anyone and everyone we met in conversation;

just as in England, she was able to find out who was who in any family straightaway. People always liked her, from the great and the grand to the poorest, most miserable mite; my Lady had the ability to make each person she met feel as though he was of great interest to her. Everyone had a story, and my Lady wanted to hear them all. Consequently, we were soon visiting more babies and old people than ruined temples and tombs, drinking cups of sweet tea and nibbling foods with strange flavors that were both sharper and sweeter than any we had eaten before. And the peculiar thing was—peculiar to me—that I enjoyed these visits as much as my Lady.

I was surprised by this transformation, this redirection of my gaze, surprised to find myself abandoning my amateur study of Isis, my once-wholehearted curiosity about the true meaning of the hieroglyphs, and instead expanding my knowledge of Egyptian farming practices. I got to the point where, if asked to choose between a visit to the ruins at Kom Ombo or a stroll through the lively village next door, I'd choose the village, every time.

And so, sated with temples and sand and tiny settlements where the women and children rushed out to greet us as though we were Pharaohs on our last journey up the Nile, we arrived at Luxor and thought—yes. We will stop here for a while. We had visited briefly on our way south and my Lady had formed the idea then of re-turning to make Luxor our base: Alexandria was too damp, Cairo too busy. We had been to view the French House on our first visit, and after that, my Lady made inquiries about hiring it. "This is it," she said. "Sally, Omar, this is our destination."

Luxor. The name itself felt warm in my mouth. Luxurious. My Lady called it "Thebes," the Greek name, she said, meaning "the most selected place." And it was, I agreed, even then, the day we arrived, the most selected place.

We disembarked, and *Zint el-Bachreyn* was unloaded—all the bags, boxes, trunks, crates, cases, all the things Mr. Abu Halaweh

THE MISTRESS OF NOTHING

and I had purchased in Cairo, everything my Lady had brought with her from Esher. The donkey boys crowded round, and we set off, in convoy. Along the waterfront and into the village, through the great pylons of the temple, past the grand stone columns, some still erect, others topsy-turvy, the mud-red dwellings perched and pitched in over and around and above, donkeys, chickens, children, rubble, gravel, dirt, sand, all higgledy-piggledy, Mr. Abu Halaweh marshaling our raggedy procession, the village women making that *ul-ul* sound, to the house. The French House. So-called because it was owned by the French consul, who had graciously agreed to lease it to Lady Duff Gordon.

The French House rose above the other dwellings at the south end of the buried temple, like a lone white turret left standing in the Tower of London after all else has collapsed. It was by far the grandest building within the village; in fact, several of its windows were glazed and some of the rooms had doors. When we had passed through Luxor the month before, the French consul told my Lady that the house had been built by the British consul, Henry Salt, in 1815; Salt had overseen many excavations and had imported a good deal of antiquity from Egypt to the museums of Europe. "You'll be interested in this, Sally," my Lady said. "The famous Italian adventurer Belzoni lived here for a time, as did Champollion, the Frenchman who deciphered the Rosetta Stone."

"The Rosetta Stone!" I said, shivering with pleasure.

"And the French writer, Gustave Flaubert," my Lady added, "for a time."

"*Madame Bovary*?" I asked. My Lady had a copy of the novel, in French, with her, which I had not read—could not read.

My Lady laughed. "We shall endeavor not to be scandalized."

Though we had been to look at the house once before, I felt almost frightened as I climbed the rough stony steps that led to the door: this is where I'm going to live, I kept thinking, and it is not like any Esher house. Both my mistress and I were relieved

to be disembarking from *Zint el-Bachreyn* now; though we loved
the boat and our floating life on the Nile, it was good to get back
onto solid ground once more, to stop being a tourist day after
day. I paused to catch my breath, stepping aside so that the bearers
could pass, and as I paused I turned round to see what was behind
me, and "Look!" I cried out with no regard of who was there to
hear. There was no one near; Mr. Abu Halaweh was back down at
the riverside already, supervising, and my Lady was still en route
on her donkey, one child from the village perched in front of her,
another at her back, all three struggling not to fall off. I suppressed
my urge to talk to a boy who was hefting an enormous case past
me at that moment; my Arabic was still too basic to express any
of what I was feeling, and besides it might not be appropriate to
speak to a village boy in this way. The Nile, that most venerated of
rivers, stretched out before me, a tableau of hills, palm trees, green
fields, and the broad stretch of glinting water. I felt so overcome, I
inspired myself to laugh: it was not as though this was the first time
I'd seen the river; I'd been living on it these past weeks. Why did
the Thames never do this to me?

The ground floor of the house was dark, windowless, the
floor covered in grit; animals had been kept there until recently—
chickens and goats perhaps—and the air was pungent. There was
no front door but a gaping hole in its place. "Yes," said Mr. Abu
Halaweh. He was standing beside me now, slightly out of breath; I
hadn't heard him arrive. "We will need a door, I'll see to it." This
was his most recent, and reassuring, English expression: "I'll see to
it right away, Miss Naldrett." Up the bare, uneven stairs—no ban-
isters—and we entered the light.

It was like emerging from a cave, like moving from the ninth
century directly into the nineteenth. We were in a large room,
with shuttered windows on opposite sides, the front opening onto
a small balcony that faced northwest and that glorious view of the
Nile. At the back there was a larger terrace, and I went out onto

it now; it was shaded by tall palms that rose from below. When I looked down I saw a walled garden, densely planted, a feature I had not noticed on our first visit; the view beyond was of orange and green hills. I was almost used to finding extraordinary vistas wherever I looked; almost, but not quite. As I turned to remark on the garden to Mr. Abu Halaweh, I realized he had gone and I heard him call for me at the same time.

My Lady was outside the house, at the foot of the stairs, smiling with anticipation. Mr. Abu Halaweh shooed away the children and helped her down from the donkey and I led her into the house and up the stairs. She did not remark on the state of the ground floor—if I have learned one thing from her on this journey, it is the importance of taking everything in one's stride—and when we emerged on the first floor she said, "Oh, how lovely. We'll be happy here, Sally, you and me."

"I think we will, my Lady."

"It needs to be cleaned," Mr. Abu Halaweh said.

"I quite like it in its current state," she replied.

He tutted. "Too much dust. Bad for the chest."

"So who's the expert on my health now?" my Lady said, laughing. "You sound just like Sally, Omar."

Mr. Abu Halaweh bowed and said he thought we should retire outdoors while the place was given a good airing.

The house was full of dust and sand—no one had lived in it for three years or more—and before my Lady had time to reply, my heart sinking only slightly as I assessed the task at hand, a great crowd of *fellahin* began to arrive up the stairs one after the other until there were at least twenty young men. I bundled my mistress back down the stairs and out to the walled garden as the men set to clearing and cleaning like a swarm of worker bees, beating and shifting carpets into place, shouldering divans up the stairs, shifting packing crates. Mr. Abu Halaweh shouted orders and my Lady and I were told to sit and contemplate the view, and so we did, well away from the dust and industry. Then they were gone. And the French House was quiet and clean and perfect around us, as though we'd been residing there calmly for weeks. We made our way back inside. Mr. Abu Halaweh prepared tea, and my Lady settled into what was now her salon to speak with her first guest, Mustafa Agha Ayat, the Luxor merchant, consular agent, and the gentleman who, it turned out, had arranged the army of cleaners. He brought with him his tiny black-haired daughter; she set up house on a carpet with her dolly, and when my Lady showed her a picture of her own little Rainey, she took it in her hands and kissed it sweetly.

THAT FIRST NIGHT IN THE NEW HOUSE, I WAS RESTLESS. I'D GROWN accustomed to sleeping aboard *Zint el-Bachreyn*; I was used to hearing the river at night, to feeling my bed move beneath me. I'd grown used to moving on, always moving on, to see what there was to see. We were back on land now, once again, and I wasn't all that certain if I liked the feeling, though I had longed for it towards the end of our journey. I got up and lit a candle; I would write a letter to my sister, Ellen, who must be back in Alexandria with the Rosses and their new baby by now. The flickering candlelight turned the whitewashed walls burnished gold. Outside the shutters I could hear bats come and go. I felt sure my Lady was awake in her room, writing her own letter home. I put on the shawl that, with Mr. Abu Halaweh, I had bought in the market in Cairo—an Arab shawl, a fine and soft cotton weave; it was the first thing I had bargained for myself, though Mr. Abu Halaweh assisted me, of course. I opened the shutters and the bats hanging from the lintel dispersed. Cold night air flowed into the room. I brushed away the sand that had collected along the sill. The night was very bright and when I looked up, I gasped out loud, then covered my mouth, hoping no one had heard. The moon was high over the Theban hills and the sky was blue and black and indigo, pricked out with stars. The river was black, the palm trees were still, and Luxor was silent. I had never seen such beauty. I stood and stared out the window until the call to prayer interrupted my reverie.

I closed the shutters—I was tempted to leave them open but thought of the bats—and lay back down. In the next room I could hear Mr. Abu Halaweh stirring and I pictured him putting on his cap and rolling out his prayer mat. I was surprised at how devout he was, how devout all the men we had met seemed to be (we had yet to actually meet many Egyptian ladies, only village peasants and Bedouin; Mr. Hekekyan Bey and his wife were Armenian). My Lady and I admired the portability of Islam with its simple dictat: face Mecca. At times on the *dahabieh*, I wished I was one of the crew, slipping off my shoes, getting down on my knees. I never felt much for religion in England, and neither did my Lady; in fact, I once heard her mother-in-law refer to my mistress as "particularly godless." My Lady had laughed and grimaced and exchanged a glance with her husband. But in Egypt, Islam was such a natural part of life, so easily integrated into the everyday, that I found myself wanting to know more, wanting to understand more deeply. I'll have to ask Mr. Abu Halaweh, I thought; we can add religion and religious customs to my Egyptian education.

TIME PASSED QUICKLY. EACH DAY WAS FULL; THERE WAS ALWAYS A task to hand and the conditions, though not harsh, were basic. The household expanded: we had our own water carrier now, Mohammed, who spent at least one hour every morning walking back and forth from the Nile with his *balaas*—a clay water-carrying pot—on his head, filling up the household *ziir*, an enormous clay water-storage urn, as tall as me, that sat in one corner of the ground floor. A little boy called Ahmed appointed himself *bowab*, doorman and factotum, and he busied himself running errands for Mr. Abu

Halaweh. Tasks that would have taken minutes in Esher could take hours in Luxor. The battle against the sand was, to me, the most pressing. I would begin each day by sweeping, forcing my Lady to shift from one room to the next while the air cleared of dust and debris.

"Really, Sally, it's not necessary," she said.

"It is," I insisted. "If we don't keep up a constant fight, we'll be buried alive!'

My Lady laughed and I heard Mr. Abu Halaweh laughing too. I looked over to where he was leaning against the wall. "Don't smile at me like that," I said.

"Sally," my Lady said, "when Omar stops smiling, it's as though the sun goes behind a cloud."

He tried to frown but could not.

"You wait," he said, "this is nothing. Sometimes in winter the wind blows half the desert our way." But after that he gave Mohammed the extra task of sweeping every morning, and Mohammed made me a special palm-frond broom to use in my bedroom at the end of the day.

The days were cooler now, though the temperature could rise quite high by lunchtime, and the nights were almost chilly. After a few weeks, we found the French House had become our home. The large room, with its back and front balconies, was the salon. Off one end, my Lady's bedroom, off the other, the kitchen, although it did not resemble any kitchen I had ever worked in before: an open fire in the smooth mud chimney, a long, sturdy workbench that Mr. Abu Halaweh had a local carpenter make, the copper pans and enormous kettle we had purchased in Cairo. During the cool evenings the three of us would sit at the table and work, candles and lamps blazing for light: my Lady on her letters, me on my sewing, Mr. Abu Halaweh at his cooking. In the salon the windows were glazed; in the kitchen the glassless window gaped directly onto the village, towards the mosque at the other end of the temple. Beyond this room, Mr. Abu Halaweh and I each had quarters of our own.

Both my Lady and I had European-style wooden beds specially made by the local carpenter with blankets we'd brought with us from England, while Mr. Abu Halaweh slept, Egyptian-style, on a thick mat he rolled out every night.

Christmas came: I had asked Mr. Abu Halaweh to make my Lady the sweetmeats in honey that I knew she loved, and I placed a few of them in a little sandalwood box I'd purchased in Cairo. "You two are always trying to fatten me up," my Lady said as she opened it, "as if I'm a big goose and you are planning to eat me." And it was true that our household went through vast quantities of Egyptian honey, the sweet black syrup the locals made from sugar cane, but we all loved it—in tea, on bread, in the sweets and cakes Mr. Abu Halaweh baked nearly every day. My Lady presented me with a set of letter-writing papers that she had ordered specially from London. She had received a thick pile of post from England: letters from Sir Alick as well as her mother, notecards and drawings from Maurice and Rainey. "Look," my Lady said, showing me, "Rainey has learned to write her name." Then she disappeared into her room for the rest of the day, having said she was not to be disturbed. At lunch, I placed my Lady's meal tray outside her door and knocked lightly. At supper, I did the same. And I got on with my own Christmas Day: the sun shone and the Nile sparkled and waved and there was no sign of Christmas in Luxor, none at all, and I found myself feeling strangely lighthearted and brave, with absolutely no trace of homesickness for the heavy dark rituals of Christmas in England. In the afternoon I went down to the garden for a while. In Esher I would never have had time to sit and stare up at the blue, blue sky, to pause and pinch the fragrant fading blossom from the jasmine that grew up over the garden wall, to pull a lemon from the lemon tree, rolling it between my palms to release the scent. Imagine! Sitting outside in the warm sun on Christmas Day like the Mistress of the Nile. Mr. Abu Halaweh must have heard me laughing to myself because, a little while later, he brought down two glasses of his sharp and sweet lemonade and sat with me.

"*Sitti* Duff Gordon misses her family," he said.

"She does. Most keenly. Her baby girl is only four years old."

Mr. Abu Halaweh shook his head. "Why isn't she here with the *Sitti*?"

I looked at our dragoman then and realized how enormous the gap was between my Lady's life and his. "It's better for her to stay in England."

He nodded. "My baby daughter, Yasmina, is six months now," he said. "She stays with her mother, Mabrouka, and my parents in Cairo."

"You must miss her too. All of them."

"See?" he said, as though he had read my thoughts. "We are alike, my Lady and me, far away from our families."

"I thought I'd be near my sister, Ellen, now that we are both living in Egypt. But Alexandria seems almost as far from Luxor as England."

"But you aren't lonely," he said.

I looked at him. "What do you mean?"

"I can see," he said, "you are not lonely. You like your life here. You have *Sitti* Duff Gordon to care for. You have the household to run. You have me. You are happy."

I was a little startled by the intimacy of our conversation. I took a breath and smelled lemon and jasmine in the air. "You're right," I said.

He raised the plate of cakes he had brought down to the garden and offered them to me. "Happy Christmas, Miss Naldrett," he said.

"*Insha allah*," I replied.

Mr. Abu Halaweh recruited an Arabic tutor from the village for my Lady; he said he felt that she would benefit from lessons in conversation with a man more learned than himself. Even after only a few weeks in Luxor, we were already accustomed to receiving guests, and Mr. Abu Halaweh had taken to introducing newcomers with a flourish before rushing into the kitchen to prepare tea. When he brought the tutor into the salon, I was sitting by the window sewing, and my Lady was stretched out on a divan working at her portable writing table. I didn't hear them on the stairs, and then, suddenly, they were in the room: "Sheikh Yusuf," Mr. Abu Halaweh announced, and he bowed to the sheikh while the sheikh himself bowed to my Lady. "*Sitti* Duff Gordon," he pronounced solemnly. "But I'm not sitting!" she'd whisper to me sometimes, but not today; the presence of Sheikh Yusuf, a straight-backed young man, an *alim* or learned Islamic scholar, was sobering.

At first we were skeptical about Mr. Abu Halaweh's choice: the sheikh was, without question, a learned man, educated at the great mosque El-Azhar in Cairo; but one so devout, and one who speaks not a word of English? But when Sheikh Yusuf enters the room, he radiates sweetness and a kind of holy light. He is very handsome, tall with refined features, and he carries himself gracefully. After he departed on that first afternoon, my Lady, "godless" and pragmatic as ever, turned to me and said, "You can feel his holiness, can't you, Sally? I am quite in awe of my new tutor."

Now Sheikh Yusuf comes to the French House every afternoon, except the Muslim Sabbath, and he and my Lady sit and converse for an hour or so. I am to serve tea at the beginning of the lesson but after that they are not to be interrupted. The only book he allows my Lady to read with him—and my Lady's first question, when it comes to learning, is always, "What can I read?"—is the Quran, which he can recite, in its entirety, from memory. My Lady said that at first it was hard going—Sheikh Yusuf insisted on teaching her in a methodical and thorough manner, quite different from the kind of instruction I am gaining through Mr. Abu Halaweh— and some days as we get ready for his visit she closes her eyes, grips my hand, and whispers, "Give me strength, Sally!" But as with any language she turns her attention to, she progresses rapidly, moving from the basics to discussing religious and philosophical issues. I hear my Lady's Arabic becoming increasingly fluid and classical, whilst mine remains of a more practical nature. Mr. Abu Halaweh doesn't like me to mimic the accent of the Luxor *fellahin,* but the Arabic they speak has a directness and efficiency I admire.

My Lady has begun to pass on to me some of what she has learned of Arabic as it is written; I memorized the alphabet, which I thought a considerable achievement, by copying the letters onto a sheet of writing paper, only to discover that when the letters are joined together to form words, they change shape depending on where in the word they are located; some letters have three or four quite separate manifestations. "And that," says my Lady, "is only the beginning. Wait until we get to the vowels!" All of this is backwards, of course, from right to left. It's so complicated that we spend half our time completely baffled and the other half laughing.

The government consuls my Lady met while we were traveling have provided a series of useful introductions throughout Egypt. Now that we have set up camp here in Luxor, my Lady has made the acquaintance of all the more prominent men in the village, including Mustafa Agha Ayat, the consul we met on our first day, who acts in Luxor for Britain, Belgium, and Russia. They say he is the richest man in Luxor. My Lady has already created for herself the kind of salon she held so regularly in the Gordon Arms, but instead of arguments in English with Mr. Thackeray and Mr. Carlyle, the debate takes place in Arabic with my Lady holding her own with the men, only occasionally requesting clarification from Mr. Abu Halaweh, who is almost always at work in the kitchen next door, watching over the company like a sentinel. The claret and port drunk in Esher have been replaced by tea and, on special occasions, the thick black coffee that Mr. Abu Halaweh has shown me how to make, and my Lady's cigar has been replaced by the bubbling *narguile.* I surprise myself by how much I understand of the conversation, which I attempt to follow as I move from room to room in the French House. Mostly I work in the kitchen with Mr. Abu Halaweh, though I have relinquished all cooking duties to him; there really is no point in my attempting to cook unfamiliar food with unfamiliar ingredients, when everything Mr. Abu Halaweh makes is so delicious. Neither my Lady nor I miss the eggy soldiers and suet pudding that Cook used to make in Esher.

These men treat my Lady with great respect and courtesy, despite the fact that we are well aware of what an odd figure she is in Luxor society, if village life can warrant such a grand word: a woman—married but with no husband present, no children with her either; an invalid who is an adventurer at the same time, possessed of an avid intelligence and a hunger for debate. Several times a week the men—Sheikh Yusuf, Mustafa Agha, the magistrate Saleem Effendi, and others—gather in my Lady's salon to recline on the divans and cushions and talk. Sometimes they stay on until late in the evening and Mr. Abu Halaweh and I hover in the kitchen, waiting for my Lady to request our help, refreshing the pipe, serving the trays of sweets that Mr. Abu Halaweh will have prepared earlier in the day.

"Sally, come here," my Lady calls out from time to time, summoning me to help her make a point. "The kings and queens of England are not divine beings, are they?" She turns back to the men. "They are flesh and blood, like you and me, aren't they, Sally?" she says over her shoulder.

I smile and say, "Yes, ma'am, just like you and me," and laugh and the men laugh, and I return to the kitchen.

Luckily for me, whenever my Lady asks me to confirm a point, something the Egyptians really cannot believe can possibly be true or, at least for the sake of the argument, are pretending wholeheartedly not to believe, I always do agree. But then again, what kind of servant would disagree with her mistress, in front of esteemed company?

ONE MORNING I ENTERED MY LADY'S ROOM AND FOUND HER AL-
ready up; we had adopted the Egyptian custom of rising before
dawn long since. This morning she had dressed already.

"This is it," my Lady said with a flourish, spinning herself
around, "this is the new à la mode."

"Lady Duff Gordon!" I said, unable to say more.

"What do you think?" she asked, and spun around again. She
was wearing the most extraordinary outfit I had ever seen. She had
on a pair of Egyptian trousers (men's trousers, brown cotton, loose
flowing, tied at the ankles) and a long white cotton tunic on top (a
man's tunic, plain) and sandals on her bare feet. That was it.

I couldn't think what to say.

"Come on, Sally. How do I look?"

I had to say something. "You look like a learned Egyptian
sheikh," I said.

My Lady pressed her hands together and bowed solemnly.
"*Insha allah*," she replied. Then she picked up her shawl and placed
it over her hair, looping it around her neck: "For propriety's sake."
She looked at me. "You can laugh. It's quite all right."

I let out a laugh then, one brief yap was all I allowed myself
for fear of being unable to stop. "It's so . . . practical," I said. We had
given up our stockings and underskirts while we traveled up the
Nile, but it would never have occurred to me to go any further, no
matter how high the temperature rose.

"It's comfortable," my Lady replied. "But here is the real rev-
elation." She picked up her stays from the divan where she had
discarded them and waggled them at me.

"Your stays!" I said, bowled over by shock; I would have sat
down if it had been appropriate.

My Lady opened her traveling trunk, threw the heavy-boned
garment down into it, and slammed the lid shut. "My stays are
staying in there, my dear, from this day forward. I've had enough

of them. The object of this exile of mine is for me to breathe more freely. That thing," she said, pointing, "was not helping."

And that was it; from then on that was how my Lady dressed, like an Egyptian man, a peasant, mind you, a *fellah*, with a dash of Bedouin tribesman thrown in when she felt inspired.

We had argued about stays in the past; whenever my Lady was ill I would try to dissuade her from wearing them, but with her it had been a point of principle—mustn't let the illness have its way, mustn't let the illness force compromise. Now she'd found a way to get rid of them. "I've journeyed this far," she said to me, "and I'm not dead yet, and the time has come for me to wear whatever I wish. Don't you agree, my dear Sally?"

That moment marked a change in my life, a change more profound than a new wardrobe, however wild. My Lady cast off her English clothes and it was as though in that moment our relationship shifted as well, in some unspoken, unpredicted way. I was not her equal; I was part of her routine, part of her life, my care for her so intimate that it was as though I was part of her body—a hand, perhaps. A foot. Something indispensable, to which you do not give much thought. But from that moment hence, things shifted between us, and life changed.

LATER THAT MORNING, AFTER MY LADY HAD BREAKFASTED, I WENT into my room and closed the door. I remembered when my Lady had purchased the trousers and tunic in Cairo; both Mr. Abu Halaweh and I had assumed she was buying gifts for her husband. I had even imagined Sir Alick thus clad; he would laugh at himself and allow her to coax him into wearing the outfit for one of their supper parties. But now that my Lady had cast aside her European clothes, I longed to do the same. I undressed, taking off the brown muslin, faded now from being put out to dry in the sun repeatedly. I took off my layers of undergarments. I unlaced my stays. Like my

Lady's, they had remained remarkably intact, as though they were a form of indestructible armor. Stained, yes, the edging slightly frayed, but intact. I folded the garment into accordion pleats. For a moment I thought about taking it into the kitchen and placing it on the fire, but I knew there might come a time when I would need it again. So, instead, I took a strip of cloth from my trunk and wrapped the stays carefully, and tucked them at the bottom, out of sight.

I ventured out to the village market with Mr. Abu Halaweh the next day. I had not gone without stays since I was a child. The first time I wore them was at my parents' funeral and, at the time, I'd felt pulled together, held up and supported by the garment, and I'd relied on it ever since. But now, in Luxor, without it, I felt entirely unwrapped and as though everyone was looking at me. My back and arms seemed loosened and free, even with the stiff brown muslin on once again. I felt odd, as though, along with the stays, I'd removed my spine and become a kind of jelly creature, supple, porous. I couldn't help but smile as I walked beside Mr. Abu Halaweh. We always did the marketing together, sometimes accompanied by Ahmed, who ran along in front of us. It was during these excursions that we enjoyed some of our most illuminating language exchanges; we had progressed from words for food and objects towards greater subtleties: religious rituals, cultural observations, and local customs. We took it in turns: Arabic on the way to market, English on the way back. It was not a long walk—modern Luxor was a tiny place, much smaller than it had been in ancient times—but we made steady progress. On this day, stayless, I felt ready to discuss anything and, once again, it was as though Mr. Abu Halaweh could read my mind.

"Why are you not married, Miss Naldrett?"

I found myself blushing. I hated blushing, which made me blush even more. "I've been in my Lady's household for many years."

"But you are not a slave."

I laughed. "A lady's maid is a special, privileged position. I stay close by my Lady. She needs me to attend to her most intimate . . ."

"I know she needs you, but . . ."

"It would not be appropriate for me to marry. I couldn't carry on as lady's maid. I would no longer be able to fulfill my duties."

"I am married, Miss Naldrett, and I fulfill my duties. And a woman must have a husband, children. Who will care for you when you are old and frail?"

I had no answer. I had never dared consider my position in this way. As with the stays and the heavy English clothes I had kept wearing, washing, mending, and wearing again, it had not occurred to me to do otherwise. I am accustomed to doing as I am told; to do otherwise would be frightening. I spoke carefully: "I will be with my Lady until she no longer needs me." Then I changed the subject.

"Mr. Abu Halaweh," I began.

"Yes, Miss Naldrett?"

"I need—" I stopped myself.

He glanced at me. We continued through the village.

"I would like—" I stopped again.

"You would like?"

"I would like to buy—" I stopped, and looked across the dusty passageway to where a woman was emerging from a doorway. She was dressed in typical Upper Egyptian style, in a simple garment draped so that it covered her body, fastened at her shoulders, se-cured at her waist; as I watched, the woman pulled a piece of the cloth up from where it hung down her back and covered her head neatly.

"You want to buy a maidservant?"

"No!" I laughed and Mr. Abu Halaweh looked at me, amused and puzzled. "I would like to dress as she is dressed. My clothes, Mr. Abu Halaweh, I am always too hot in my English dress."

"You want to dress like a *fellah*?"

"No, but—you've seen Lady Duff Gordon and what she is wearing."

"*Sitti* Duff Gordon is wearing men's clothing." Mr. Abu Halaweh smiled. I could see he was amused and only slightly disapproving.

"My Lady will do as she sees fit. But what do Egyptian ladies—what I mean is, where can I buy—"

Mr. Abu Halaweh held up his hand to silence me. "You should dress as my wife does, Miss Naldrett. I will ask a woman in the village," he said. "She will come and see you. It is better this way."

And so it was that Umm Hanafi and her two daughters arrived at the French House one morning, their donkey laden with baskets of cloth. In the salon my Lady lay back on a divan that was covered with great soft cushions and pillows to watch while I was measured and prodded and draped. Mr. Abu Halaweh remained in the kitchen, out of sight, but within hearing, translating when necessary, while the women discussed my hair ("so fine, so straight"), my skin ("so clear, so white"), my figure ("so tall, so strong"), my English dress ("so hot! so heavy!"). They stripped me down to my underwear, which they studied with great incredulity; my Lady said, "Those are the most heavily repaired and restitched knickers I have ever seen, Sally." Mr. Abu Halaweh translated from the kitchen and everyone laughed, including me, who hadn't the heart to remind my Lady that what I wore under my clothes was what she had deemed no longer fit for her to wear under her own. I pulled my dress back on and went to my room to fetch the stays which Umm Hanafi and her daughters examined like three men of science given their first opportunity to handle a new species.

And then the process of re-dressing began. Mr. Abu Halaweh was told to fetch my Lady's accounts notebook—she kept a careful tally of all household expenses—and a complete set of Egyptian lady's clothes was ordered for me: two long, full shirts or tunics, one of colored crepe, the other black; two pairs of very wide trousers, tied around the hips and just below the knees, one in colored striped silk, the other in plain white muslin; one long dark outer vest, with long sleeves, buttoned up the middle to below the bosom, and one short outer vest to alternate, buttoned in the same manner; one embroidered shawl to tie around the waist; one long outer coat of blue velvet, called a *gibbeh*. "Surely I'll be just as hot as ever with all of this on," I wailed, but my Lady said, "Hush. You will look magnificent. You can peel off the layers as the temperature rises." A *tarhah* to cover my head, and a pair of slippers in yellow morocco with high, pointed toes. I balked at the last piece, a long outer gown to be worn when I left the house to go to market, its sleeves also reaching to the floor—"No one covers up to this extent here in Luxor," I said—but my Lady insisted we have it made. "You never know when we might need you to be able to move freely through the city without being seen to be European, Sally, to pass as Egyptian; this way, you'll be able to accompany Omar, unnoticed." I couldn't imagine the circumstances in which such a thing would be necessary, but I did not continue to object. The walking cloak, the *tezyerah*, would be made of violet silk, and Umm Hanafi also insisted on including a veil. "And a new set of undergarments as well," my Lady said, "please."

I, who had never possessed a single item of new clothing in my entire life, looked at the gorgeous pile of fabric on the floor at my feet and, unable to speak, made a kind of involuntary noise in the back of my throat and, to my horror, began to cry. The three women stopped working and stared at me in wonder and consternation.

"What is it, Sally?" asked my Lady.

"I'm not—I won't—you'll have to take it out of my wages, my Lady."

"Sally, I'm buying these things to give myself the pleasure of seeing you wear them. It's the least I can do," she said, "after all you do for me every day." And that made me cry even more.

During the fitting, I had been able to examine Umm Hanafi and her daughters as closely as they, in turn, were examining me. Their black eyes were rimmed with kohl, their glossy black hair was done up in plaits, and they had intricate henna patterns tattooed on their hands and their feet. "Do you like them?" the elder daughter had asked, smiling and holding out her hand so I could look more closely, and I nodded, unsure of the correct reply. When the women were finished measuring and discussing, the elder daughter disappeared into the kitchen and reemerged carrying a bowl of henna paste. "Oh Sally, you must," my Lady exclaimed, and before I could make up my mind whether or not it was a good idea, the girl had taken my hand and begun to paint a pattern of diamonds and stripes on it. Mr. Abu Halaweh emerged from where he had been sitting behind the door. "Now you are a true Egyptian, Miss Naldrett," he said, smiling.

5

I LEARNED TO READ WHEN I WAS EIGHTEEN. MY MOTHER HAD begun to teach me when I was young, but then my parents were taken from me. My Lady taught me, though I doubt she'd remember; she teaches all her household staff to read; she says it's a practical skill no servant can do without. The Esher house was full of books—books in German and French as well as English, books my Lady had translated and published, as well as all the books she had ever read and, indeed, books she had not yet got around to reading. She was always surrounded by pens and ink and piles and piles of paper, even when she was ill. And here in Egypt, in place of her work as a translator, she has her letters home. Her letters home have become as important to her as any paid translation work might have been, and not just because they are her only true link to her beloved family; there is already talk of publishing them in book form one day.

I write to my sister, Ellen, in Alexandria twice a week, as she does me, and her letters are full of the British colony there and the Rosses' life within it. Mr. and Mrs. Ross played bridge with this consul or that, Mrs. Ross hosted a wonderful supper party to which Mr. Ross's colleagues at the bank were invited. Ellen fills me in on the gossip about what the other servants are getting up to, talk that I would have spurned had we been in England but that I find entertaining to read here, now that I myself am so far beyond gossip's reach. Sometimes I find it hard to believe that my sister and I are living in the same country; it's as though there exist two Egypts—the one my sister lives in, looking across the Mediterranean to Europe, and the one that my Lady and I inhabit, our gaze fixed firmly on the Nile.

We have only a few books here with us in the French House, and when a new parcel arrives from England, my Lady falls on it avidly. Whenever European guests come to call, and now that the season is upon us they do come to call, once or sometimes twice a week, my Lady begs them to leave behind whatever books they have with them, and so, in this way, the novels find their way to me. Recent acquisitions include the most recent books by the "three Georges" as my Lady calls them, her great friend George Meredith, George Eliot, and, indeed, Georges Sand, though I can't read that one. When we were traveling we fell into the habit of sitting and reading together, for the companionship. My Lady liked to see what I was reading so that we could discuss it; I was forever having to implore her not to give away the plot. With the French and German novels, she used to summarize the stories to me as she read. I'd assumed that once we'd settled in Luxor the sessions would end; I had a household to run and plenty to be getting on with. But most afternoons, once she'd had her rest, I'd hear her call out for me. "Sally," she'd say, then more loudly, "Sally! It's time."

When I entered her room I discovered she had put all of her many cushions ("You can never have too many cushions, my dear!" she'd say to me each time she spotted a new one to purchase in a market) into a great gorgeous pile on the floor, and she was sitting in the middle of it.

"I'm your new Pasha," she declared. "The Sultana of Pillows. Sit, and read to me."

So I sat, and we read, and this became our new habit. If I'd written home to our old Esher household and described this scene, no one would have believed me. But here I thought nothing of it.

Sometimes when it was my turn to read, my Lady would take it upon herself to brush my hair, which she claims is longer and darker than she could have thought possible: "Are you sure you weren't an Egyptian in some former life?" she asks me. When Mr. Abu Halaweh brings us our tea, I don't even try to get up to help him, the reading and the hair brushing make me feel so lazy. Some days my Lady tries to persuade him to sit with us but he always says the same thing, "Too busy."

In the kitchen one day when we were clearing up after lunch I asked him why he never joined us in the salon. "My Lady would like it if you would sit with us for a while." But as soon as I said it I saw how unlikely it was to happen.

He shook his head. "If I sat down with you and Lady Duff Gordon, I might never get up again."

Our sojourn on the cushions ends when the men from the village begin to arrive for "my Luxor parliament," as my Lady calls it, and I return to my duties. My life here in Luxor, now that we are settled, is much easier than my life as lady's maid has ever been. There are no bedroom fires to attend to now that it is growing warm once again, and our conditions are so basic that all my duties are much lighter. My Lady's clothes are simple to care for; she has kept to her preferred à la mode and favors the loose tunic and trousers exclusively. What our esteemed guests make of her attire is beyond me, but my Lady is comfortable and she breathes easily and that's all that matters to me.

While the men and my Lady converse, Mr. Abu Halaweh not only provides a concise translation when I need it but also explains the content of the discussion to me. The political situation in Egypt is complex and changing rapidly and my Lady mines the men's knowledge of it deeply, often provoking heated exchanges. The Khedive, Ismail Pasha, is a grand modernizer, and in England

I heard Mrs. Ross speak of him as a true progressive in the Arab world; indeed, that is how the majority of *Frangi*—the Egyptian word for Europeans—see him. He has made great progress in modernizing the country's railways, bridges, roads, and irrigation. However, here in Upper Egypt, the perspective is somewhat different, and we hear of the true cost of the Khedive's monumental program: he subjects his people to the corvée, the lash, enforcing labor on his huge building projects with immense cruelty. His great ambition is concentrated on building the canal at Suez, to provide a shipping route between the Mediterranean and the Red Sea, thus linking Europe and the Far East and generating income for the country. Construction began more than three years ago, but it will take many more years to complete. However, this project, and others like it, is enormously expensive and requires a huge labor force. The *fellahin* are being abducted from their villages and forced to work; in some villages virtually all able-bodied men have been taken away, often for years, to work as slaves, without food or pay. All the young men who, under Mustafa Agha's command, helped us move into the French House the day we arrived have gone away over the past few weeks. "But surely this must have been how the Great Pyramid itself was built," my Lady says mildly one day. "I don't condone it—far from it. But needs must, as they say."

"*Sitti* Duff Gordon," says Sheikh Yusuf solemnly, "in ancient times workers labored with love and devotion for their Pharaoh and the promise of reward in the afterlife, but the Khedive inspires none of this loyalty."

"Sheikh Yusuf," says my Lady, "I didn't know you were of such a radical opinion."

"Common sense," replies the sheikh, and without looking in the room I can hear that he is blushing.

"It won't seem so common the day they come to arrest you," says Mustafa Agha, laughing.

My Lady is eager to learn more about the current situation

and its history, and our guests speak more and more freely. Mustafa Agha always takes the view that the Khedive acts in the best interests of Egypt and its people and that the canal will ensure Egypt's future role in the world of commerce and trade, while the magistrate, Saleem Effendi, and Sheikh Yusuf continue to express their doubts that the interests of the Khedive and the Turkish Empire he represents are truly one and the same as the interests of the Egyptian people, despite the independence from Constantinople that Ismail Pasha claims. The men keep their voices low when they are talking, as though they are afraid of being heard beyond the walls of the French House, but it is clear that they want my Lady to hear what they have to say. These discussions remind me of the arguments she used to enjoy at her supper parties in Esher, where she would feel the evening had been especially successful if at some point absolutely everyone present was shouting. Universal suffrage was a particularly popular subject in Esher and even I found myself warming up with the debate, though of course I was never called upon to express my ideas. In Esher the claret had its influence on the politics, but here everyone remains sober at all times and, indeed, they seem to find the discussion itself sobering and sometimes the evenings end on a somber note, though my Lady claims they've simply worn themselves out with the arguing. "Wouldn't have it any other way," she says.

Whenever these contentious topics arise—and they arise more and more frequently—Mr. Abu Halaweh stops in the middle of whatever task he is performing (chopping herbs, grinding beans into a paste, rinsing dark ripe tomatoes in a basin) and goes very still, listening. I first noticed this when I asked him a question and, unusually, he did not reply immediately. I looked up from my work and was surprised to see him standing rigid, not moving, as though he'd spotted an asp on the floor. Afraid to move myself, I tried to see what he was seeing, until I realized he was not looking but listening. And I shook myself from whatever reverie had been occupying my thoughts—watching a boat pass softly up the Nile—and attuned myself to the discussion taking place in the next room. Now that he sees I am following the conversation as attentively as he does, Mr. Abu Halaweh supplements his translation with his own commentary: our dragoman is firmly on the side of the *fellahin*. This does not surprise me. It's not for me to have an opinion on these things; what do I know of Egyptian politics? But it seems to me that these discussions are becoming more and more intense, as well as more frequent.

The heat increases daily now, and I find it an inspiring and awesome thing. It has made sense to me of the Egyptian habit of rising before dawn, sleeping in the afternoon, and socializing in the early evening. Some days after lunch when I've settled my Lady in her room with her letters and books, knowing that she will soon sleep, I leave the house to wander through the village. I wear my summer bonnet, which remains the last vestige of my English dress, as I like the shade it affords and I'm not fully accustomed to wearing a headscarf yet. I'm sure I make an odd spectacle. I try to get the layers of my Egyptian clothes in the right order, and I attempt to hold it all together with the shawl tied around my waist as Umm Hanafi and her daughters showed me; I'm sure I get it very wrong, but the villagers are used to me and it is, indeed, much cooler and lighter than my English dress could ever be.

The French House sits at the far end of what was once a great temple, and the modest mud houses around it rest on top of layers of rubble and sand. If you look carefully you can spot remnants of the temple decoration; not far from us the top of a monumental stone head sticks out of the ground, and the outside wall of one dwelling is comprised of a slab of rock carved with an intricate tableau of ancient gentlemen and ladies and hieroglyphs. The colors of the paint, though faded, are clear, and I almost always pause to study it when I pass by. Two figures, a man and a woman, reach out towards each other with graceful elongated arms, while the sun casts its rays over them; beneath their feet, the rows of hiero-glyphs. I have no idea if these are gods or Pharaohs or both, but their pose, formal and yet intimate, speaks to me, although I'm not entirely sure what it is saying.

There's an Englishman who is staying across the Nile, but he has not been at all friendly to my Lady and has not paid the French House a single visit. I came upon him one day over in the ruins at Karnak; he was wearing a great sunhat tied under his chin with a scarf and he was sketching with absolute concentration. For a brief moment I considered speaking to him (the village grapevine had already informed us of his nationality), but he looked up at me with such surprise and horror that I wanted to vanish. He folded his sketchbook, got up from the broken column on which he was seated, and walked away without speaking. I reported him to my Lady, of course, and the next time she had one of her salons, this man and his business were the sole topic of conversation.

"Antiquities Service," said Mustafa Agha, "he's been sent to spy on me."

"What?" said my Lady.

"Mariette has accused me of stealing and selling antiquities! It's most insulting," said Mustafa Agha, looking both puffed up with anger and deflated with shame at the same time. I knew the name François Mariette; he was the head of the Egyptian Antiquities Service in Cairo.

"But you do steal antiquities and sell them on the black market, Mustafa, my dear friend," said my Lady. "Everyone does, don't they?" My Lady herself was forever parceling up things we find in the rubble of the temple—scarabs, small statuettes, even bits of antique jewelry—and sending them back to friends and family in England. "Just last week," she continued, "a *fellah* brought me a very nice silver ring he had stolen out of the new excavations. 'Better you have it than Mariette, who will sell it to the French and pocket the money himself; if I didn't steal it, he would,' he said to me."

"What did you do?" asked Mustafa Agha.

"I bought it from him, of course. Here it is," she held out her hand for everyone to see. "It's lovely."

Mustafa Agha admired the ring. "But you must not speak to this man," he said. "You must not tell him any of this; he'll have me arrested."

"Well, don't worry about me speaking to him, Mustafa; he ran away from Sally the other day. Spooked, he was, clearly. We won't be inviting him for tea."

RAMADAN ARRIVED, THE HOLY MONTH OF FASTING FROM DAWN TILL dusk. All activity in the French House slowed to a snail's pace in the daytime as no one had the energy to do much of anything, except me, and I found I could think of nothing but food all day, even though I was not fasting. Mr. Abu Halaweh continued to cook for us, which both my Lady and I thought was beyond the call of duty, but he wouldn't have it any other way.

"Besides," he said to me one morning when I tried to relieve him, "you might poison her with your food."

"Omar!" I shouted, and I attempted to swat him with my spoon but he ducked down low and got away. Then I realized I had used his Christian name, not his Christian name of course, but his given name, and said, "I'm so sorry, Mr. Abu Halaweh." I bowed my head and placed my palms together, the way he did when he was showing respect, and wished I had a veil to draw across my face. In Esher there were always a few servants with whom I never progressed beyond formal address; Sir Alick had a butler everyone, including Sir Alick, called Mr. Roberts, even after he had been in the household for more than a decade. There were others with whom I used first names straightaway, and others still who didn't really have names but were known by their position, like Cook, of course. But as soon as I'd said it, "Omar" felt right to me.

He shrugged. "This is my name. You may use it, I'm happy."

"Please," I said, "you must call me Sally." Of course I blushed, and I paused for a moment at the thought of impropriety, but I shook this off quickly. Our complicity had deepened, and after we began to use our first names, it was hard to believe we'd ever done anything differently.

While Ramadan continued, visitors to my Lady's afternoon salon dropped away, and Saleem Effendi and Mustafa Agha sent gifts of incense and scented soap by way of apology. Luxor was very quiet. At sunset Omar was able to break his fast; he would have laid a small plate of dates and a glass of water for himself earlier, in anticipation. While my Lady was unable to persuade Omar to join us among the cushions for our afternoon reading session, during Ramadan he did consent to share the evening meal with us, such was the sense of occasion. We took to eating together in the salon as the sky over the Theban hills went from deep and starry blue to black. I would carry in a basin of water, soap, and napkin for my Lady to wash her hands—cleanliness is highly valued in Egypt, so much so that I've begun to think we English must appear rather grubby when we travel in this country—then I prepared basins for myself and Omar as well. I lit the many candles while Omar brought the food into the salon on a large silver tray that he set upon a low stool, and we three sat on cushions around it. We had both become accustomed to eating in the Egyptian manner, using the right hand only to scoop up the rice and beans with the delicious herbed and salted bread that he makes. We drank lemonade and tea and toasted each other and all our best qualities. My Lady told jokes and, more often than not, we'd have to explain the punch line to Omar, which would prove even more amusing. We'd laugh and shout and every once in a while I'd allow my Lady to persuade me to do my impression of the dancing girl houri whose performance we had witnessed in Edfu. I don't know why or how this had become my party trick, but it had. Dancing for an audience, however small and familiar: no one in all of England would have believed me to be capable of such a thing. And the most peculiar thing was, I enjoyed it. I enjoyed it enormously. It was a very bad impression, I was clumsy and slow on my feet, but it never failed to make us all roar. My Lady and Omar reclined on their cushions and they applauded me.

We'd grown so relaxed and familiar with each other; I see now that this was extraordinary, that the shifts and changes in our relationships to one another were, for all three of us, unprecedented. My Lady had always treated her staff well, but now we'd moved beyond any of the formalities left between employer and employee. Omar had stuck to the old structures for longer than me, but it was as though the devotion required during Ramadan had produced in him a license, a new sense of freedom.

During Ramadan I expected Omar's appetite to be enormous, but in fact, as the days went by he seemed to eat less and less and, like everyone else in the village, approached life with increasing languor. My Lady took ill, which was hard for us to bear given how well she had been feeling. Not the usual coughing and spitting, but something else, as though the fast-induced sleepiness of the village had worked its way inside her. She said she felt tired, bone tired, but more than that, I think homesickness had overtaken her once again, unexpectedly. Whenever I entered her room I'd find her either looking at the photographic portraits of her children and Sir Alick that had been sent to her at Christmas or sleeping with the photographs laid out next to her divan, on her writing table.

Those evenings that my Lady was too unwell to join us, Omar and I continued with our new tradition of sharing the meal, the windows of the salon flung open to the night. As well as bats, the eaves of the French House were populated by tiny owls that looked as though they had hopped straight from a hieroglyphic frieze, and there was one that would sit on the windowsill and watch us eat. By now the night air was warm and soft but still cool enough to provide a welcome contrast to the day. Omar and I would lie back on the cushions and talk late into the evening; I think we were both surprised by how much we had to say. And we said most things at least twice, once in English, once in Arabic, with many digressions and explanations along the way. I had never spoken so freely with a man, and Omar had never spoken so freely with a woman: I know this because he told me.

"I never met my wife," he told me, one evening, "before the day I married her."

"That doesn't seem to me like such a bad way of doing things," I said. I found myself thinking of the little maid, Laura, who had got herself into such trouble in Esher. "What was it like," I asked, "the first time you saw her?"

He smiled and shook his head and, when I did not understand his reply, said, "I don't have enough words in either language."

I marveled at the conversation: a man had confided in me. The night breeze ran across my skin; the little owl hooted, then flew away. I felt as far from Esher as it was possible to be; it was as though not only did I inhabit a different land, but I inhabited a different body.

LUCKILY MY LADY RECOVERED FROM THIS LATEST BOUT QUICKLY AND needed none of the special treatment that we all so dreaded. She decided to mount an expedition to the Valley of the Kings before the nights grew as hot as the days. Omar organized the little ferry-man to take us across the river in the late afternoon, and donkeys to carry us once we reached the other side. The path to the Val-ley is long and winding, and for a time we traveled alongside the fields where the crops were ripening. The soil is so enriched by the annual summer inundation of the Nile that farmers can plant two or sometimes three crops in rotation, and once the barley and lentils have been harvested, they sow follow-on crops of maize and cotton and sugar cane; they use an ingenious system of canals for irrigation, waterways built in ancient times. The soil is black and rich and pungent as far as the annual Nile floods reach, but beyond that, as though a line has been drawn, the ground turns scrappy and hard as the desert begins. I find the division between the voluptuous green flood plain and the white stony hills quite alarming, as though the land has issued a warning: go beyond here and you are doomed; beyond here you will not survive. My heart sank as our little procession turned away from the plain to head up into the Valley, and I struggled not to show my apprehension; my Lady and Omar were so engaged in their discussion of the landscape and the farmers that she had met and spoken with on previous outings to this side of the river—several of whom came out to greet us as we made our way past their smallholdings—that they did not notice the grim look on my face.

The sun began to go down and the hills turned as red as hot coals in the dying fire of the day; we reached the Valley at twilight, which in Egypt gives a glorious, soft, warm light. Now that we had been in the country for more than half a year, I felt I should be accustomed to its beauty and its mysteries, but I was not, nor would I ever be. The Egyptian people live among the ruins of their former selves and they accept as given the strange and monumental remnants of their past. A whole valley, high up in the hills, where the tombs of kings and queens have been carved deep underground into the stone, filled with treasure, then opened and plundered and sealed and reopened and plundered yet again. The bearers had brought torches with them and we entered the tomb of the Pharaoh Sety. The walls were painted in exquisite tableaux and the colors were perfect and bright. Omar pointed out to me the ceiling with its painted vultures flying towards the back of the tomb, and Sety himself standing before falcon-headed Re, the Sun God. I felt awestruck by what I was seeing; the air in the tomb was very dry and the torches were burning hard, throwing out an intense yellow light. I turned to my Lady to say, once again, that I wished I could read and interpret the hieroglyphs, but my Lady was deep in conversation with one of the bearers. Instead of discussing the tomb and its elaborate and meaning-laden decoration, as usual my Lady was asking the bearer about his family: how many children, where did they live, were they all healthy?

When it was time to return home, we made our way out of the Valley of the Kings and mounted our donkeys, my Lady and myself both complimenting each other on our dress sense, which made riding a donkey if not comfortable, at least a little less perilous and a little more dignified. The bearers extinguished the torches and, for a moment, we were blinded by the night. But night is not dark in Egypt; the moon and stars were so bright and the night sky so clear that as we came down from the Valley, the Nile was laid out before us in the distance, more dreamlike and sinuous than any tomb painting. We picked our way out of the hills back down the stony lane and the night was so quiet we were reminded of where we'd just been: the realm of the dead, a valley of the dead, a place where the dead had been disturbed in their rest over and over again.

6

R AMADAN CONTINUED, AND AS THE DAYS PASSED I COULD SEE that Omar was finding it more and more difficult to rise in time for the dawn prayer, to rise at all, in fact. One morning as I dressed in the half-light before sunrise, I heard the muezzin call to the faithful from the minaret in the mosque of Abu el-Haggag on the other side of the village. I was accustomed to hearing Omar respond to the call to prayer in his room next door to mine, and I was always careful to move about the house as quietly as possible during this time. But this morning I did not hear him stirring, and so I went to his door and saw that he was still sound asleep on his mat. I had never woken a sleeping man before. I was not sure how to go about it; I took a step into his room and whispered his name, but that had no effect whatsoever. I took another step, and Omar sighed and shifted his position, his dark hair falling across his face. Then I had an idea: I began to recite the call to prayer myself. I had heard it so often, I found I could recite the words even though I understood less than half of their meaning. "Prayer is sweeter than sleep," I said, in English—I knew this part because Omar sometimes greeted me with these words first thing in the morning— then I stumbled through the Arabic, starting at the beginning with *Allahu Akbar, Allahu Akbar*, God is Great, God is Great.

Omar shifted once again, and I saw he was waking, and I

stepped backwards through the door, out of his room, and stood in the corridor continuing with my call. I heard him roll out of bed; he sat up and coughed and cleared his throat and was about to perform his ablutions, pouring water from the jug into the basin, when he stopped. He poked his head out of his room and saw me standing there, "Are you my muezzin now, Sally?" he asked, smiling.

"*Allahu Akbar*, Omar," I repeated. "*Allahu Akbar.*" And I went back into my own room, where I threw open the shutters and looked out across the Nile as the sun rose over the hills on the other side.

THE EARLY HEAT THIS YEAR, COMBINED WITH RAMADAN, EXHAUSTED the people of Luxor, and as the religious month came to an end with the festival of Eid el-Fitr, many villagers fell ill with a contagion that swept through the village. The first I knew of it was when Ahmed, the little boy who appeared every morning to fetch and carry for Omar, failed to turn up for the third day running.

"The boy is lazy, Sally," Omar said, when I mentioned Ahmed was still missing. "How many times have we found him sleeping in the sun just when we need his help?"

"Sleeping in the sun, yes," I admitted, "but here, in the French House, where he knows we can find him."

Omar was not concerned. But Ahmed's absence was so out of character that I felt sure something terrible must have happened to the boy. I set out on my own to find him.

I knew where Ahmed lived; I was often greeted by his mother as I made my way to market with Omar. She would emerge from her little one-room dwelling to take me by the hand, offering endless thanks for allowing Ahmed to work in the household of the great *Sitti* Duff Gordon. She was blind in one eye and had very few teeth, but—I realized one day with a shock when she announced her age proudly to Omar—she was younger than me. After that I was bold and addressed her as Umm Ahmed, Mother of Ahmed, which delighted her and everyone else who was listening (I was always surprised to discover just how many others were listening). She and Omar would engage in a lengthy series of greetings and blessings, which Omar would translate for me before Umm Ahmed released my hand and allowed us to continue on our way. Our passage to the market now consisted of a series of encounters like these, blessings exchanged, news passed on. I understood that my Lady and I were figures of great interest to the villagers, but I saw also how their curiosity was transcended by their adherence to the rituals of greeting and respect; Egyptians were unfailingly polite.

This morning, when I arrived at Ahmed's house and called out my greeting—"*Ahlen, ahlen Umm Ahmed*"—no one came forward. I stepped closer; no sound emerged through the gaping open hole that functioned as a doorway. I called out again and still received no answer, so this time I stepped right up to the threshold of the house and peered in. The air was putrid with the stench of vomit and death and I barely controlled my impulse to flee. Despite the smell I felt convinced that there was someone inside the house, though I couldn't make out any shape or form in the gloom. I thought I heard something stirring, and I leaned forward further still, not wanting to step inside the house without having been invited. "Ahmed?" I found myself whispering.

Someone tapped me on the shoulder and I stifled a shriek. It was Mohammed, the water carrier. "I followed you," he confessed, "I am so worried for Ahmed." He spoke to me slowly, in his clearest Arabic, enunciating carefully. "Umm Ahmed died, from fever," he said. "Ahmed is already very weak. Half of Luxor is sick with this dreadful epidemic. You must help him," Mohammed said, and he spread his hands. "*Insha allah*—God willing."

"Why didn't you tell us earlier—yesterday or the day before?" I asked.

"We did not want Ahmed to lose his position in the French House."

"Where is he?"

Mohammed turned and looked towards the dark and low doorway.

"Fetch clean water and bring it to me," I said. And, no longer hesitant, I entered the tiny house.

The ceiling was so low the top of my head brushed against it, and I shuddered at the unexpected contact. I took three steps forward and stopped, allowing my eyes to adjust to the darkness. I could make out a pallet against the wall to my right and, on it, a pile of clothing, but after another moment I realized that the pile of clothing was, in fact, Ahmed. I took a few more steps and was beside him. In the dim light I could see that he had grown very thin: he was a small boy, a child of eight or nine, ten at most, and there had been no substance to him when he was well, running after Omar. His lips were cracked and his clothes were filthy and the smell was terrible. Was he dead? Had they left him here on his own to die? There was a jug of water next to his head. I thought to pour a few drops onto his lips but then wondered how long the water had been sitting there, stagnating, colonized by insects from the Nile. Still not sure if he was dead or alive, I placed my hand on his forehead and felt the fever burning on his skin; it was already hot outside, despite the early hour, but the heat emanating from Ahmed's forehead was terrifying. I took off my headscarf and dipped one end of it into the water and slowly, carefully, washed Ahmed's face. I pulled the pile of dirty clothes away from his body and, my scarf now fully wet, washed his limbs. His arms and legs seemed elongated in their skinniness, his elbows and knees painful interruptions, his ribs showing themselves to me plainly. He was a child, just a young child, despite the pleasure he took in the mischief he made, vexing Omar several times every day; he could be my child, I found myself thinking before I wondered aloud where that idea had come from. "Fancy that," I said, "my boy." He was not as dirty as the smell suggested—someone was caring for him, there was no doubt about that—and I pictured Ahmed's mother, holding my hand as she talked with Omar, so grateful for the work we had given to her son. Dead now. Doubtless buried already, as Muslims bury their dead quickly.

Mohammed arrived with fresh water. "Help me," I said, and together we propped him up using the pile of dirty clothing as a pillow. Once we moved him, he began to cough weakly, and he opened his eyes. "Missy," he said, using the name he'd adopted for me. He continued speaking in a broken voice.

"What's he saying?" I asked Mohammed, who repeated the boy's words using the same slow and careful enunciation he had used earlier.

"The little brown owl, he said, the little brown owl came to his door and looked at him and flew away and he knew then that you would come to find him, Missy."

"See if you can get him to drink. I'm going to fetch Lady Duff Gordon's medicine box." As I stooped to clear the doorway I realized that I'd spoken Arabic without pausing to think, without first formulating the English, then planning the translation.

Life in the French House went from calm and slow to urgent and fast-paced that day. A strange epidemic was upon the village, a gastric condition that produced as its symptoms chronic stomach pain, constricted bowels, and terrible fever. Left untreated, one simply weakened, poisoned, then died. Though I went home with the sole intention of getting her medicine box, my Lady herself insisted on returning to Ahmed's house with me. "I've nursed my share of sick children," she said, "and I know the contents of this dreadful box of tricks better than anyone." In fact, there had been several occasions on *Zint el-Bachreyn* during our Nile journey when a boatman had been injured and the medicine box produced, its poultices, tinctures, salts, and wraps providing far more sophisticated treatment than any of these men, the *reis* included, had received or witnessed elsewhere. My Lady had become quite adept at treating minor injuries and ailments, and my own skill at physicking when she was ill was already well established.

However, Omar and I spoke at the same time: "You must stay here, my Lady, you must not—" We stopped speaking and looked at each other, shaking our heads and frowning in agreement.

My Lady folded her arms firmly. "I want to see Ahmed. We shall go together, Sally, you, and me."

My Lady was aghast when she saw Ahmed's condition and heard what had happened to the boy's mother. She insisted we transport him to the French House, where a bed was made up for him in a cool and quiet alcove. There he could be nursed properly.

When the villagers heard that Ahmed was receiving treatment, they began to arrive at the door of the French House to ask my Lady to treat their own families who had been brought low by the epidemic. Mustafa Agha came to the house that afternoon to warn my Lady not to treat them. "You'll contract the fever yourself," he said, to my relief. My Lady might pay heed to Mustafa Agha's advice.

"Nonsense," she replied. "How do we know this disease is infectious?"

"Half the village is sick!"

I had wondered myself how the disease was transmitted, but I kept quiet; my Lady had a theory that the villagers were eating too much green corn and green wheat and this, combined with the religious fasting, had led to the sickness.

"I'll dose them with castor oil and that will clear out the digestive tract," said my Lady.

"Lady Duff Gordon," Mustafa Agha replied, and his expression was very serious—Mustafa Agha was rarely entirely serious—"if your treatments do not work for the *fellahin*, they'll accuse you of poisoning them, or giving them the evil eye."

"Don't be ridiculous! Is it better to leave them to languish with terrible stomach pain? Sally," my Lady ordered, "go and fetch my lavement machine." The machine, a collection of tubes and sacks and pumps and funnels, was stored in a cloth bag at the bottom of the largest trunk; while I unpacked it I could hear my Lady arguing with Mustafa Agha in the next room. "We'll give them castor oil," she repeated, "and if that doesn't work, we'll treat them with my lavement machine."

My Lady and I knew all about stoppages of the digestive tract; laudanum also caused this problem and I had had to administer this expensive but effective sedative—kept in a special bottle in its own lined wooden box, for desperate emergencies only—to my Lady on several occasions. And laudanum invariably led to castor oil, and if that failed to work, to the gruesome lavement machine.

Omar and I spent the rest of the day, when we were not tending Ahmed, cleaning and emptying the ground floor room of the French House; this would be where we would treat the villagers. It had been a while since animals were last kept there, but the floor of the windowless room was still covered in straw and ancient dried dung; we swept and cleared and threw water on the rough surface to keep the dust down. As I swept the stairs, I saw that the stones were ancient temple building blocks, shifted and rearranged, something I hadn't noticed before, despite cursing the uneven steps whenever I tripped on my way up. On the third step from the bottom I found a single row of hieroglyphs. When I showed Omar he shrugged and kept working, as though to say, they are everywhere, these markings, they are ordinary, and indeed, in Luxor it was commonplace to live one's life surrounded by indecipherable messages from the past. The work was hot and dirty and we were both forced outside into the sun from time to time, coughing and spluttering, gasping for breath like my Lady on one of her bad days.

THAT EVENING BEFORE SUPPER I DRAGGED THE TIN BATH TO MY ROOM and filled it with hot water, my body ached and I was avid for a hot bath even though the evening was warm. I added a few drops of the perfumed oil I had bought in Cairo to soften my skin; my hands were so dry, the skin between my fingers had begun to crack and bleed. I opened the shutters wide, and as I sat in the steaming water, I looked out over the Nile. My body felt different from before, as if not wearing stays had effected a long-term physical change; my limbs felt longer and straighter, my back stronger, my neck more flexible; even my hands felt more capable. I ran the soap over my skin and closed my eyes. When I got out I covered myself in a good layer of the oil. I was slippery, and clean.

At dinner the three of us sat on our cushions and talked, planning our makeshift clinic. My Lady was vivid with the challenge of our undertaking and had already written a letter to her daughter, Miss Janet, requesting more medical supplies from Alexandria and Cairo, anticipating what we would use, what would need to be replenished. It was late when we finally extinguished the candles and went to bed. The dawn call to prayer arrived in what seemed only moments after I'd gone to sleep. I got up, splashed clean water on my face, drew my shawl around my shoulders, and went next door to wake Omar, who had slept through the call once again.

Instead of standing outside his door and mimicking the muezzin myself, I entered his room. The shutters were open and the room was full of cool night air though the sky outside was pink and fading to blue-white already. He was asleep on his back, breathing evenly. I knelt down beside him and began the call to prayer.

Omar opened his eyes. He did not look at all surprised to see me there so close beside him. He sat up slowly, stretched his arms above his head, then took my hand. He brushed my hair away from my face; I had not put it up yet that morning. He ran his fingers across my lips, very lightly. Then he brought his face close to mine, and kissed me.

I had never been kissed, never, not once; I had never dared allow that to happen to me. I had spent my entire life avoiding kissing. He was whispering in Arabic and stroking my hair and the truth of the matter is that I did not hesitate. It was as though I had waited so long to lie down beside Omar that I had forgotten why I was waiting. All I can remember thinking was, Yes, this is it, this is right, this is what I want, this is what I've spent the past months wanting. He kissed me again and this time it was a long kiss and I moved towards him as he moved towards me. Then he drew my nightdress over my head and I gasped out loud to be so revealed and he kissed me in order to help me be quiet, and his warm hands on my body reassured me. He took his own nightshirt off. And we sat there, on the carpet in the middle of his room, next to his sleeping mat, the cool air pouring over and over our skin, and we looked at each other for a long time. He was wonderful to look at; I had never thought that a man—a man's body—could be a thing of such dream-filled beauty. Then he drew me down beside him on his sleeping mat and we began. We began and we began and we began and it was perfect. I had not known it could be so perfect.

My Lady had come to Egypt to evade death, but in Egypt I found life.

7

WE SET TO WORK, THE THREE OF US, AND ALMOST IMMEDI-
ately the work was overwhelming. My Lady and I opened
our clinic at the French House that morning, seeing villagers early
before it grew too warm. Over the next few days the epidemic
increased in viciousness; as many as four villagers were dying every
day. If patients were brought to us before they were too poisoned
by the sickness, the castor oil, combined with the lavement machine and the internal wash it afforded, proved to be a very successful treatment. My Lady took the role of doctor, with me as her
assistant; we fell into a working rhythm quite naturally. Instead of
tiring with the increasing pressure of the task at hand, my Lady
thrived, though I was careful to bear the brunt of any physical
labor—heating kettles in the kitchen and carrying the water down
the stairs, lifting patients, cleaning and sterilizing the lavement machine. Omar and I worked out how to extract oil from the leaves
of the enormous castor plant growing in the garden and he spent
a large part of every evening pounding the leaves with his pestle
and mortar. Rather than curse her with the evil eye, villagers proclaimed my Lady their new *hakima*, or healer.

News came from farther up the Nile at El-Moutaneh that the
sickness had spread through both the people and the cattle and
that they were losing eight to ten people every day and double

that number of animals. In Luxor, only a few calves had died. One afternoon I walked down to the Nile on my own, to get away from the house for a time, and thought the surface of the water had somehow been altered before I realized the river was crowded with dead cows, so many head of cattle floating downriver that, should I choose, I could walk across to the other side without wetting the hems of my Egyptian trousers.

The next day I walked out onto the balcony to find that the sand in front of the French House was thronged by people and camels. I called my Lady to come out and look; we stood together and marveled at this inexplicable gathering of men and beasts. My Lady spotted Sheikh Yusuf in the crowd and called to him to come up. "The camels are being sent off to transport the Pasha's troops in Sudan," he explained as he stood with us surveying the scene. "They'll head south in convoy. The poor owners will not see their animals again." As well as the camels, the owners had been ordered to supply two months' worth of feed per animal, so the village was crowded with camels, their beleaguered owners, and great heaps of maize and hay. Bitterness and resentment rose off the men like a great black cloud of fleas.

"How are they meant to live and work without their camels?" my Lady asked.

Sheikh Yusuf gave one of his expressive shrugs. "*Alhamdulillah.*"

Later, after the sheikh had gone back down to the crowd, my Lady and I went into the kitchen to beg Omar for more information. He explained that all the land in Egypt is owned by the Khedive, Ismail Pasha. "There are no Egyptian owners," he said, "only tenants, each paying a tariff according to the value of the land; when they die they can pass their tenancy on to their children."

"Thus the passion for babies," my Lady said to me, nodding.

"If you are childless, you lose your land," Omar continued. "The Pasha can take it from you, with payment or without."

"Without payment?" I said.

"Yes, in fact, the Pasha can take the land any time he wants—to give to someone else more favored perhaps, or for one of his grand building projects, or some other, more obscure purpose. And I have seen it happen, I have seen families stripped of their land, their animals, their . . ." Omar stopped himself. We urged him to continue, but he declined. "We must leave you to rest, my Lady," he said. Then he bowed and left the room.

My Lady looked at me. "I suspect Omar has politics," she said, "but he doesn't want to share his views with you and me."

I nodded. Talking about Omar made my throat tighten.

"Or does he talk to you, when I'm not around to hear?" she asked.

"There's a lot to learn," I said. I could feel myself beginning to blush and I hoped my Lady would not notice. "There's a great deal about this country that I can't begin to comprehend."

Omar and I did talk about the situation in Luxor; we talked about it endlessly; it was not difficult to get him to talk about Egypt, especially when it came to the Pasha's ill-treatment of the *fellahin*, and he was amused by my curiosity. We talked as we worked in the house, we talked as we walked through the village, we talked all day every day. But I was unwilling to confide this to my Lady. She knew that Omar and I spent our days together: we were with her as well, for much of the time. But now, for the first time in my life, I had a secret. A real secret, not just another tiny piece of information I kept to myself out of longing to own something, anything. And for the first time in my long years of service, I did not tell the whole truth to my Lady.

"Well," my Lady said benignly, as she returned to her seat on the balcony, where she could observe the scene, "we are lucky to have Omar here with us."

And I scuttled back to the kitchen, where I could continue my conversation with Omar, in private.

⤸⤷

AND IT WAS OUR SECRET, OUR WONDERFUL SECRET, SOMETHING THAT Omar and I shared with no one else. We were my Lady's devoted servants. But in the nighttime everything changed. Everything was altered.

After that first dawn, I wasn't sure what to do; I spent much of the day the first day of our clinic (and I was grateful for all the activity)—in a kind of self-induced fever. I wondered if I had in fact fallen ill myself and the whole thing was a hallucination. Omar looked at me, spoke to me, behaved towards me exactly as he had the day before; his deference and charm had no additional note of sweetness. In the evening we took our meal together with my Lady and made yet more excited plans for our clinic; I helped my Lady to bed, then went to my own room. I kept a single candle alight and opened my shutters to the Nile and got ready to go to sleep. I sat on my bed and rubbed a few drops of oil into the dry skin of my hands. Then I heard a tiny knock on my door. And he came into my room and into my arms and I felt a happiness so great that had someone else described the sensation to me, I would never have believed them.

I BEGAN TO RECEIVE MARRIAGE PROPOSALS FROM THE FATHERS OF THE young men of Luxor and the surrounding villages. I can see now there was a horrible irony to this, although at the time I found it bewildering, as though the whole of Upper Egypt had suddenly decided to take notice of me. I was not used to being noticed. It was my Lady who gathered onlookers and admirers; the fact was that she herself, let alone anyone else, scarcely noticed me: that was the whole point of being a good, faithful, and hardworking lady's maid.

The first proposal was a direct result of what my Lady and I were doing in our makeshift clinic; as the epidemic at last began to ebb away, the household was overwhelmed with gifts: a woven shawl, clay pots full of black honey, a chicken stuffed with green wheat and roasted with dates—delicious—from people too poor to spare such things. But on this occasion, instead of offering a bundle of wheat or maize, an old man from the village asked to speak in private to my Lady. I took him upstairs to the salon. In the kitchen next door, I asked Omar to brew the tea while I picked up my sewing.

"My son, *Sitti*," we heard the man say simply, after a few opening pleasantries, "my son for your Missy."

I stabbed my finger with my needle and it began to bleed.

Omar dropped the tray he was carrying with a huge clatter. We both stood still as a stone Ramses, afraid to move in case we missed anything.

Though I couldn't see her, I could hear my Lady was lost for an appropriate reply; my Lady was never lost for a reply.

The old man in his tidy worn clothes mistook my Lady's ongoing silence for interest in his proposal. "A woman needs a husband and children," he said. He was on uncertain ground, unaccustomed to discussing such important matters with a woman, let alone a *Frangi* woman. I could hear the hesitation in his voice. There was much confusion in the village about the husbandless *Sitti* Duff Gordon, although this confusion had been alleviated by my Lady's growing stature as the host of regular salons with her important male friends and village *hakima*. In fact, she was well on her way to becoming an honorary man. The old *fellah* continued, despite his lack of confidence. "We are not wealthy people, but we would give a good home to Missy."

Now my Lady began to cough, but I could tell this was in an effort not to laugh. We knew this man and his family to be very poor, possessing nothing, not even their own smallholding. I knew the son in question as well; he was one of the village donkey boys, though the broken-down and decrepit donkey he hauled tourists around on during the season was not his own beast but one that he hired from Mustafa Agha.

Omar, having pulled himself together, picked up and rearranged his tray. He crossed the room to me, leaned down and kissed my cheek. Then he entered the salon bearing the sweet tea.

Left behind in the kitchen on my own, I gripped the sides of the wooden bench. Oh my God, oh my good God, no, my Lady, no, please.

"Omar," my Lady said in English, "I need your help with answering this man with the proper degree of respect. You heard his offer?"

"Yes, my Lady." His voice was strained.

"Please, Omar, please speak for me; my Arabic is bound to fail me now. How best to turn him down? I must not offend him. What is the right thing to say, the thing that will not result in Sally having to marry one of our lovely village donkey boys?"

Omar cleared his throat and took a breath. "I will tell him you are honored by his offer."

"Yes. That sounds right."

"And I will tell him that Miss Naldrett came to Egypt with you from England, and that she belongs at your side. And that your own husband has asked her to stay with you always, that she has promised she will never leave you." He paused. "She is spoken for already."

At that, my heart felt light.

"Good," she said. "Will he think I'm wicked for not letting Sally marry his son?"

"He will accept it, my Lady. You and Sally are a great source of puzzlement to the villagers. This refusal will be one of many unanswerable mysteries."

"Thank you, Omar. Please."

When the old man rose to leave, I came through to see him out. He bowed his head graciously, and my Lady offered him her hand. He took hold of it as though it was a strange and fragile glass replica of a hand, not real at all. He smiled shyly at me.

When we returned to the kitchen I held up my finger, still

bleeding from where I had stabbed myself with my needle, for Omar to see. He got a bowl of water and washed away the blood, then wrapped the finger in a clean cloth, neither of us speaking.

When I emerged from the kitchen, my Lady saw that I had gone so pale I looked gray. "I think you've started something, Sally," she said. "I have a distinct feeling that this won't be the last offer of marriage that comes your way."

"Thank you, my Lady," I said, and I curtsied to my mistress for the first time in a number of months, our manner with each other having become so informal and easy. "I'm grateful to you for sending him on his way."

My Lady laughed. "Did you think, even for one moment, that I might accept his offer?"

"I did," I said. "I was convinced that you would agree immediately!'

"Sally," my Lady said, her voice soft, chiding.

"I know, my Lady."

Omar came into the room; he stood with his hands on his hips. "The donkey boy," he said, in English. "The donkey boy." And I began to laugh and soon was laughing so hard I had to sit down on the divan next to my Lady, who pulled me into an embrace.

"No one is going to take you away from me, my dear," my Lady said as she stroked my hair. "No one is taking away my Sally."

I was safe; Omar stood there and watched us, a big grin on his face.

And, as predicted, after that the marriage proposals began to arrive regularly; fathers representing their beloved eldest sons, widowed mothers hoping to find a good wife for their much-favored boys. The most serious proposal came from Mustafa Agha himself, on behalf of his eldest son, Seyd. Seyd was a good-looking young man who sometimes accompanied his father to my Lady's salons, where he must have had a good look at me on more than one occasion; in the better Egyptian households the unmarried daughters are hidden away from the world, more rumor than reality to outsiders, and Omar told me that catching a glimpse of a girl was always a great challenge. I, of course, was not my Lady's daughter but her servant, not a girl but an ancient spinster, and yet the fact that I was English seemed to count for a great deal. My Lady knew she must treat Mustafa Agha's proposal with the utmost consideration; he was the wealthiest and one of the most important men in Luxor, in all of Upper Egypt in fact, and he was good-humored and well disposed towards my Lady, his friendship a valuable and useful thing.

"The very idea," my Lady said, once he had departed. She had promised him she would consider his offer carefully. She paused for a moment and looked at me. "Would you like to marry him?" she asked abruptly. "This is, quite possibly, the best offer you'll ever receive."

I gasped. "No! Of course not!"

"Of course not," my Lady agreed. "What was I thinking? How ridiculous." She shook her head and frowned and laughed at the same time. "For an Englishwoman to marry an Egyptian man. Unthinkable. But still," she said, and she studied me, "I should not take it as read that you will be with me always."

"Yes, you should," I said, but my thoughts on the subject did not resemble my Lady's. I was not interested in the suitability or otherwise of the young Seyd (who was, it transpired, all of nineteen), nor of any of the men who had requested my hand in marriage. As far as I was concerned, life would continue just as it was, until the end of all our days.

The next time Mustafa came to visit, the proposal was rebuffed, like all the others, gracefully.

8

IT WAS OMAR WHO TOLD ME. I WAS TOO IGNORANT TO RECOGNIZE the signs in myself, though I would have spotted them in another woman right away; I was already too astonished by my body, too overwhelmed by sensation, to notice yet more changes. It was, after all, very warm during the day now, and the heat made it difficult to eat, and not eating made my head ache, and that made me dizzy and nauseous, especially first thing in the morning. Late one night, as I stood before him, full of desire, happy in the knowledge of his desire for me, Omar said, "You are going to have a child."

I laughed, not understanding, then felt amazement flood through me. Was this what he wanted? To father my child?

He got up from the divan and ran his hand across my stomach. "You are going to have a child," he said, once again.

I looked at him. Of course. My knees buckled and he caught me as I slid toward the floor.

This was it. Here I was, trapped, like a foolish girl who has let things go too far in the alley behind the big house where she works.

I turned quickly and threw up in the basin that Omar keeps in his room for his early morning ablutions. What will happen? What will happen to me?

Then I felt his warm hands on my back and he drew me

towards him, whispering, "Don't worry, I'll take care of you. I'll take care of you and our baby."

AT NIGHT, OMAR AND I LAY TOGETHER AND DISCUSSED OUR PLANS TO marry.

"We can't tell her," I'd say.

"We must tell her," he'd reply.

"We can't tell her," he'd say.

"We must tell her," I'd reply. "When the time is right."

"You're already married," I'd say.

"I can take another wife. It is permitted."

"We'd have to tell my Lady first."

"We can't tell her."

"We must tell her."

"We will tell her. When the time is right."

But, of course, the time was never quite precisely right. Perhaps tomorrow, we'd say. We'd find the right moment on the right day.

And our secret grew more elaborate every day.

I was not used to deception and it did not come naturally to me. However, it would never occur to my Lady that Omar and I could be anything other than her loyal servants; it hadn't occurred to me before the moment it happened. And, truth be told, we remained her loyal servants; together, as apart, she was our main priority. Nothing had changed; everything revolved around our mistress. Nothing would change; nothing needed to change. At least that's what I told myself; that's what Omar and I told each other.

I wasn't afraid. I wasn't worried about the future, mine or the baby's. I trusted Omar absolutely. I trusted my Lady; she was my guide, my mistress; she would always stand by me. We'd find a way to tell her, and when we did, she'd pause for a moment before moving onward, taking it in her stride. She'd find a way to help us through; our happiness would make her happy. We'd gone far beyond the normal roles of Lady, lady's maid, and loyal dragoman; this was just an extra step in our journey.

And, besides, it *was* hard to believe. Every day I had to pinch myself; this man loves me. This man desires me. I am carrying this man's child. This man has asked for my hand in marriage. We are going to be married; we are going to have a family. It was all so far removed from the realm of what was possible for a woman like me, at my time of life, in my position, that it was completely unreal to me. Perfectly tangible, but absolutely unreal. It was remarkably easy to go about my business every day as though nothing unexpected—untoward—was happening. I deceived my Lady, I know I did, and in the process I deceived myself as well.

TOWARDS THE END OF APRIL, I WAS OPENING THE SHUTTERS IN MY Lady's bedroom one morning when I noticed a young Englishman coming up the footpath towards the house. I called my Lady to the window. Just then, he looked up and spotted us, and we both recognized her cousin. "Arthur," my Lady cried, "Arthur Taylor." She ran down the stairs and out the front door of the house as though she'd never been ill and greeted the young man as though she'd been deprived of human companionship for months. Once again, I was reminded of how much my Lady missed her own family. Once again, I was reminded that, for her, life away from England was full of loss and deprivation, however brave a face she showed to the world, however wholeheartedly she threw herself into village life.

That night as I was preparing the salon for the evening meal, my Lady entered the room and said, "Mr. Taylor has returned to his *dahabieh* to get ready for supper. He and I will take it here, together, Egyptian-style." There was a hardness to her tone that I hadn't heard in many months; it was a tone she used in Esher when speaking to servants with whom she was annoyed.

I looked up at her. "Of course, Lady Duff Gordon," I said. "I wouldn't have it any other way Omar"—I paused, and corrected myself—"Mr. Abu Halaweh is preparing a most wonderful meal."

She smiled then and I could tell she was relieved. "Thank you, Sally," she said.

Though he slept on his *dahabieh* at night, Mr. Taylor spent much of his day with my Lady, and the household ran on English rules once again; Omar and I took our meals in the kitchen and my Lady rang a little bell when we were needed. This restoration of our old ways felt odd at first but, in fact, its rhythm was natural to me, second nature, and besides, it gave Omar and me more time to ourselves. Mr. Taylor was full of news and gossip from England and my Lady was overjoyed to discover he had seen every member of her family before he departed, less than two months previously.

"And my little Rainey," I heard her ask, "tell me about her again. How did she look? What did she say? Tell me everything."

Mr. Taylor was en route, up the Nile, stopping at all the sites along the way, despite the lateness of the season. It had been months since my Lady and I had done any traveling and the whole household had worked throughout the village epidemic to a state of near exhaustion. But no one had presented themselves at the house for treatment for a while, and no one in the village had died for even longer, and so when Mr. Taylor told my Lady of his plans to travel on to Edfu, she asked if she might join him. He was traveling alone in his large *dahabieh* with only one servant apart from the crew, a Copt, a former tailor who, Mr. Taylor said, had turned out to be rather useless, not even able to sew. "Aunt Lucie," he said, "I would be very glad of the company."

"Good!" she replied.

There was confusion in the village over Mr. Taylor's arrival; gossip traveled quickly through the warm Nile air. Mustafa Agha was convinced that my Lady's cousin, whom he had heard referred to as the son of my Lady's uncle, must be her long-lost husband at last come to reclaim his wife. My Lady was greatly amused by this as Mr. Taylor was not much beyond twenty-five years of age, and she quelled this rumor quickly. Mustafa Agha and Sheikh Yusuf both appeared at the door of the French House one afternoon; Mr. Taylor had set off on an expedition to the Valley of the Kings, and my Lady had decided against joining him. The two men must have watched him go. I could see they had something pressing they wanted to say to her.

I ushered them into the salon. "*Sitti* Duff Gordon," Sheikh Yusuf said, bowing. He was blushing and now seemed unable to speak; I wondered what on earth he had come to say.

Mustafa Agha stepped forward, clearing his throat. "Madam," he said, "forgive me."

"What is it, Mustafa?" my Lady said.

"Setting sail with a man who is not your husband," he replied, his tone both apologetic and serious, "unaccompanied . . ."

"I see," said my Lady. "He is my cousin, Mustafa, a young man of high standing, and I assure you . . ."

Omar stepped forward. "If I may, my Lady?"

She raised her eyebrows and nodded.

He turned to Sheikh Yusuf and Mustafa Agha, and a long conversation about the propriety of the situation and the manners and customs of English people took place. Omar went so far as to take the men down to the river for a tour of the boat, where they were shown that Omar's cabin was situated between Mr. Taylor's and my Lady's (and next to mine). He assured them that my Lady would come to no harm and face no embarrassment, and they went away, mollified. When he returned to the house he informed my Lady that all was well.

"Thank you, Omar," she said, "you have restored my reputation."

"They were very concerned, my Lady," Omar replied. "And they were very keen to have a look at that boat."

When word got out of my Lady's imminent departure, there was a great fuss in the village. My Lady and I reassured everyone that we would return to Luxor soon; women whose children's lives we had saved brought presents of bread and eggs down to the *dahabieh* for our journey and our send-off was quite ludicrously sentimental and grand. As the boat pulled away from the riverbank the villagers fired their weapons—hunting guns and rifles—into the air and Omar responded with Sir Alick's old horse pistols that my Lady had packed in England and since forgotten about. My Lady and I both shrieked, ducked, and, too late, covered our ears.

"We'll be back in less than two weeks," my Lady called to Mustafa Agha, who was seated on his horse amidst the crowd.

"We will find it hard to continue without you," Mustafa Agha replied.

I was glad of the idea of change, getting away from Luxor for a brief spell, reimmersing myself in that floating life on the Nile. I had almost forgotten what it felt like to be free of the land, free of the house and its attendant responsibilities, the village and our ever-increasing involvement in village life. From the moment we embarked, the temperature soared and by the second day out the thermometer on the *dahabieh* registered 110 degrees. The heat turned the day on its head; Mr. Taylor and most of the crew slept all day, and the boat came to life at night when the temperature dropped enough to allow languid attempts at conversation. "*Omar cooks the meals amphibiously,*" my Lady read aloud the letter she was writing to Sir Alick, "*bathing between every meal. The silence of noon with the white heat glowing on the river which flows like liquid tin, and the silent Nubian rough boats floating down without a ripple, is magnificent and really awful.*"

At Esna we entered the temple through a huge portico that had been partially dug out, a narrow set of mud steps leading down into the gloom; once my eyes grew accustomed to the darkness I could make out the enormous columns on either side, carved and painted, though it was too dark to see any detail or color. While Omar sat with my Lady at the bottom of the stairs—the temple was dank and damp-smelling but wonderfully cool—I paced out the length of the excavated portico: three rows of six columns, each column as big as a house, or so it felt to me. The roof of the portico pressed down from overhead, as though threatening to collapse in on top of us. At the far end, dirt and rubble were heaped up high, blocking access to the temple itself. "Hallo!" I turned and called towards the light at the entrance, and my words felt flat and muffled by the great weight of stone all around. "*Ahlen!*" I heard my Lady reply, and I made my way back to them, feeling both relieved at going towards the light and gleeful at having ventured inside the ancient, still buried, ruin on my own.

"Do you think this is what lies beneath our house in Luxor, my Lady?" I asked.

"I don't know, Sally," she replied, "but when the house collapses in on itself, I'm sure we'll find out."

After accompanying my Lady and Mr. Taylor to the boat, Omar and I made our way to the village—like Luxor, a tumbledown affair in the midst of the equally tumbledown temple—to buy supplies for our journey, sugar, tobacco, charcoal, but discovered that, this far south, goods for travelers were not available in summer. Indeed, we had seen no other foreign travelers on our journey thus far. The villagers treated us as though we were migrating birds who had returned during the wrong season; they looked at me with round eyes, their mouths falling open in amazement when they heard my Arabic. As we walked back to the *dahabieh*, we ducked beneath the long swaths of blue linen that had been dyed and hung out to dry on lines that crisscrossed above the street. By now it was nearly ten in the morning and it was as though the temperature rose a degree with every step we took.

From Esna we sailed down to Edfu, where the roof of the great old temple was crowded with mud huts and the people who lived in them. I persisted with my sightseeing, though I left it until the evening, and only Omar would agree to accompany me, more out of kindness than any other motivation; I tried to persuade him to let me go on my own, but he would not hear of it. I wandered through the temple in the brief Egyptian twilight while he sat on a broken-down column and fanned himself; I could hear the bats beginning to come out, and I could hear Omar panting in the heat, and together the two sounds were reassuring.

At Aswan there were traders from Darfur passing through in the opposite direction, bringing with them animal skins and Ethiopian slaves to sell down the Nile, also bringing with them a taste of Nubia, of an Africa at which the rest of Egypt only hinted; Omar was able to trade with them for supplies. We passed a group of young female slaves sitting beneath a palm tree cooking maize cakes on a small fire.

"If you want," Omar said, "we could purchase one of these girls in exchange for a couple of handkerchiefs or a loaf of bread."

I shook my head. I suspected he was teasing me.

"Then you wouldn't have to work at all," he said.

"Are you suggesting I don't work hard enough?"

"No," he said, laughing; and when he laughed I could not help but laugh as well and I slipped on the stony footpath. Omar took my hand on the pretense of steadying me, but he was careful to let go of it well before we came in view of our *dahabieh*.

The next day Omar arranged the hire of donkeys to transport our party the short distance up the river to Philae. We left Aswan in the night and reached the ferryman at dawn; he agreed to take us across the river and to tend the donkeys while we remained on the island overnight. We set up camp in the temple itself; we had passed this way the year before but had not stayed for more than a few hours. "This is where Isis found the heart of her dead husband, Osiris," my Lady explained to me, though I knew this already; the God of the Underworld, Osiris, was killed by his brother,

Seth, who scattered his dismembered body throughout Egypt; Isis roamed the country to find and re-member his body. The home of his heart was a special place, and the island temple at Philae one of the most serene in all of Egypt. My Lady and I decided to make our beds in the Osiris chamber, where it was dark and felt as though it should be cool, though of course it was not, and Mr. Taylor and his Coptic tailor set up home at the foot of the great temple pylons. During the day my Lady and I did not do much more than nap in the shade and take turns to bathe in the Nile in the tentlike awning that Omar and the crew had become adept at rigging up for our privacy. Mr. Taylor spent most of the day in or near the water; my Lady came upon him in the afternoon, asleep, his head anchored by a scarf and hat tied to a conveniently placed rock, the rest of his body floating. At night the stars came out and the enormous basalt rocks in the cataract just beyond the island hissed and whispered as they cooled in the light breeze. But it re-mained hot as an oven in the Osiris chamber, so after tossing and turning on our mats for a while, my Lady and I gave ourselves up to the night and went outside and lay down between the columns of the temple. From there the view was dreamy and the stars cast a light that was deceptively cool and watery, and the tall palms on the far side of the river waved gracefully.

"Have you ever seen such a . . . ," my Lady said, her voice trail-ing off.

"No," I replied, "nor ever imagined I would find myself in such a place." After a while my Lady lay down to sleep, but I sat up, my arms wrapped around my knees. Omar came over from where he'd positioned himself to sleep, just outside the Osiris chamber, on guard duty (though we'd stepped over him when we came outside and he hadn't stirred), and together we watched as the dawn broke, a deep crimson, ever-widening slash across the sky. We sat side by side, without touching, without speaking, but it was as though we were in one another's arms all night.

In the morning my Lady bathed in Omar's bathing contraption and then walked down to inspect the colonnade. She sat on a rock looking up the Nile at the First Cataract, and beyond that, in the invisible distance, Nubia. When I arrived to fetch her for breakfast she said, "We'll go farther up the Nile once again, Sally, another time."

Despite the beauty of the night I had a woolly head and was beginning to feel unwell. When we got back to the temple, where Omar was preparing our breakfast, I suddenly felt a terrible sensation of dizziness: I couldn't stop myself from crying out. Omar rushed towards me and everything went blank.

I woke again after a few minutes to find I was lying in the shade on mats and cushions with the Coptic tailor standing over me, fanning vigorously. Omar was hovering with a cup of water. My Lady was seated nearby. I tried to sit up, embarrassed to be the focus of so much attention, but had to lie back down once again.

"It's the heat," my Lady said, "and the fatigue from not sleeping, and the cucumber we had for supper last night. Don't worry, Omar."

"But she's never unwell," Omar said, and I could hear he was anxious.

"You're right," said my Lady, laughing, "it's usually me. We'll nurse Sally well, you and me, after all she has done for me."

"Stop talking as though I'm not here," I said. "I can still hear." Incapacity made me bad-tempered.

I forced myself to sit up. My head was aching. "Stop that," I said to the Copt, who had kept up his manic fanning. "Stop that now, and go away." I lay down once again with my feet—what had happened to my shoes?—and hands in bowls of water that Omar had fetched from the Nile, but then had to sit up and put my head between my knees. Omar fussed and both my Lady and I were annoyed by his attentions; I was out of sorts with the world and myself and I could see that she was annoyed at not being the center of attention, and even more annoyed with herself for feeling that way. Of course I should have been afraid that she would guess at my condition, but I was not. I had come to rely on the fact that she trusted me. But now I knew I would need to be more careful.

THAT EVENING WE CROSSED BACK OVER THE NILE TO WHERE OUR donkeys were waiting and made the journey to Aswan through the night. We were all pleased to get back on board the *dahabieh* and planned to make our way downriver to Luxor quickly.

Beyond Aswan we moored the boat in the early evening so my Lady could bathe in the river; Omar and the *reis* rigged up the tent-awning and my Lady submerged herself in the water, sighing with relief. "You should come and join me, Sally," she called out, but I couldn't summon the energy, even though I knew the water would cool me. I was at the back of the boat on a divan in the shade. It was peaceful; my Lady paddled, Omar pottered, I dozed, and the crew went about their business.

Then Omar came upon the Coptic tailor on his tiptoes peeping at my Lady through a gap in the awning. He let out an almighty roar. "*Kelb!*" he shouted. "*Ya ibn el kelb!* Dog! Son of a dog!" And he called to the *reis* and his crew to come. "Should I cut his throat?" Omar asked. "He has defiled my noble Lady with his pig's eyes. I will cut your throat and then drown you!" he shouted.

The sailors had grabbed hold of the Copt and were half strangling him already, when my Lady, still in the water at the side of the *dahabieh*, raised her voice in protest: "He does not deserve to die for this . . . ," she paused, "trivial crime." Omar shouted out his protest, but she raised her voice once again: "In the scope of things, this is unimportant." And, in fact, to my amazement, I could hear she was struggling not to laugh. When I asked her why later, she said, "So audacious. The little tailor. Who'd have thought he'd have it in him to peep at me that way?" But at the time she allowed the crew to lead the tailor away. Omar helped her out of the water, his dignity as well as hers restored. I accompanied my Lady to her cabin; we chatted about nothing in an effort to block out the noise as the Copt was beaten.

Our journey home after that was quick, only stopping to obtain supplies. Omar had to bribe the *nazir* at Edfu to sell him some charcoal; we had had no means to brew tea or cook for several days. When we arrived back in Luxor we were greeted like returning heroes. Mustafa Agha came bearing a stack of letters from England for my Lady and two for me from my sister, Ellen. Sheikh Yusuf was there, beaming with pleasure at seeing his assiduous student once again, Mohammed had made fresh loaves of bread with the new season's wheat, the gardener had distributed flowers throughout the house, and little Ahmed, fully recovered from the contagion, a child of the village now that he was parentless, rushed around and around wildly, catching our hands in order to cover them with swift kisses. "The French House," my Lady said, as we reached the front door, "this is our home now, and what a homecoming!"

In May my Lady took the decision to stay in Upper Egypt for the summer. It was the most economical thing to do, she said. Mustafa Agha told her that she would be the first *Frangi* in living memory to remain in Luxor through the hottest period of the year; not even the most devoted Egyptologists and adventurers were inclined to stay. My Lady reported this to me, laughing: "So we are pioneers, after all, in our way. We will stay here, to bake." Sir Alick was planning to come to Egypt for a visit in November: "I'll write to him now," she said, "and ask him to come earlier, and we can go to Cairo to meet him in the autumn."

I was happy at the idea of staying in the south. My Lady's fragile health had been stable for more than two months and the sun really did seem to be helping her to heal. And it suited me to re-main in Luxor, tucked away in familiar obscurity. Mr. Taylor had departed and we had returned to our relaxed, easy ways. I spent my days at my Lady's side, and my nights with Omar.

And so, the heat. Throughout May each moment felt hotter than the last. By June our days took on a stately quality; Omar and I attempted to complete the necessary domestic tasks in the early morning light and then kept our movements to a minimum for the rest of the day. My Lady did as little as possible, morning, noon, and night. Venturing into the sun required preparation, and soon she gave up on going out entirely. By this time neither she nor I cared much about the color of our skin; one afternoon my Lady turned to me and said, out of the blue, "You look as though you've been dipped in walnut juice, my dear, like a true Arab." I laughed and then caught sight of my hands and thought, Yes, it is as though I am entirely henna-stained. It was too hot to eat but Omar kept up a constant stream of delicious morsels from his kitchen; he saw it as part of his duty to make sure neither my Lady nor I lost any weight despite our lack of appetite. Before the sun came up we closed all the shutters in the house against the heat; after sunset we opened the shutters and moved outside, my Lady sleeping on the balcony at the front of the house, overlooking the Nile, both Omar and I on the terrace at the back. Inside in the dark during the day, outside in the dark at night; we began to feel like creatures of dark-ness, cowering from the intense sunlight that streamed in through the smallest gap in the shades. Candles could not be lit, as they at-tracted huge swarms of vicious little insects and even a single tiny flame felt like an inferno. "My one loss now," my Lady said to me, "is that there is never enough light to read."

These conditions, on their own, were not too terrible; there was an awe-inspiring intensity to the heat to which we surren-dered, giving ourselves up to the awkward luxury of doing noth-ing. But then the sandstorms began, when full days and parts of weeks were lost as the *simoom* whipped up the desert and deposited great swaths of it on the village. I understood now how so many of the temples and monuments came to be up to their necks in the stuff; if I had sat outside during one of these storms, I would have been covered up like an ancient monument myself, only fit to be dug out at some distant future date. The *simoom* brought nothing with it that resembled a cooling breeze, only dust and sand filtering through the shutters and under the doors, and yet more heat, and some days everything we ate, everything we drank, was full of it. I forgot what it was like not to feel grit in my mouth, between my teeth, under my tongue, all the time.

The afternoon was the most difficult, when the heat plateaued and settled down to stay, and something approaching boredom threatened to impinge on the day. Both my Lady and I migrated to the kitchen, where Omar would get on with his duties, very slowly, all the while quizzing us on our vocabulary, correcting our pronunciation. My Lady spelled words for me, using Omar's wooden spoon to draw the script in the wheat flour he had spilled on the floor. "Repeat after me," he would say in his special tutorial tone; if either of us had had the strength we would have teased him, but instead we repeated each word dutifully, my Lady on a divan against the far wall, me lying flat on the floor beneath the workbench. Sometimes he'd ask a question with his back to us, but when he turned round, expecting an answer, he'd find us both asleep. My Lady tried to write letters home, when she could find enough light, but even letters to her beloved husband that she would ordinarily write in an hour or two took a week to complete.

By now we had lost all sense of modesty inside the French House and dressed in the minimum amount of clothing required, my Lady in a long, loose shirt, me in my lightest Egyptian trousers and tunic, my feet bare, my hair tied back and pulled away from my face. Only Omar made any real effort to look respectable but even he made do without a sash, without a waistcoat. My Lady

demanded I cut her short hair shorter still, until it was quite man-
nish, shot through with gray. Mohammed and Ahmed came early
and did their chores as quickly as possible before heading off once
again. The linen of our sweat-soaked shirts and trousers grew thin
with the washerwoman's constant pounding and rinsing.

In running the house, I had come to rely on Omar more than
ever; while the heat was terrible for anyone, at least Omar had
a little more experience of living in it and, indeed, surviving it.
I watched him carefully and copied his movements, which were
even neater and more minimal than before. I relied on him to help
me complete most tasks, especially during the days when the air
outside was full of swirling sand; now only the most intimate tasks
of my Lady's toilet were mine and mine alone. While she rested I
retired to my room to sew (though mostly I napped), and when
Omar came in he would lie on the floor at my feet, rising only to
roll out his prayer mat when the call to prayer came. I watched him
pray, feeling a pure and precious ease.

The cattle murrain in Upper Egypt continued to rage, long
past the season when it normally abated; virtually all the cattle in
Luxor had been infected now and were dead or dying. Men were
having to do the work of oxen, turning the water wheel, dragging
the plow over the fields, all through the hot season. Though we had
been able to help with sickness in the people, my Lady and I were
powerless to help with sickness in the cows, and Omar reported to
us daily of the losses; Mustafa Agha had lost thirty-three head and
had only three left in total. On the rare occasions when I ventured
out of the French House, I would see small groups of women, boys,
and the few men the Pasha had not taken away to work on his
grand schemes dragging the dead animals through the village and
across the fields to the burial site. The town elders, Mustafa Agha
among them, struggled to cope with the disposing of the carcasses
and took to burning as well as burying the cattle. When the wind
changed direction, the smell was terrible.

The Nile rose, and rose, and rose further still, inundating the valley, at places growing as broad and placid as a lake, its scenic beauty giving no indication of the havoc it would wreak if it rose above expected levels this year. All we could do—my Lady and I included—was wait and see.

But the dust storms did not rage continually, and there were days when the sky was so clear and blue, the sun so pure and strong, that I thought I would weep with happiness, despite the heat. When the wind came in from the north, the air cooled slightly. On these days Omar and I got out to market early, as did all the people of Luxor, and the mood was light and clear in the village, everyone greeting each other, gossiping and arguing with great relief. Because of the cattle disease, prices of milk and meat in the market had soared, and so Omar turned his cooking skills to the vegetables and grains available—stewed apricots with nuts and raisins, cucumber minced with watermelon and mint, fresh lime from our garden squeezed over everything.

When they could move from their houses, my Lady's friends returned for the salon; Omar served tea with the *narguile*, which my Lady now used as though puffing on a communal water pipe had been part of her routine all her life. After the conversation and exchange of views—slightly less vehement than had been the case in the cooler part of the year—were finished, Sheikh Yusuf stayed on to give my Lady her Arabic lessons, but even Sheikh Yusuf, normally so formal and restrained, kept his clothes to a minimum upon entering the house and lay on the carpet while delivering his lesson, sometimes falling asleep.

And I grew. I do not mean that I grew larger. I grew within myself, as the baby grew inside me.

It was easy to hide the changes in my physical self; for the first few months I became thinner than before with the sickness and the heat; once I began to round out a little I simply adjusted my Egyptian clothes, which are, after all, made for modesty, made to disguise the true shape of one's body. I'm tall for a woman, and I have a good strong frame, and I can carry extra weight easily. One afternoon my Lady said to me, "You are looking particularly well, Sally, your skin, your shape; obviously this climate suits you as well as it suits me." But that was the closest she came to noticing that I was different, that I was changing.

I felt him kick in June, like a little owl in my womb, gentle, flickering. Omar would lie with his head pressed against my belly, whispering. "Your mother is very beautiful," he would say. "She carries you as if she is a Queen—"

"A Pharaoh," I'd interrupt. "A lady Pharaoh, if there ever was such a thing."

"A goddess. An ancient goddess. And we both know that you will be a good, strong man when you grow up . . ." And our whispering would continue late into the night until we'd roll into each other's arms and begin where it all began, once again.

We took such pleasure in each other. We took such deep and abiding pleasure in each other's bodies.

I whispered to Omar, "We won't tell her now."

He stroked my hair.

"We can't tell her now, with the heat, and her plans for Sir Alick's visit in the autumn. She's so well, we must not disturb her in any way."

He did not reply.

"We both know—we both know how much she loves children. Look how she dotes on Ahmed." I paused. "When the child arrives, all will be revealed and celebrated."

"We won't tell her now," I continued.

"No. We'll tell her later," I said.

Omar had fallen asleep.

9

By the middle of August, we had had enough of baking ourselves. It was time to travel to Cairo. The trip down the Nile was arduous, the heat debilitating for even the *reis* and his crew on the *dahabieh* my Lady had hired for the journey. Being out on the water had no cooling effect; instead the surface of the Nile was like an enormous mirror, intensifying the sun, burning. The days and nights merged and we did not sightsee but stayed on the deck beneath the awning, discussing ice and snow and other chilling topics when we could summon the energy.

Despite my Lady's letters to her husband telling him of her plans, Sir Alick was not in Cairo waiting when we arrived at the end of September.

"He's not here, is he, Sally?" she said when we disembarked at Boulak and found no one there to meet us.

"Perhaps the letters didn't reach him in time for him to change his plans, my Lady."

She looked at me calmly. "Perhaps not, Sally, perhaps not," she said, but I could see what she was thinking: I've been gone from him so long it's as though I am dead already. She swallowed hard and blinked, and frowned, and showed no other sign of the tremendous disappointment I knew she was feeling.

And, in fact, there had been a death: my Lady's friend, Mr.

William Thayer, the American consul who had been so good to us when we arrived in Alexandria, who had found Omar for us. This was sorrowful news for my Lady. Omar quickly located another house for us to rent—we had planned to stay with Mr. Thayer—but after the silence and peace of Luxor my Lady and I found Cairo an abrupt and not altogether welcome change. The house, though cool and compact, with an inner courtyard full of fragrant orange trees and its own water supply, was in the middle of the *Frangi* quarter; whenever my Lady and I ventured out, we were assailed by French and Italian voices as well as English, which my Lady found jarring. "I've traveled so far from Europe now," she said, "it disturbs my Muslim nerves to be reminded of it." We had forgotten what it was like to live in a noisy, busy city, and while I acclimatized and began to enjoy the bustle and fray of Cairo with its great bazaars and mosques and crowded streets, my Lady retired to her divan, her spirits as low as when we first arrived in Alexandria and thought we had come to an awful place.

The day after we moved in, Omar knocked on the door of my room first thing. We'd had less privacy on the *dahabieh* than in the French House, but now we were settled, our rooms chosen carefully, I knew we'd soon be together in the night once again. I was getting dressed and I called to him to come in.

"You don't need to knock," I said, laughing, but I stopped when I saw his face. "Omar? What's wrong?"

"Nothing is wrong, Sally," he said. "Today I am going to visit my family. I've spoken to *Sitti* Duff Gordon, who has given me permission."

"You have?"

He nodded. "I'll go after breakfast. I'll be back in time to cook the evening meal. I know there is a lot to do in the house, but much of it can wait until tomorrow. I've prepared lunch, all you need do is serve it—"

I held up my hand to stop him from speaking. We were in

Cairo, the city of his family, his parents and wife and child: Omar's city. I'd somehow got very good at not facing up to the truth, at denying the facts even when they were presented baldly to me. We were in Cairo, and Omar was going to see his wife and his child. I would stay behind with my Lady. "That's good," I said, and I kept my voice light. "I hope it goes well." And Omar was on his way.

It was a long, dark day for me. My head began to ache and the dizziness and sickness I hadn't felt for several months returned. Omar's wife. The phrase repeated itself over and over again in my head: Omar's wife. For a moment—a long, terrifying moment—an abyss opened up before me: I am an unmarried woman, a spinster, a lady's maid, and I have got myself into a position of absolute insecurity. I couldn't be more compromised. Omar is married already; Omar is married to another woman; he has a child. Maybe I should tell her now. Maybe I should tell Lady Duff Gordon that I am going to have Omar Abu Halaweh's child. I will tell her today. I calmed myself down by whispering over and over again, "I am loved, I am loved, Omar loves me, Omar loves me, and my Lady will protect me."

I was in my Lady's room helping her dress for supper: we agreed that Cairo might require a little more formality than Luxor, though my Lady still refused to wear her English clothes. I'd chosen my words carefully; I would start by reminding her of how long we had been together. I would remind her, tactfully of course, of my absolute loyalty. Then I would tell her my wonderful news. And she would be so pleased.

But before I could say anything, Omar returned. We heard him moving through the house. "That will be our man, home from his family," said my Lady. "You know," she added, "I've grown so used to our little threesome, I found myself missing him today." She laughed. "Silly."

"Me too, my Lady," was all I was able to say.

I avoided Omar for the rest of the day, which was much easier in our Cairo house than it would have been in Luxor. I excused myself from supper by claiming my lunch had not agreed with me and attempted to busy myself elsewhere. But I was drawn to the room where they were sitting together to eat; I could not keep away. "How sweet your child sounds!" I heard my Lady say to Omar. And I heard in her tone a wistfulness for her own family.

When Omar entered my room that night I shocked myself by pretending to be asleep. But when I felt him lie down beside me—so cool and clean-smelling—I turned towards him once again. "Did it go well?" I asked.

He sighed heavily. The circumstances weighed on him as well. "Yes. It went well." Before I could speak again he placed his finger across my lips, then moved close, kissing me.

The weather was considerably cooler in Cairo already, which was both a relief and a disappointment; summer had brought out the reptile in me. Suddenly my Lady was ill with a high fever, coughing up phlegm, the pain in her side becoming increasingly acute with each new day. She'd been so well throughout the spring and summer that the illness was like a bad memory, returned to haunt us. I treated her carefully with all the old cures, to no avail; before long she was coughing up blood as well. I inspected my Lady's handkerchiefs, showing the bloody contents to Omar, who turned a pale shade of green. I brought the vial of laudanum out from its inlaid wooden box and dosed my Lady, alternating with the castor oil that Omar and I had made earlier that year, during the village epidemic. The effect of the laudanum was almost instantaneous and she slept more easily for a while; while she slept I wrote a letter to Sir Duff Gordon myself, detailing my concerns for my Lady's health: *The climate in Cairo is not good for her, she cannot linger here for long, we must return to Upper Egypt soon, Sir.* I'd written to Sir Duff Gordon before, at the behest of my Lady, during periods when she was too unwell to write herself, but this was the first time I had written to him with a direct request this urgently expressed: *You must come to Egypt now if you want to see her.* I hoped he would not receive the letter, that he had left England and was en route already.

But our wait continued. Omar was able to find more time to visit his parents and his wife and child, though he went only on the days he felt my Lady was well enough and there were weeks when he didn't go at all. I tried my best not to feel relieved. "I should like to visit your parents, and to meet Mabrouka," my Lady said, and Omar promised to arrange it, but nothing was done to set up the event, and I was relieved about this as well. My Lady needed to conserve her strength for when Sir Alick arrived. For the first time ever her illness was useful—advantageous even—for me.

With my Lady an invalid once more, there was plenty for Omar and me to do; as well as run the Cairo house, we needed to lay in supplies for when we returned to Luxor. In the market one day I was on my own buying almonds and dates—Omar had gone off to purchase eggs—and I was addressing the stallholder in Arabic, as was my custom, discussing which dates were most fresh and sweet, when I became conscious of two women staring at me.

"Look at that one," the younger woman said, in English; she was wearing a bonnet and a stout dress and was perspiring heavily, despite what felt to me a cooler-than-usual day. "What an odd costume."

"She could almost be English," said the older woman, "if you look at her face."

"Very brown-skinned though."

"She's looking at us."

I turned away quickly, my heart pounding, and strained to hear the women, who had lowered their voices. Omar arrived at my side and relieved me of the heavy bags I'd been carrying. Still the women continued to speculate.

"Do you think she's a European, gone native?"

"Oh! To think of marrying one of them "

"Disgusting!'

"Are you finished?" Omar asked, in Arabic.

"*Aywa*," yes, I replied, pulling my *tarhah* up to cover my hair. Then, "I want to buy some cloth; we'll do that another day," in English, loudly. I glanced back at the women, who stared after me dumbly.

The days passed and my Lady's health gradually improved but her mood remained dark. "I'm as homesick for Luxor as I've ever been for England," she said, and I wondered at this, understanding that my Lady felt nervy and anxious over Sir Alick's forthcoming visit. She had achieved an astonishing equilibrium in Luxor, her love for the village and the country, her interest in the people, her good health in the dry air almost balancing out her longing for her family, her children Maurice and Rainey, and her own mother, her dear husband. But her sangfroid vanished as she waited for Sir Alick to arrive. I worried that a visit from him would be as damaging to her health as it was longed for and anticipated.

News came from my Lady's mother, Mrs. Austin, that the idea for a book of my Lady's letters home to England had been accepted by her publisher. Mrs. Austin would select and edit the letters herself, and my Lady was to write a preface. The book would be published in spring, next year. "Let's raise a toast," my Lady said after she had read the letter, though she was lying in bed, and I couldn't remember the last time I had taken a drink of alcohol. "Omar," she said, "make us tea!"

Mr. Hekekyan Bey was a frequent visitor to our Cairo residence. He came bearing gifts, perhaps an ancient amulet for my Lady, a smooth blue scarab for me—pilfered, no doubt, from the Antiquities Service—bestowing these trinkets as he swept into the house in his red fez. He was fond of Omar's lemonade and would drink an entire jug of it as he sat with my Lady, perspiring heavily.

"What do you need, Lady Duff Gordon?" he'd cry. "I can get you anything your heart desires."

"An elephant," my Lady said one afternoon. "Don't you think, Sally, that an elephant is what we actually need?"

Mr. Hekekyan Bey laughed.

I nodded. "Yes, my Lady."

"If we had an elephant with us in Luxor, we could get so much more accomplished!"

Mr. Hekekyan Bey removed his fez, wiped his brow, then popped the hat back on again. "African or Indian?"

"African, of course," said my Lady.

"You tease me, Lady Duff Gordon," he said, "but I would never let you down."

"I know that, Hekekyan," she replied.

FINALLY, IN MID-NOVEMBER, SIR ALICK WAS DUE TO ARRIVE. THIS was the original date he and my Lady had planned to meet; either our letters had not reached him or he was unable to change his plans. We were to go to the port at Boulak to meet him; for the first time in many months my Lady allowed me to fuss over helping her dress. I had fetched her English clothes from the traveling trunk and spent several days repairing and preparing them, but in the end, my Lady said she couldn't face wearing any of it and decided on a pair of harem trousers and a white linen shift, freshly washed and pressed.

I pulled my old brown muslin English dress out of my traveling trunk in honor of the occasion. I put it on but, to my horror, was unable to do up any of the buttons or laces. Panicked, I took all my clothes out of my case and attempted to assemble a decent European-style outfit, with only partial success.

The Cairo house had a mirror in the entrance foyer which both my Lady and I had been carefully avoiding; my Lady stood in front of it now and said, "He won't recognize me. I don't recognize myself! I'm neither English nor Arab; I've become a kind of creature in between. I look a kind of man/woman, don't I?" My Lady laughed and I tried to disagree but it was too true; she was thin and brown and had shorn gray hair and in no way resembled the woman her husband had said goodbye to in Marseilles, the woman in the portrait that Henry Phillips had painted more than a decade previously.

"And look at you, Sally," she said. "You've got fat! Omar's cooking is clearly too good for you." She continued to laugh as she put on her hat, while I felt as though someone had just walked over my grave. There was nothing I could do or say; "fat" was better than "disgraced."

Omar was very excited about meeting Abu Maurice; to refer to Sir Alick as my Lady's husband discomfited his Egyptian sense of propriety. Abu Maurice—father of Maurice—suited my Lady as well. "I've shown you his photograph so many times," she said to him, "I'm sure you know his face as well as do I."

And then, there he was, disembarking from the steamer: my Lady's beloved Alick, looking the same as always, tall and straight-backed, wearing glasses and the type of hat common to English travelers in Egypt. "Too hot," my Lady said, taking it off his head and putting it onto her own, and laughing, "too *serious*. We'll take you to the bazaar, my dear, and we'll kit you out, like an Egyptian, won't we, Omar?" she said over her shoulder as she led her husband away, her arm through his.

But I had seen how Sir Alick had paused when he found his wife in the crowd, paused and taken in her appearance. He paused and, in that pause, he did not smile; a moment passed, a moment as long as a heartbeat, a moment as long as the year and months he had spent wondering if he would ever see his wife again, and here she was, and she was so utterly changed. Then he drew a deep breath and opened his arms and let her remove his hat and smiled a great warm, happy smile and I felt myself hoping, hope against hope, that everything was going to be fine for my Lady, and yet thinking it might not be.

With the arrival of Sir Alick, everything in the household changed again, and the hot dusty complicity between Lady, maid, and manservant was altered, and we lost our easy ways with each other. Omar jostled us all into place: Abu Maurice was the master of the household now; our will would bend to his. We spent a happy week; my Lady made herself into Sir Alick's guide and showed him the famous mosques in the city and the great citadel on the hill, and we rode out into the desert on donkeys and finally visited the Great Pyramids at Giza, which filled me with wonder and glee. My Lady showed off her Arabic and instructed me to show off mine as well. Omar cooked from dawn until dusk every day, preparing his most flavorsome and delicate dishes. Sir Alick smacked his lips together and ate everything he was given and praised our Arabic and our knowledge of Islam and marveled at the wonders of the city.

But then the temperature dropped one night as November drew on and I overheard my Lady saying to Sir Alick that perhaps it was time they traveled to Luxor, there was so much she wanted him to see up the Nile, and the French House—the French House!—how he would love Luxor, and how the people of Luxor would greet him as one of their own and—

Sir Alick interrupted his wife. "I don't think I'll travel with you to Luxor after all, my dear."

I was moving down the corridor, away from the room where Sir Alick and my Lady were talking. I stopped.

"Janet has made plans; we've been invited to visit Suez, where they are building the canal, in a party led by de Lesseps himself. And after viewing the construction, we'll hunt gazelle in the desert. Janet has set it all up; we leave in a few days."

I couldn't move.

It was a few moments before my Lady spoke, and then her voice was low and hoarse. "I'm not well enough for that kind of expedition."

"Oh no, my dear, we weren't expecting you to come."

I moved away, not wanting to hear any more.

Omar had set mint tea and sweetmeats on a tray. I stopped him from interrupting my Lady and Sir Alick. After ten minutes had passed, I took the tea tray into the room myself. Sir Alick was on his feet, looking through the wooden screen that shaded the window. My Lady was sitting at her writing table, clutching a handkerchief but looking entirely composed. "Thank you, Sally," she said, when I put down the tray. "I'll ring if we need anything."

Two days later the Rosses arrived in Cairo, Miss Janet and her husband, Mr. Ross, accompanied by various staff, including my sister, Ellen; they had left their baby behind in Alexandria with his nanny, which seemed a shame given that my Lady had never met her first grandchild. "Oh, Mummy," Miss Janet said, in lieu of a greeting, "what have you done to your hair? And what on earth are you wearing?" She heaved a great sigh and gave her father a look that said, See, didn't I warn you?

Ellen and I were so pleased to see each other that we couldn't stop smiling and we snatched every moment possible away from our duties to sit with each other and talk. I couldn't help but feel uneasy; my secret was on my lips constantly. I hadn't worried about seeing Sir Alick, as I knew he'd benignly ignore me in the way he'd always benignly ignored me. But my sister was different; here was someone who really would look at me.

Ellen was full of gossip about the English people the Rosses knew in Alexandria and she was appalled at the state of my wardrobe, as unimpressed with the native dress I was wearing as Miss Janet was with my Lady's clothes. "You look as though you've been cast in a West End play," she said. "And you've got a bit—well—fat, Sally." She laughed.

I blushed. "I left my stays behind in Luxor, I'm afraid."

Ellen widened her eyes and lowered her face. "I'm scandalized," she said. "Anyway, you look well enough on it. Arab food makes me sick. You're lucky. But listen. I'm going to get married."

"You're what?" I shrieked.

"Shh," Ellen laughed, "keep your voice down."

"To whom?"

"Oh, I don't know yet, but I've decided. I'm going to line some fellows up when we are next in England—either that or I'll nab one of the young men passing through Alexandria."

"But you'll have to leave your position with Mrs. Ross."

"I know that. But I can't be a lady's maid for the rest of my life. I'm not like you, Sally."

I almost told her. I almost told her then, but she kept on talking.

"I want to have my own house one day. I'll find a man with a good position in a good household, or maybe someone who has a trade—or a soldier! We'll live in England—that's what I want. I'm tired of this life. I hate Egypt. It's dirty and hot and crowded and noisy. Don't you hate it, Sally?"

"No," I said, "no, Ellen, I do not."

"Don't you miss England? Don't you miss your trips into London to see the sights? Don't you miss a good strong cup of cocoa by the fire while the winter rains pelt down outside?"

"Winter," I repeated, amused by my sister's unexpected nostalgia. "No. Not one bit. I could stay in Egypt for the rest of my life."

"Lady Duff Gordon is very lucky to have you, Sal, I hope she knows that. There's not many Englishwomen who'd be willing to bury themselves in the sand like you have, for the sake of a mistress and her health."

"It's easy for me," I said. And I stopped at that, full of guilt over what I was not telling my sister. We frowned at each other for a moment but then couldn't keep ourselves from smiling.

THE NEXT DAY THE ROSS PARTY DEPARTED, WITH SIR ALICK IN TOW.

My Lady, Omar, and I were left behind in Cairo. She decided we would stay put and wait for Sir Alick to return; she didn't say why, but I knew it was because she hoped her husband would change his mind about Luxor after he'd been hunting, that he'd fall in love with Egypt and decide he must see more of the country. The temperature continued to drop and my Lady's health faltered once more. The days seemed endless, and it was not a joyful time; we were caught between missing our Luxor life and hoping Sir Alick would return early. My Lady sent Omar off in the afternoons to sit in the coffeehouses and see his old Cairo friends. And, of course, to spend time with his family.

The days were hard for me; my Lady's spirits were so low she was not good company and, what's more, she did not want to be kept company but preferred to pass her time on her own, which was highly unusual, if not unprecedented. Omar was off with his friends—discussing politics, no doubt, in a coffeehouse full of men like him, all worried about being overheard by the wrong person, a government official or a member of the Khedive's police force, but unable to stop themselves from defining and refining their strongly held opinions nonetheless.

And, of course, he visited his family. I found I could not bring myself to think about this; it made me feel too alone. I forced myself to ask him questions when he returned home in the evening: "What are your parents like, Omar? Tell me about your mother." I wanted him to believe I was calm and poised. However, this pretense of mine didn't stretch as far as to allow me to ask questions about his wife and child.

"I will take you to meet them," he said, but then he ducked his head in the way he did when offering to do something he did not actually want to do, "whether or not my Lady can join us."

I shook my head. I had to stay with my Lady when Omar was gone, she could not be left on her own, and, truth be told, the idea of meeting his family was alarming. When he was with them I felt a rising tide of desperation and unhappiness and an awful sense of foreboding that I had to push hard to make go away. When he came to my room after a day away, we were awkward and slow and shy with one another. I could not bring myself to ask any further questions for fear of what might be revealed to me. Our conversation stumbled and tripped and we crashed into each other, but then we stopped talking and took solace in another way. If anything, our passion burned more intensely on those nights, our desire mixed with my confusion and anxiety. My life felt more constricted and circumscribed in those weeks in Cairo than it had for a long time.

And when Sir Alick did return, it transpired that he had been unwell during the expedition. He looked haggard and worn, as though he'd been on a forced march through the desert with the indentured *fellahin* instead of accompanying a grand party. My Lady and Sir Alick spent many hours behind closed doors, their voices low, talking, and neither Omar nor I were any the wiser; we worked extra hard on keeping the house running smoothly as a way of dispelling our worries. I could see that Sir Alick's curiosity about Egypt and the life his wife had adopted here had turned to distaste; he did not like Omar's cooking, he did not relish the bazaar, he complained about being woken up by the call to prayer, he claimed Cairo was crumbling and inconvenient. "Yes, it is," I heard my Lady say, "but that's not the point."

Another week, and he was on his way back to England. When they said farewell, no one said what was plainly on everyone's mind: this might be the last time husband and wife would meet. We knew it would be a considerable time before Sir Alick could afford to make the journey to Egypt again, if he was so inclined. And as for her two younger children, Master Maurice and Miss Rainey, no one dared to mention them, to ask if my Lady hoped ever to see them again. The truth was that she might never be well enough to travel to England. But she told Sir Alick she planned to return next summer and went as far as to begin to plan some kind of family reunion in a spa town, perhaps Germany? They made their goodbyes lightly and turned away from each other as if they would meet again in a few days, not as if it might be the end of what had been, in better times, a loving marriage.

AFTER THAT, MY LADY WANTED TO GET BACK TO LUXOR straight-away; it took Omar a while to secure a boat and, when he did, the price was much higher than anticipated, but there was no choice in the matter. It was cold, and my Lady's spirits were low, and we needed to be on our way "home," she said, and I heard my mistress trying to convince herself that there was such a place for her now. We traveled as quickly as possible, and my Lady said that she felt a little better with each mile. It was as though she was attempting to slough off and forget all the hopes she had had for Sir Alick's visit as we moved farther and farther south, away from Cairo.

PART
2

DEATH

10

WE SAT BY THE OPEN WINDOW OF MY ROOM IN THE FRENCH House in the evening, to watch the sun set on the Nile. It was January—we'd been back in Luxor for only a few days—and the nights were chilly still, so I wrapped us up together in my heavy patterned shawl. Having him there with me was the most tremendous feeling: I felt warm and soft and tired and sore and shocked and bewildered and happy, so wonderfully happy, all at the same time. My baby—even now these two little words give me a start of surprise and wonder. My baby in my arms: nothing—I'll say it again—*nothing* could mean more to me. My baby was bonny and hungry, with dimpled hands, brown eyes, black hair, pale skin, and round cheeks. He was clean and swaddled, and his hand came to rest on my breast as he fed. He nibbled at me, tiny and strong. Our room smelled of sweet milk and sleep and that extraordinary, indescribable smell—baby.

Omar brought in a tray of food he had prepared specially, things he said would build up my stamina, everything smooth and pure and clean, nothing too spicy or sharp. He leaned close to kiss my hair and I caught his hand in mine and he smiled. Since that night on the Nile when my baby was born I had felt my motherlessness most acutely; having lost my own mother when I was twelve, I had no idea how to be a mother myself. But Omar moved around the room quickly, as he always does, swift and precise, reassuring, putting everything in its place. "The washerwoman will come in the morning," he said, and he went to fetch Ahmed to help with the great pile of laundry the baby and I had accumulated. "Don't move," he said when he returned; he knew I felt compelled to help even before I realized it myself. No one had ever taken care of me before; I was not accustomed to having things done for me. They filled the basket, and Ahmed dragged it away. Omar came to sit beside me.

And then we heard her. Her voice traveled through the house faintly, "Omar? Omar!" I smiled. "Why don't I go to her?" I said. "I'll take the baby with me."

"Don't move," he said, again. "Everything is fine." And he made his way through the French House to my Lady. I leaned back on my cushion and pulled my shawl close and looked down on my baby, the most beautiful child in Egypt, and he opened his eyes and closed them again, and we were at complete peace.

I didn't know it yet, but that peace was not mine, and would never be mine, to enjoy. And out of nowhere, that evening, I suddenly thought, I suddenly found myself thinking, Everything is fine? But why would he say that? Why would he need to say that? Everything *is* fine. It must be.

I WAS SO PLEASED TO RETURN TO THE FRENCH HOUSE, TO THE LOVELY rooms, the beautiful garden, that I was deaf to what was going on around me. On the first day back, I settled the baby in my room and was able to help with the unpacking: a great horde of village children had greeted the *dahabieh* when it landed and they were now running back and forth from the *dahabieh* through the village, transporting everything to the house. "One cup," Omar said, "one spoon at a time." It felt good to be up and moving around, working once again. My Lady had been taken by a happy greeting party

straight from the boat to Mustafa Agha's house, where she was to
be fed and watered and kept away from the chaos. I sorted out my
Lady's room for her, knowing she'd be glad to find all her familiar
things around her as I set them out—her hairbrush, her hand mirror, the kohl she sometimes played at wearing around her eyes, her
writing table, her papers, her books. Little Ahmed was overjoyed
at our return and kept sneaking into my room to peer at the baby,
then leaping out into the salon and dancing madly. Already all of
Luxor knew about the child. One of the villagers appeared at the
door with a woven basket that she said was for the baby to sleep
in; it was decorated prettily with fine white cotton and lace. The
woman watched while I placed the sleeping baby in it, then she
exclaimed over his pale skin, and blessed me before leaving.

"Wait till my Lady sees!" I said to Omar once the villager had
left, "wait till she sees him, a little Egyptian prince in his basket!"

Omar did not reply. I looked at him but he would not look at
me.

I hadn't spoken to my mistress since the night the baby came
into the world and, truth be told, I hadn't thought to worry. I was
occupied with the baby and sleeping and eating, and while we
were traveling Omar would not let me get up from my bed for
more than a few minutes every day. He tended me and the baby
and our every need, and he tended my Lady as well. I wasn't thinking of anything beyond the baby and the pains and sensations of
my body. I had had a good birth—I had attended enough bad ones
to know it—and I had not sustained any permanent injury, but I
was battered and felt as though I'd come through a great trial. But
the baby! There he was for me to hold, for me to care for, for me
to wonder at, for me to share with my beloved Omar. And that's
what we did for long moments on the *dahabieh*, we huddled close
together in my cabin and smiled at our baby and talked about what
life would be like once we were back in Luxor, once we were
married.

We chose the name Abdullah for our child, the name of the father of the Prophet Mohammed, Abdullah Abu Halaweh. "And that makes you Abu Abdullah Abu Halaweh," I said to Omar at the time, laughing and poking him in the chest with my finger. He grabbed my hand and pulled me to him, kissing me.

Now we were back in Luxor, I still had not seen my Lady. All the fears and worries we had discussed during the past few months came rushing back to me. Where was she? Where was my Lady? Why did Omar discourage me from taking Abdullah to her? Why had she not been to visit me? In my cozy fug aboard the *dahabieh* I had expected to take up my duties as lady's maid once we returned to the French House; in fact, I was looking forward to spending my days with my Lady once again. I had pictured Abdullah in his basket on the floor of her room, my Lady looking up from her writing to coo at him from time to time, while I bustled about the place, a model of maternal efficiency. When he woke and cried out, my Lady would pick him up and bounce him in her lap and then carry him through the house to me. Abdullah would be a most welcome, a most venerated member of our Luxor household, our Egyptian family. A baby and, best of all, a boy.

But this picture I had created was beginning to crack in its frame.

ABDULLAH WAS SOUND ASLEEP IN MY ARMS, THE SUN HAD SET, AND the starlit night was upon us. I tucked him into his basket and lit a lamp in the far corner on the little table I used as a writing desk. I hadn't written to Ellen in Alexandria about the baby yet; she knew nothing of him, despite the fact that I had seen her less than two months past. I would write a letter and tell her everything.

I look back on our time in Cairo that autumn with a kind of amazement. There I was, almost fully at term, and no one noticed. Not even Ellen. Like her mistress, Mrs. Ross, my sister did not approve of the way that my Lady and I were living, did not approve of the way we dressed, the way we'd adopted local customs, the way I shopped with Omar in the market, the way we ate our meals together with my Lady seated on the floor around a silver tray, and she was blinded by her disapproval from truly seeing me. Even my Lady's new English doctor, Doctor Patterson, who saw me in Cairo just a few days before Abdullah was born, did not come near to guessing; he was more concerned with my Lady's health and making sure our medicine box was up to date, and rightly so.

I began my letter: *Dear Ellen, I have something to tell you, the most wonderful . . .* , but I could not continue. Why had my Lady not been to see me and the baby? I knew her too well; she must be longing to see us, she must be dying of curiosity, she will want to know everything. It had been more than a fortnight since that night on the Nile, nearly three weeks. Suddenly my doubt had grown to dis-ease, blossoming as rapidly as jealousy. I checked that Abdullah was still sleeping soundly and left my room.

Omar was coming down the corridor; he was carrying a candle and it flickered in the draft. The house was full of drafts, given its many glassless windows and doorless doorways; on windy evenings we could not keep any of our lamps alight.

"Is my Lady awake still?" I kept my voice low though I knew it wasn't late. "I thought I might speak to her."

"No" was all Omar said, and he said it wearily.

"What do you mean, no?" I asked; I was still tired enough from the birth and the journey to be easily pricked and annoyed and to feel justified in wanting to have things my way.

"My Lady has said . . ." He hesitated, and I felt my heart sink, as though it knew already, well before the rest of me. "My Lady has asked . . ." He paused again, trying to find the words. "She has given me instructions for the household."

I didn't understand.

"I am in charge of the household now."

I took a step back. It was my household. Even in Egypt, where we were often on uncertain territory, it was my household; I was Lady Duff Gordon's maid and thus, in the absence of an English housekeeper, responsible for the smooth running of the household. I was in charge here, answerable to no one, apart from my Lady.

But, of course, everything had changed. Omar was the father of my child. We had plans to marry. He would be my husband; he would have dominion over me. But it was my household. He was an Egyptian. I was English.

"What do you mean?" I didn't want to feel this way.

Omar sighed, as though his new role weighed on him heavily.

"My Lady has said . . ." Again he stopped, and turned away to fuss over the candle, which was burning a little blackly.

"What has she said?" I asked, my voice harsher than I intended.

"You are to stay in your room with Abdullah. This is what she has said."

"But I am feeling quite well and restored already. I can tell her that myself."

"Sally," Omar said, taking my hand, turning me around, guiding me back into my room. "Listen to me."

I did not like to see him looking so grave.

He kept his voice low. "My Lady does not want to see you, or the child."

I was too blasted by his words to reply. My Lady does not want to see me, or my child. My Lady will not see me. I have been by her side for years and years, but my Lady will not see me.

"She does not want—she believes that . . ." He stuttered and stopped.

I gasped out loud when I saw that he was weeping.

"She blames you entirely." He swallowed hard and forced himself to speak. "She will not listen to me. She will not allow me to defend you. She says you have corrupted me; she says you have led me astray."

Now I could see that Omar was angry as well.

"I have told her that I am a man and that I knew what I was doing and that I take full responsibility. That we have made our plans. That we will marry. But she will not hear me, Sally. She will not let me speak in your defense; she has used terrible words; she has said terrible things about you to me."

"She will not see me?"

"No."

I remained confused. We should speak in English. Or were we speaking English already? "When we are married . . ."

He shook his head. "It will make no difference to how she feels."

And if I thought that was the worst he could tell me, I was wrong.

I thought, my Lady isn't thinking straight, she can't be. She is so full of anger and sadness and fear over losing her own family that she can't allow me to be happy in this way. But she'll come round, she'll calm down, and she'll remember that it's me, her faithful servant, her devoted lady's maid, Sally Naldrett, her Sally; she will remember herself, her good strong fair self, and then she'll remember me. She'll see Abdullah, and she'll love him; how could anyone fail to love him? She'll see the baby and then she'll know she must do what is right. That's what I thought. That's what I kept on thinking.

"She wants you to leave the French House."

"To leave?"

"Not now, not right away, it is too early, the baby is too young. But she does not want to see you, and then, in two or three months, when you are both strong and fit, she has said you must leave. Abdullah must go to my wife Mabrouka in Cairo and you must return to England."

In that moment, my life was ruined. With her words, relayed to me by my lover, I was destroyed.

11

I NEVER THOUGHT I COULD BE SO HAPPY. I NEVER THOUGHT I COULD be so frightened of what the future would bring. To feel both these things at the same time exhausted me.

That night on the boat my Lady helped us bring Abdullah into the world and she was as gentle and skilled and unhurried as any midwife; when first she arrived in my cabin I forgot the torment for a moment and felt ashamed to have my Lady see me so plainly, my nightdress shoved up around my shoulders and me there, screaming, but she did not blink once, nor even hesitate, and I felt a surge of relief almost as profound as the waves of pain passing through my body. It will be all right, I thought, my Lady is here now, my Lady can deal with almost anything.

It was Christmas Eve, and a dark and moonless night on a long, dull, unpopulated stretch of the river. All day I'd been feeling peculiar, itchy almost, heavy, restless, and tetchy. Of course, I didn't recognize what was happening: I was too stupid, too bovine with pleasure, as though I might stay pregnant forever and be happy that way. And neither did Omar, despite the fact that we had prepared ourselves for this to happen while we were on the *dahabieh*: we had laid in secret supplies; we had readied ourselves like good midwives; I had coached Omar in all I knew about childbirth and labor. It began in the early evening and I kept it to myself, walking up and down the boat, pursuing every task I could think of, until every fixture and fitting on the *dahabieh* was shining. I saw to my Lady, got her ready for bed, and went back to my pacing, until Omar came to ask me why I wasn't coming to bed. It was late, and my Lady had been asleep for several hours, she was sleeping heavily at that time, during the day as well as at night, her lungs like lead, the ache in her side continuous once again.

It stepped up then, the pain; it came upon me as a full-force gale comes upon a ship at sea. We were in my cabin and I was trying to keep quiet, I was working hard to control myself, to prevent myself from screaming as I was battered by the waves. But after a few long hours—how long, I have no idea—I could no longer hold it back and I was transformed, as all women are transformed at this time, into my animal self, raw and beyond sensibility. I know I made a most terrible racket. And Omar was frightened. He has never admitted as much but I know it must be true because, though I was not aware of it at the time, he went to fetch my Lady. Midwife was not a role he had performed in the past, and all our talk and planning proved to be feeble and wrongheaded when it came to the real thing. There came a point when he needed help with helping me, and he went and woke up my Lady.

It would have taken her a while to surface. Even if she'd heard my cries far off, muffled, she was sleeping too soundly for the sound to register fully. She would have turned in her bed—What was that, an animal at the riverbank?—then rolled back into sleep. But she was forced up again before long: What is it? And then, right then, Omar began to shout "My Lady! My Lady!" and he pounded on the door of her cabin with his fists. She got out of bed and wrapped her shawl around her shoulders and opened the door, where she found Omar, distraught, shivering. "*Sitti* Duff Gordon! Come! Sally needs you! Come with me!"

My Lady rushed behind Omar down the narrow passageway and they entered my cabin, Omar first, my Lady behind him, fearful of what she might see.

What she saw was not what she feared, but something very different. I know this now. Something much worse.

She saw me, in the throes of labor. Her maid, Sally Naldrett, spinster, age of at least thirty, crying out, hunched up on the bed, sheets and nightdress streaked with blood, wild with pain and concentration.

"Help me, my Lady," Omar said, stronger now, knowing I needed him to be strong for me. "Help me deliver my child."

And that was how my Lady found out that I was pregnant. That was how my Lady found out about Omar and me.

THE REST OF OUR JOURNEY DID NOT GO WELL. THE DAYS PASSED LIKE a long slow convoy of *dahabieh*; they slipped by quietly, one at a time. It was winter, but the afternoon sun was still warming and my Lady continued to spend most afternoons outside on the deck of the boat, watching Egypt slide by. The *fellahin* labored in the fields and brought their produce to sell in the villages. A millennium passed and it looked as though nothing had changed. But, in fact, change was rapid, on the land, for the people, and on our *dahabieh*. Nothing remained the same.

LATER OMAR TOLD ME THAT WHEN HE WENT TO MY LADY'S CABIN bearing fresh water and a clean basin the morning after the birth of our child, he apologized for being late. "I am sorry, my Lady," he said, "once I knew Sally and the baby were fine, I fell asleep. I slept for much longer than I intended."

"That's all right, Omar," said my Lady; she had dressed and readied herself for the day without my help for the first time since—well, it was beyond remembering. When he told me this I felt both shame and sorrow. "I'm quite capable," she added.

"Of course, my Lady."

"I'll take my breakfast on the deck."

"Yes, my Lady."

"One of those eggs that we picked up the other day." She waved a hand to dismiss him, but he was not familiar with this gesture, he told me: "Like this," he said, and he waved his hand airily, and I almost laughed at the look of indignity on his face. He stood there, he said, waiting. "That's all, Omar," my Lady said, "thank you."

He tried again later that day. "He's perfect," he said when he was helping my Lady get ready to go to bed, a task made awkward by the fact that it was the first time he had performed it.

"Who?" said my Lady.

"The baby," Omar said, and I imagine he smiled so sweetly that my Lady could not help but smile in return.

But she tucked the smile away quickly. "Oh yes," she said, "the child."

"Would you like me to bring him to you?"

My Lady cleared her throat. "No. Thank you, Omar, but no. I don't want you to bring him to me."

Omar was puzzled. "Sally will rest. I can carry out her duties for her; I don't mind. I'm more than—"

"I have no doubt that you can do Sally's job as well as your own, Omar. That's not what I'm saying. I don't want to see the baby."

Omar stood still, looking at her.

"Is that clear?"

"Yes, my Lady."

"Thank you, Omar. Good night."

It was Christmas Day. Omar had forgotten, which was not surprising, and I, of course, had forgotten as well. Neither of us thought to mark the day in any way, and my Lady did not say a word about it to Omar. She must have been very tired after the hours she had spent with us in the night. If she thought of crying, she probably felt too worn out and, besides, that wasn't her way. I imagine she felt quite ill; she hadn't been well, and now this shock on top of everything. Finding me racked with the pain of child-birth on a boat on the Nile on Christmas Eve; this shocked her but it was not the worst of it. She had seen women labor before, she had given birth herself, and she knew what it was: a horrifying, unruly, and dangerous mess of hope and agony. But to not know, to have not been told, to have been lied to, by me, Sally Naldrett, her loyal maid—it was too much. She could not abide not know-ing. I think this was what caused her the most pain. How could I, her constant companion these past few years, her devoted servant for more than a dozen—how could I betray her confidence in this way? How could she have not known, not guessed? I think this, as much as any of the deception, hurt her pride. How could she have not seen what I was up to? How could I have not told her? The whole thing, the entire *affair*, as she would have it, took place right under her nose and she did not catch so much as a whiff of it. This was too much. It was my Lady to whom people turned when they were in difficulty—servants, friends, and family alike. At home in the Gordon Arms it was my Lady who was expected to step in and sort out whatever problems the staff were having—personal, finan-cial, or otherwise. That girl, Laura, the young one, who got herself into trouble in Esher just before we departed for Egypt, I told her to go to my Lady for help, and she did. And my Lady helped her. My Lady found her a place in a household in Esher—a lowly place, it has to be said, a humble household where she would be the only servant—but they agreed to take her in, along with her child. That young girl went to my Lady for help, and my Lady gave it freely. In Luxor the villagers came to her when they needed advice and assistance; they came to her with their sick children, with their dis-putes, their trials. People came to my Lady for help; they told her everything, all their troubles, all their woes. They asked for her advice, they asked for her assistance, more often than not they asked her to intervene in their lives. They didn't lie to her; they didn't go out of their way to hide the truth. They didn't conspire to hide an entire pregnancy!

And on finding me in labor, well, there was nothing else for it: my Lady had rolled up her sleeves and helped her dragoman deliver his child. She held my hand and reassured me calmly; she told me to shout out, shout out the pain. She woke the *reis* and shifted the boatmen into action, delivering hot water, clean clothes, hot drinks, clean sheets, a sharp knife that had been sterilized in the fire. She was not surprised to find me as sturdy and stoic in labor as I was in the rest of my life. She told me so, and it is, in fact, the last thing I remember her saying to me when I was at my lowest in my labor: "I'm not surprised, Sally Naldrett, to find you capable of this." And when the baby finally battled its way into the world, my Lady placed him in my arms and declared him fit and hale.

"I'm not surprised, Sally Naldrett, to find you capable of this." At the time I heard one meaning. Now I hear another.

It was too much; it was too much to expect her to bear this turn of events. To expect her to take it, like everything else, in her stride: illness, years of it, dogged illness that couldn't be shaken off or willed away, and then exile, voluntary exile—well, it was either that or death—far away from England and all she held dear, her friends, her children, her husband, her mother. At times on our travels I fancied us a tribe of thieves, my Lady, Omar, and me. We were stealing time, creating our own world, new lives for us all together, in Luxor, on the Nile, in Egypt. We three. But I smashed all this; I destroyed my Lady's peace. It was an illusion all along and I exposed it thus, irrevocably.

That night, once my Lady was confident that mother and child were both fine, she went back to her cabin. She stripped off her bloody clothes and washed my blood off her hands, arms, and face.

She did this without my help, without the assistance of her devoted lady's maid. Then she lay down, exhausted. But I imagine that she was unable to sleep.

The time with Sir Alick in Cairo had gone badly. She had so longed for his visit; she had had such plans and hopes and ideas; we had talked about it endlessly. The things she would show him! The conversations they would have! He would love Egypt as she did, he would love Luxor even more, she was convinced. To be with him once again, her husband, the man she had married when she was eighteen and had loved ever since, all those years, all those happy years. And then his visit was spoiled. Sir Alick did not fall in love with Egypt. He did not love Luxor even more: he did not travel with my Lady to Luxor when she asked him to. And she fell ill once again, of course she did, her lungs growing tighter and tighter, the pain in her side like being licked by flames, she told me so, the coughing and spitting and the blood—years of it, blighting everything. Sir Alick's visit was a failure, a dismal failure, their goodbye at Boulak a melancholy end to a miserable time. My Lady thought of her son, Maurice, almost a man, and her baby Rainey, five years old—nearly six—at home in England, without their mother, without any prospect of seeing their mother; she thought of them, and she was bereft. She turned away from me once Sir Alick was gone and, I could see, she was immolated. Buried alive. Here she was, in Egypt, alone, without her children, without her husband, without her family; Miss Janet was in Alexandria but, frankly, the distance between them was so great, my Lady's daughter might as well have been back in England.

And perhaps then—I don't know, I couldn't see into her mind, even though I once felt as though I did so on a daily, hourly basis— my Lady had a thought that had never occurred to her before, a thought that shocked her as deeply as the birth of my baby: it might have been better to have stayed in England to die with those she loved around her, than to have come here to live out her Egyptian afterlife. It might have been better to die. And that thought was enough to destroy what remained of her equanimity, to annihilate the picture that my Lady had painted for herself and the world of the sweet harmony of her Egyptian domestic life. That, and the baby.

And whose fault is it? my Lady asked herself, though it wasn't a real question because she knew the answer already: it was my fault. Sally Naldrett. Me.

I SOMETIMES WONDER NOW IF THINGS WOULD HAVE TURNED OUT differently if we had told her about the child early on, from the beginning. Perhaps then she would have had time to become accustomed to the idea, to find a way to reconcile herself to the situation. If Omar and I had married early on and not kept our secret, perhaps the disaster could have been averted and, as the months passed, my Lady could have joined us in our happy anticipation. Perhaps then she would have come round, she could have been part of our conspiracy, instead of feeling conspired against. Abdullah's birth came at the worst possible moment, a lonely Christmasless Christmas Eve on the Nile, just days after my Lady had made her farewell to Sir Alick. But it seems likely to me now that her reaction would have been the same, no matter when she discovered the truth of my—our—situation. And if we had told her then, in the spring, our time together might have been cut even more cruelly short, and Omar might not have been nearby at the time of the birth of his child. That was why we never did find a way to tell her; we knew inside our hearts that the risk was very great. So we deceived her, and now the consequences were ours—mine—to bear.

THE JOURNEY UP THE NILE AFTER THE BIRTH OF THE BABY WAS SLOW; when we crossed the invisible line that divides Lower and Upper

Egypt, at Asyut, the wind deserted us almost entirely. In my cabin, we felt becalmed, Abdullah and I, along with the *dahabieh*. One afternoon the crew were forced to get out and tow the boat with a rope along the riverbank. I could hear their shouts and the *reis* issuing sharp orders from his place on deck; the baby was asleep so I decided to go up, stretch my limbs, and see what there was to see. I came out at the stern of the boat, and I could see my Lady up ahead, in her seat beneath the canopy, the *reis* at her side. Omar was at his pots and pans below in the galley.

I stood and watched the men, envying their brown-limbed strength; the sunshine was warming; as always, it warmed the aches in my body. I'd speak to my Lady in a moment or two, but for now it felt good to be in the open air. I stared down at the still, green Nile, when something in the water caught my attention. Next to the hull, midship, something had risen to the surface. For a moment I thought it was a crocodile.

It was a woman. A dead woman. Silver bracelets glittered on her arms, which were raised up and stiffened as though in self-defense. Her knees were drawn up as well, and she was naked, and her breasts floated on the water beneath her young face. "*Beni Adam!*" the men shouted, spotting her only a moment after I had. The *reis* immediately offered a prayer. "God have mercy on her."

"What on earth . . . ?" I heard my Lady exclaim. "Is she dead?" But of course we could see she was.

The *reis* replied, "Murdered, most likely. She still has her bracelets, so she has not been robbed. Let us pray for her father."

"The poor girl," said my Lady, and I wanted to rush to her side, "why would anyone want to murder her?"

One of the boatmen was attempting to push the woman away from the *dahabieh* with a pole; the body spun round in the water, making an ugly sucking noise. I began to feel faint. I was relieved that no one had noticed me. I'd go back down to my cabin to rest. But before I could go I heard the *reis* speak. "We are in the Saeed, Upper Egypt, *Sitti*. Most likely the woman was an adulteress, she has blackened her father's name—his honor—and he has been forced to strangle her. Poor man."

"An adulteress," said my Lady. "I see."

There was a strange note in my Lady's voice; I heard it and I thought, that woman in the water is me.

I gave an involuntary shriek. "My Lady," I said, and I began to move along the ship towards her. Just then, Omar came up from the galley, cutting off my progress. He placed a shawl around my shoulders and I slumped against him as he murmured to me, herding me back to my cabin, steering me away from my mistress, though of course I did not realize this at the time.

That night I was restless, unable to sleep, the dead woman bobbing in the water before my eyes, that word, "adulteress," repeating itself over and over again. I was an adulteress. Omar already had a wife and a child, though it suited me to ignore this fact. We planned to marry: Egyptian law would allow us to do so; he would not have to divorce his first wife. But for the time being, I was an adulteress. Would my punishment be as harsh as that of the woman we had seen?

"Keep her from my sight, Omar."

In Luxor, late at night, Omar told me about the conversation that took place between himself and my Lady on our *dahabieh* that night.

"Pardon, my Lady?" Omar was tidying her cabin, one of the many duties that had previously fallen to me.

"Keep her away from me. I don't want to see her."

"But, my Lady—"

"Don't answer back to me!"

Omar took a step away from my Lady and straightened. She had never spoken to him this way.

"I do not want to see her."

"Yes, my Lady."

"Thank you."

Omar nodded.

"That will be all." Again, that unfamiliar gesture of dismissal. Omar bowed and left the cabin.

A few days later, Omar told me, he took it upon himself to plead our case.

"We plan to marry."

"You are already married!"

"Egyptian law allows me to take more than one wife, my Lady."

"You will not marry her. What will become of Mabrouka?"

"I can carry out my duties as the husband of two wives; this will not be difficult for me." Omar kept his voice low, while my Lady's rose and rose.

"She came to Egypt in service to me; it is I who will determine her fate. She is my employee."

"I will marry her, my Lady."

"Omar, she has tricked you into this. She is clever and quick and she has taken advantage of your—your kindness. You do not understand European women. I will not give my permission."

Omar listened, his head bowed as though in obedience. After a moment, he looked up at his mistress. "I will marry her," he said. "I will be father to my child." Then he left the room quickly.

I don't doubt that Omar's stand made my Lady furious. No member of her staff had ever defied her in this way. The next time he dared to raise the subject of our marriage, my Lady gave up any pretense of calm and shouted at him. "She has tricked you, Omar! And she has tricked me as well. She will not get away with this deceit. She must leave. She can't stay with us in the French House. The French House, where I have been so happy. The French House, where I will live out my ruined life in peace."

"I've made a plan," she said, "I've written to Janet already. I'll pay Sally's passage. Yes. I will send her away. I will send Sally Naldrett back to England."

And Omar? What did he say? He said nothing. But he would find a way to change my Lady's mind. "I will find a way to keep you in Egypt," he said, as he held me in his arms in the French House, after having told me that my Lady was determined to send me away.

12

I SPENT LONG HOURS ALONE IN MY ROOM WITH ABDULLAH, WORRY-ing. Long hours—pacing with anxiety or sunk into myself, de-spairing. For Omar's sake, I tried to keep a brave face, but it was difficult. To tell the truth, I felt as though I was twelve years old, I felt as though my parents had only just died, I felt as though I had been abandoned all over again. Abdullah distracted me, with his warm little body, with his hunger, his need, and Omar would come to see me late at night. But I always ended up prodding him for information, wanting him to tell me it was going to be all right, willing him to say once and for all, "Listen. Everything is fine." But he did not. He could not. And after an hour or two with me and Abdullah, he'd show his impatience with my questions and slink away, back to my Lady.

I COULD SEE HER IN MY MIND'S EYE, ON THE FAR SIDE OF THE FRENCH House. Omar told me she was unwell, although in fact her health was much improved from what it had been on the *dahabieh* before Christmas. "She's not well," he said, and I took that to mean she'd gone a little bit crazy, like me; it seemed I couldn't stop myself from sharing things with my Lady. I could picture her, with great clarity, lying back on her divan, next to her writing table. Her papers are in disarray, and she has spilled ink across her stack of clean note-paper. She can't get on with anything or anyone; she is making no progress with the preface for her book of letters—the book that is due to be published in just a few weeks—and she must send something to her mother as soon as possible. Her head hurts and her side aches, but worse than that, she is annoyed. Very annoyed. The shutters are open; she wants them closed. The fire in her room needs stoking. She is hungry and cold and thirsty and uncomfortable. Nothing is as it should be, not in the French House, not in all of Egypt.

"She calls you 'That wretched girl and her bawling baby,'" Omar told me. "'Omar!'" he mimics her. "'Omar!' she says, 'Come here.' I go to her. Of course I go, I am loyal. But then I ask her when we will be allowed to marry."

My Lady was surprised to find Omar so obstinate, so determined, on the subject of our marriage. "Why?" she asked him. "Why persist with this foolishness? You are risking everything you have worked for. You cannot marry without my permission. And I will not give it."

"She will be my wife. Abdullah is my child," Omar replied.

"You have made a promise to her," my Lady said, "and it's beneath your dignity to break it. You are afraid you will lose face. This is Sally's cleverness at work," she said. "She has you trapped, we both know it. This was her plan from the very beginning."

Omar told me he did not reply to this. She spoke of his dignity, but it was beneath his dignity to argue with his mistress. She could batter him with words, but he would not bend. I loved him all the more when I saw the truth in that. It did not occur to me that he might see marriage to me as useful in any way, as part of his plans for his future, an addition to his lengthy list of skills and accomplishments in life.

❧

I DID NOT DARE TO HOPE. I HAD NOT BEEN RAISED TO DARE TO HOPE for anything beyond my fated lot in life. I could have become sour and dour and long-faced but for Abdullah; he lifted my spirits over and over again each and every day. I had never thought I would have a child; even when I was pregnant I had not understood what having a child would mean to me. I loved Omar with an unexpected passion that opened the world, but I loved Abdullah in a way that was larger, fiercer, more complete than the world itself could ever be. Lady Duff Gordon's decree—that I was to give up Abdullah to Omar's first wife and take myself off to England—was like a death sentence to me.

And then one day at the end of January Omar entered my room and said, "Sally, my love. Tomorrow. We will be married!" His words sent me swirling around the room with Abdullah; we did a little dance together before I passed him to his father and the three of us did a quick turn. Married, at last: a small victory. Perhaps this was the first step towards finding a way to ward off my fate as determined by my Lady.

On the day itself there were no musicians and there was no singing, no procession through the village, no sisters and cousins to paint my hands and feet with henna, to help me hold up my veil. Sheikh Yusuf performed the ceremony in the front room of the French House, Lady Duff Gordon our reluctant witness. I wore a red shawl that I had draped over my head, copied from the country weddings that my Lady and I had attended together. Afterwards Omar served the meal himself. He had filled one corner of the salon with cushions for the baby and me; Sheikh Yusuf and my Lady sat and conversed on the other side of the room.

Sheikh Yusuf, though unfailingly polite, was clearly puzzled by the lack of ceremony. "Why has no one else been invited?" he asked my Lady, and he smiled across the room at me. I, of course, did not dare to speak.

"This was what they wanted," my Lady replied, "given the inauspicious arrival of the child prior to the wedding day."

I was shocked by how easily she lied. Sheikh Yusuf took his cue and asked no further questions. I continued to sit in silence and my Lady did her best not to look at me while she discussed village matters with the young sheikh.

Later that day Mustafa Agha arrived with his gift of a slaughtered lamb, prepared, cooked, and displayed most beautifully, but by that time I had retreated to my room with the baby, and Omar served tea to my Lady and her friend as though nothing had taken place, as though it was not his wedding day.

"The baby will go and live with Omar's wife Mabrouka," my Lady informed Mustafa Agha, who puffed on the *narguile* comfortably.

He nodded. "And Sally will also be welcomed into the house of Omar's father."

"No," my Lady said. "She will leave the child in Cairo and return to England."

"No no no," Mustafa clucked as though they were having a minor misunderstanding. "Omar's first wife will welcome the second: the mothers of my children have done the same. The Egyptian household is expansive. They'll be fine."

"It is not fine," my Lady replied.

Omar told me that Mustafa Agha put down his pipe as my Lady continued to speak.

"Sally has disgraced herself; she has disgraced her family; she will not be allowed to ruin Omar as well. She will return to England."

Mustafa Agha shrugged. He gave her a look, a look that meant that Mustafa Agha thought the *Frangi* were beyond understanding, even those as sympathetic as Lady Duff Gordon. He resumed smoking. She laughed lightly and tried to pretend it was all precisely as it should be. Omar took himself back to the kitchen.

After Mustafa Agha was gone, my Lady spoke to Omar one more time. "I agreed to your marriage in an effort to ward off further scandal in the village. I will continue to live here and I do not intend Sally Naldrett's disgrace to become my own."

Omar had no reply. But that night, our wedding night, he came to my room immediately after settling my Lady and did not leave again until after sunrise.

My Lady did her utmost to make sure my marriage day was as penitential and joyless as possible, but she did not succeed. My heart flew that day, and uncontainable joy bubbled up inside me. Truth be told, I could not have cared less about the ceremony and its trappings, Egyptian or English. Omar and I were married! He took my hand in marriage, we made our vows, and I believed those vows would be cherished. I had no idea what shape our marriage would take, nor what our future together could possibly hold, but we were married. Me, Sally Naldrett, spinster Lady's maid no longer; all the sun in Egypt poured down on me. On that day I believed I would never be cold again.

THE DAYS DRIPPED BY. THE BABY THRIVED, WHILE WE ADULTS WITH-ered and twisted. On my Lady's insistence I remained in my room with the child. We were not to venture from the French House; we were not to show our faces in the village. At night, again at my Lady's bidding, Omar slept on the floor outside her room, the door open, in case he was needed. She seemed to fear the night now—she had never been afraid at night before, not even at her most racked with illness—and she often woke and called out for her dragoman, and he went to her quickly. She was ill once again, weakening daily, the familiar symptoms returning one after the other, but she would not allow Omar to fetch me to help treat her. When the baby cried, the sound muffled by the distance between our rooms, she railed against it, "What *is* that caterwauling? Will someone *please* restore my quiet?" No effort on Omar's behalf to tempt her into wanting to see and hold the child made any difference to her hardness of feeling.

It was an awful thing, her disease. Of course this goes without saying. But the fact that it came and went at its own pace had always made it seem especially cruel to me. She'd been battling it for years now; she would weaken and weaken and get more and more ill, coughing up blood, rapidly losing weight, her lungs rattling in her chest like two bricks of splintered wood, slipping further and further away, until we all thought surely she must die, surely she must be almost dead already, and then it would retreat. A few months' recovery, wrapped up in a blanket in the sunshine, her color gradually returning along with her appetite, and then she would be almost well once again, she'd be almost hale and hearty and robust, or rather, she'd be able to do a passable impression of feeling that way. And this was how it went, in an endless cycle. After each round she'd emerge a little more frail, her recovery would be slightly less complete. But there was no telling how long or how tough each bout would be; at times it was as though she was on the edge of becoming seriously ill, then she'd rally. And on and on it went. It was gradual, it was unpredictable, and it was nasty. And there can be no underestimating the toll that it took on her. Sometimes now I think that perhaps the disease was more responsible than my Lady herself for what she did to me. But the fact is that I had too much at stake to be quite that forgiving.

One afternoon, my Lady returned to the house early, after an excursion to visit Mustafa Agha at his home across the Nile. Her arrival was not preceded, as was usual, by a breathless Ahmed, who liked to be first to arrive anywhere as well as first to leave;

he'd been distracted in the village and had fallen behind the small procession. My Lady found the baby asleep in his basket in the middle of the salon; she must have known at once that Omar was with me. The first thing we heard was her annoyed exclamation. Omar threw on his clothes and rushed out to greet her, his shirt not tucked in completely. I stood in the doorway of my room, listening.

My Lady was standing over the baby's basket, staring down at him. "An ugly child," she announced. "He doesn't even look like you, Omar. Are you sure he is your son?"

My gasp was audible to them both.

Omar paused for a long moment; then he said, "Are you ready for a cup of tea?"

I closed the door of my room. Any hope I had conjured after my wedding receded rapidly.

In the week that followed this incident, my Lady convinced herself that I was trying to persuade Omar to divorce Mabrouka so that I would be his only wife and my marriage could be recognized by English law. Nothing Omar said, none of his denials, would persuade my Lady otherwise. I pleaded with him to persuade her to hear me out, to allow me to speak to her; he tried his best, but she would not agree, saying, "Do not ask such things of me." At the salon one evening—the regular salons continued and were as jovial and convivial as ever, as far as I could hear, as though there was no domestic drama taking place within the French House—my Lady insisted that Sheikh Yusuf and the magistrate Saleem Effendi oversee her latest decree: she asked Omar to stand in front of her while she laid down the law. "You will not divorce Mabrouka, Omar," she said. She looked at her guests, adding, "You are my witnesses. Such a cruel injustice will not take place; and if it does, I will make sure, Omar, that you are discharged from your position in my household. English law recognizes only your first wife, her alone, and your marriage to Sally is not recognized as such and never will be. In the eyes of English law, Sally Naldrett is an adulteress."

The magistrate chuckled, not noticing the look Sheikh Yusuf gave him. "There is no need for this, *Sitti* Duff Gordon," he said. "English law doesn't apply in Egypt. It's the Khedive you need to worry about, and Omar Abu Halaweh's having two wives is not going to bother Ismail Pasha too much."

Omar stood with his fists clenched behind his back, composed and still, saying nothing.

He did not come to my room that night. He did not come to my room the following night either. I paced, desperate with worry. Would I lose him now, despite the marriage? When he came in to collect the washing the following morning, he tried to leave again without taking the time to speak to me, without greeting his son. As he went towards the door, I grabbed his arm. He pushed me away, hard.

"What are you doing?" I said. My breast hurt where his hand had struck me.

"I have my duties," he replied.

"Why are you not coming to see us?"

He hissed at me, "You ask too much of me."

"I ask too much?" I said. "I ask nothing."

He stooped, beaten. "She has humiliated me."

"You must stay strong, Omar. You must stay strong for me, for Abdullah."

Omar left the room again then. He did not return to my bed for more than a week.

I did not want Omar to divorce Mabrouka; I had never suggested such a thing. I will admit to thinking about it, to wanting to have Omar to myself, especially during those months we were in Cairo waiting for Sir Alick to arrive. When he felt able to get away, Omar would head off to spend the afternoon with his family. He'd return from those visits smelling clean and fresh, as though he had bathed in water made fragrant with rosewater and orange oil, his mood light, and he'd give me the news from his home, smiling, laughing, chasing away my jealousy. He told me all about his parents and his little girl, Yasmina, and Mabrouka as well, whom I imagined to be dark and petite and pretty; he took it for granted that I'd want to hear about them. "She is very shy," he said, "very quiet. A good wife," and then he'd look at me and laugh, teasing. "You will meet one day, when we are married, and we return to Cairo with my Lady. Next summer, I think." From this I guessed that he hadn't told them our secret either, and that he continued to fulfill all his marital duties, and I said to myself that Egypt was not England, everything in Egypt is entirely unlike anything in England, including Omar, his marriage, and his relations with me. We assured each other that everything—*everything*—would be fine. We promised each other that the future looked grand, as though we were master and mistress of our own fates. And, in fact, Omar was master of his own household, however infrequently he was able to attend to it, while I was mistress of nothing.

That autumn the Cairo house, like the French House in Luxor, had afforded us great privacy. My Lady was laid low, first by illness before Sir Alick's arrival, and then by—what is the right word?— deep melancholy after Sir Alick departed; she retired early and rose late, leaving the long and sparkling Cairo nights to Omar and me.

In the beginning, I was a stranger to passion. I was a stranger to love itself. And I'll admit, I was greedy; once I'd tasted both, I was hungry for more. After my parents passed away, my aunt Clara had not been able to care for me and my sister; I was sent into service early and there was no one in the world who looked out for me, just me. Had I been asked, I might have ventured that my Lady was possessed of a distinct fondness for me after all the years I had been her maid, but I wouldn't have dared to stake my claim in her affections; after all, I was paid for what I provided. Had she been asked herself, I don't doubt that she would have claimed to love me; my Lady bestowed love and kindness freely and graciously, inspiring the same in those around her, and she was good to the people in her household. It was characteristic of her servants, in England just as much as in Egypt, that we felt privileged to serve her.

But now it was over. My best instinct was to continue to do all I could in the household, while staying out of my Lady's way, but my best instincts were corroded and corrupted by humiliation, my own and Omar's beside me. I stayed in my room and lost myself in Abdullah and waited for Omar.

MY ROOM BECAME MY CUSHIONED PRISON. FINALLY, AFTER WHAT felt like an eternity, late one night when my Lady was asleep, Omar returned to me. When I saw him at my door, I rushed into his arms, and he whispered to me, "My wife. My love. My wife."

13

THE PUBLICATION, IN ENGLAND, OF MY LADY'S BOOK OF LETTERS home came and went as though it had happened to someone else. She told Omar she was glad of the income, but the world of books, the sparks and flare-ups of London literary life, was distant to her now, as unreal as Luxor itself had once been. When she lived in England an event like that would have been a highlight, a huge cause for celebration, marked with parties and suppers and outings. She would have fretted about the critics; she would have sought out the opinions of her writer friends. But in Luxor the day of publication had passed before she remembered to mark it. Instead, she took a glass of mint tea and remarked to Omar, "I feel more Arab than European," and told him that this feeling, this knowledge, meant as much to her now as any publication.

That spring, unwelcome guests kept arriving; the Nile tour was as popular as ever and, once my Lady's book was published, it was as though the French House had become a destination as worthy as the Valley of the Kings.

"The truth is that my book," my Lady said to Omar and Omar reported to me, "will help Sir Alick pay my bills. The more copies they sell, the better. But I never meant for it to serve as an invitation to the whole of London: come and visit the old ruin herself."

"Of course not," said Omar. "You do not like to entertain, after all."

"No," my Lady laughed, "don't tease me!"

And, of course, the guests were a diversion and most days it was good for my Lady to see friends, and friends of friends, and friends of those friends even. Baroness Kevenbrinck and Lord and Lady Hopetown passed through and were duly received by Lady Duff Gordon; they, in turn, invited her to supper parties aboard their *dahabiehs*. My Lady traveled by donkey down to where the Hopetowns were moored, led by Ahmed, who told me later that he found a "lovely restful spot" on the riverbank to nap while he waited for his mistress. On the occasion of Lord Dudley's visit, my Lady threw a great dinner, sending Omar into a cooking frenzy. She invited all her grandest Luxor friends, who dutifully appeared to take a look at the latest English nobleman to journey through their country, but the party was not a success. Omar reported that Lord Dudley amazed everyone present with his lack of manners, his haw-haw laugh and his overboisterous talk; he brooked no ceremony and talked over Mustafa Agha when the consul stood to greet him, as though he couldn't even begin to imagine how one might address, let alone be addressed by, the natives.

The fourteen-year-old heir to the Rothschild fortune arrived, traveling like a royal prince in a grand steamer with a huge entourage, his expenses paid by Ismail Pasha. Rothschild's own dragoman, Mohammed Er-Rasheedee, was a respectable elderly man who had fallen ill during the journey up the Nile. Despite the fact that there was a doctor traveling with the party, the young Rothschild took the decision to cast the old man out at Luxor, abandoning him with only his bare wages and a small sum to take him back to Cairo. My Lady was struck with sympathy for the old man and took him into the French House, where she and Omar nursed him. He was racked with high fever and died quietly one day, at noon. My Lady laid his face to the *kiblah*, and those present,

Omar included, chanted a prayer, *La illaha illa'allah*. His body was washed and within an hour and a half he was wrapped in linen and carried by the men to the burial place. I watched from my window as everyone in the village made their way through the broken colossi and pylons of the temple to the mosque for prayers; when they finished, they went out to the graveyard to bury the old man, my Lady in her Frankish hat and scarf, the village women veiled and wailing. When they returned to the French House, a boy from the village recited the Quran in the room where Er-Rasheedee had died, his young voice unbroken and clear, and later on, Omar described the day to me. I was as hungry as always for news of the household and village.

Omar also reported that many of these friends, and friends of friends, of my Lady seemed to know all about me and my situation and took it upon themselves to offer their advice to my Lady. Some thought her decision too harsh, others too lenient, and the only real consensus, Omar said, was that no one thought that my Lady should even consider continuing to live in Egypt without a lady's maid. "Unheard of!" Omar mimicked Lady Hopetown. "A catastrophe!"

As well as this, Omar told me, letters on the subject had begun to arrive from my Lady's family. Mrs. Ross—Miss Janet—was particularly adamant. "She thinks my Lady is wrong," Omar told me. "Wrong to send you away."

My heart skipped a bit. Miss Janet, taking my side? "Really?"

"Yes! My Lady read me the letter."

"What did my Lady say?"

"Oh, she dismissed that. But Miss Janet also insists that my Lady engage a new lady's maid straightaway." And it was this issue—not my misfortune, not my fate—that had become the issue of the day. I hadn't expected any member of the Duff Gordon family to be my advocate, not seriously. But even so, to hear that news of my predicament had traveled down the Nile astonished me.

THROUGHOUT ALL THIS, I REMAINED OBEDIENTLY IN MY ROOM WITH Abdullah. I cared for my child with all the methodical devotion I had once given to my Lady. I sewed his clothes and kept him clean and did everything in my power to keep him content and happy. Content and happy and thus, quiet; my goal now was to make her forget that the child and I were in the French House, to make my Lady feel as though we had already departed and gone away. "If she doesn't see us," I whispered to Omar late at night, "doesn't hear us, never thinks of us, it will be as though we don't exist, and if we don't exist, we won't have to leave." I asked Omar to bring me extra work, so that I could help with his duties; I knew how much had fallen on his shoulders. At first he resisted, wanting me to be able to give myself fully to our child, but eventually he relented, and he brought my Lady's clothes for me to repair. And so I sat and sewed and fed my child. I opened my windows and let the spring sun into the room in the morning; I hoped it would melt my loneliness away. To be in a busy household, yet shut away, what fate could be worse for a skilled and industrious lady's maid?

Abdullah was growing fast; he lay on his back and examined his own fingers and toes as though they were objects of wonder and, indeed, to Omar and me, they were. He smiled all the time and looked around expectantly, wriggling with pleasure every time someone entered the room. He'd found his baby voice and gurgled incessantly, as though partaking in an ongoing conversation. The day he accidentally rolled himself over from his back to his stomach, clonking his chin on the floor, crying out with surprise at the new position as much as at the pain, it was all I could do to restrain myself from rushing out of my room into the French House to tell everybody. Instead, I scooped him up and cuddled him and sang and stood by the window where we could both look out and see what we were missing in the village.

I screamed the night Abdullah was born; I made more noise

that one night than I had during the whole of the rest of my life put together. But after that, I fell into silence. And that silence deepened and darkened and grew heavier and thicker, until my days were as dark and silent as my nights.

Omar whispered to me and his Arabic pierced the night—each word like a star, flaring out, then falling. I spoke no English now, heard no English spoken in fact, and it was as though my mother tongue was shriveling, growing faint. I'd mouth words to myself, I sang Abdullah English nursery rhymes and lullabies, but conversation—what was conversation? Something my Lady prized, and practiced avidly, something now denied to me.

Those lullabies—they surprised me. It was as if they'd lived inside me all these years and now they were emerging. I found I had a small store of them, and they were not the same as those I had heard my Lady sing to her children, they were not the same as those I had heard other women sing to their babies; they were songs my own mother had sung to me, my mother, long dead, faded in my memory, but fresh to me once again through these songs, through the way I found myself loving and caring for my child, my own mother, reembodied.

AND WHAT COULD OMAR DO? HE WAS EVERYTHING TO ME AND YET we discovered that meant nothing. There was nothing he could do to save me. He took on the work of two people and was cook, housekeeper, valet, and nursemaid to my Lady. The endless stream of guests added to his workload but he didn't mind; he was as interested as the next man in the parade of *Frangi*, and besides, they helped take my Lady's mind off the domestic situation, provided I wasn't the chosen topic of conversation. While my Lady was diverted, I imagined Abdullah and I were safe.

OMAR LIVED SO MANY DIFFERENT LIVES SIMULTANEOUSLY THAT HE said he sometimes worried he would become confused and say the wrong thing to the wrong person in the wrong place. But he did not. I watched him as he slipped between worlds like a spirit, as and when required. Like any domestic servant worth his salt, he'd long since grown accustomed to being one man for one set of people and quite another man for the next.

His first life, before he met me, was that of family man—son, husband, father. Though he and his wife, Mabrouka, were apart most of the time, she was at the center of this world, in Cairo where she lived with his parents and his little daughter, Yasmina. This was not difficult for me to accept; it had been this way since the first day we met. Omar had always had this other life, but given our distance from it, it was both easy to accept and easy to forget.

He had other lives as well, other roles, including dragoman to Lady Duff Gordon. Attaining this position was a great achievement, one Omar had spent his life working towards. His father's business struggled to survive under its heavy weight of rent and taxes, and his family relied upon him to secure a decent income. Omar knew that his place in my Lady's household, if he carried out his duties with enough love and talent, would continue to bring him many opportunities. He had worked for *Frangi* before, in Cairo and Alexandria, so he was familiar with that world, but he told me he never imagined that he'd find himself in a household like ours. Lady Duff Gordon was not like any woman he'd ever met before, *Frangi* or Egyptian; he told me she was more serious, and more scholarly, than most of the men he knew. She liked to argue and discuss; she sought the company of men who could inform and teach her; she grappled with Islam in a way that made him look again at his own pale faith. And she kept her illness at one remove with teases and threats and bargains and a strength of will that surpassed his reckoning.

And in yet another one of Omar's many lives: me. He tumbled

into that headlong, without thinking: I doubt he had ever done anything so without thought before or since. Everything about our relationship was as new to him as it was to me. I was full of passion, he said; I had always been full of passion, he said, I'd just never had a chance to display it before. We displayed ourselves to each other, Omar and me, in secret, in private. He could not understand why I was not already married, did not have my own family, so when the chance came to show me his heart, he said, he seized it.

He blamed himself for what happened, of course he did, no matter how I objected. And it was true, it would never have happened had it not come from him. But once it started he let it continue, we both allowed it to continue, without pause, without thinking. "That's my defense," he said to me one night as we lay together, "though I've never been given a chance to produce it, certainly not by my Lady. We did it without thinking. And because I wasn't thinking," he said, "I wasn't afraid."

The same was not true of me, not once I realized I was carrying a child. I didn't show my fear to him during that time, but I held it, clenched inside my gut, along with the baby.

"Twins," I said, "the baby and its future."

"If there is one thing I understand now," he said, "it is this: you are very brave."

The baby was a secret life, hidden within the life that we led together without my Lady's knowing, and that life in turn was hidden from Omar's wife and parents in Cairo, who looked on him as the good son, the able provider. *Insha allah.* God willing.

And there was a whole other life for Omar, another layer of living that no one in either of his households knew much about, not even me. I had seen hints of it but the pregnancy and the birth of our child made me keep my eyes averted at the very time there was the most to see.

The mistake that both the ruling Ottomans—the *Osmani*—and the *Frangi* make when they think about this country is that

they believe it never changes. They are deceived by this perception because it is partially true: since the time of the Pharaohs
Egypt has been invaded and occupied and ruled from a distance,
and even now, the *Osmani* Khedive, Ismail Pasha, who claims his
independence from Constantinople, oversees the people as if they
are his personal possessions, not a land, a people, in their own right.
And yet they continue, the Egyptians endure, like the Nile itself,
through the eternal calendar of abundance followed by famine,
famine followed by abundance. But while all of this is true, it is a
mistake to think that the people are so preoccupied with the Nile
and its inundation of the land—an inundation that destroys while
at the same time rebirthing—that they will continue to labor
under the sun, oblivious to the passing of the centuries. Instead,
they lie in wait, like a scorpion on a rock, like a crocodile among
the reeds, and from time to time they rise up and they bite.

Omar is a man from the green delta of Lower Egypt and he has
no particular allegiance to the people of Saeed who live wedged
between the Nile and the desert, between the wet black mud and
the bone-white sand. But in Luxor he witnessed the corvée, the
brutality meted out to the *fellahin*, his fellow Egyptians, by the
Osmani Pasha in his palace in Cairo. He watched as the villages
around us lost their men, drafted to Suez to dig the enormous
wide trench that will one day become the canal; he watched as
the crops they grew and the animals they tended were stolen from
the women and children who were left behind. He watched as the
camels and horses were abducted for the troops who'd been dra-
gooned into fighting the Pasha's battles in Nubia and Sudan, in the
Gulf, and even farther afield. When he returned to Cairo with my
Lady, he saw the fevered pitch of the building program; they said
that Ismail Pasha would make Cairo into a city to rival Paris with
his boulevards and his palaces and his gardens. But in Luxor Omar
witnessed the real price of the Pasha's ambition.

And so in Cairo in the autumn, before our baby's birth, Omar found his old friends in the city who felt as he did and he began to do what he could to help. It was not a lot. He passed on messages. He talked to people. There were rumors, in the army, of rebellion among the troops, discontent at the very top, among the generals— only rumors, yet Omar and his friends knew that, when whispered loudly enough, it was possible for rumors to become truths. Like most things in Egypt, it would take a long time to happen, perhaps another twenty years, thirty years, one hundred years even would pass before they would see real change, but—here's another partial truth, Omar says, about himself and his country—"We Egyptians are patient; we Egyptians know how to wait."

Omar whispered fragments to me late at night while we waited for my fate; he kept these thoughts hidden from my Lady, of course. But my Lady spent many hours on her balcony watching over the people of Luxor, and she had many friends among both the *fellahin* and the men of importance in the village; Mustafa Agha the consular agent, Saleem Effendi the magistrate, and Sheikh Yusuf were frequent visitors to her salon, and they talked politics all the time. I heard them but, at the time, I wasn't interested; my Lady talked politics wherever she was—Egypt, England, Germany. She saw what was happening in Luxor and the villages nearby, she saw the fields empty of men, the animals rounded up and driven away, and she took note. She did what she did best—she raised her voice in protest. She argued with her friends in Luxor and, when she saw how little they were able to do, as subject to the Pasha's whims as any lowly *fellah*, she wrote letters home; she sat at her desk in the French House in the mornings when the light was strong but not too bright. One day Omar brought a partial draft of one to me to read:

> The whole place is in desolation, the men are being beaten, one because his camel is not good enough, another because its saddle is old and shabby, and the rest

because they have not money enough to pay two months of food and the wages of one man, to every four camels, to be paid for the use of the Government beforehand. The *courbash* has been going on my neighbours' backs and feet all the morning. It is a new sensation too when a friend turns up his sleeve and shows the marks of the wooden handcuffs and the gall of the chain on his throat. The system of wholesale extortion and spoliation has reached a point beyond which it would be difficult to go . . . I grieve for Abdallah-el-Habbashee and men of high position like him, sent to die by disease (or murder) in the prison at Fazoghou, but I grieve still more over the daily anguish of the poor *fellahin*, who are forced to take the bread from the mouths of their starving families and to eat it while toiling for the private profit of one man. Egypt is one vast plantation where the master works his slaves without even feeding them. From my window now I see the men limping about among the poor camels that are waiting for the Pasha's boats to take them, and the great heaps of maize which they are forced to bring for their food. I can tell you the tears such a sight brings to one's eyes are hot and bitter. These are no sentimental grievances; hunger, and pain, and labour without hope and without reward and the constant bitterness of impotent resentment. To you all this must sound remote and almost fabulous. But try to imagine Farmer Smith's team driven off by the police and himself beaten till he delivered his hay, his oats and his farm servant for the use of the Lord Lieutenant, and his two sons dragged in chains to work at railway embankments—and you will have some idea of my state of mind today. I fancy from the number of troops going up to Assouan that there is another rising among the blacks. Some of the black regiments revolted up in the

Sudan last summer, and now I hear Shaheen Pasha is to be here in a day or two on his way up, and the camels are being sent off by hundreds from all the villages every day. But I am weary of telling, and you will sicken of hearing my constant lamentations.

I READ IT AND SAT BACK AND LOOKED AT OMAR, WHO WAS LOOKING at me expectantly. The letter was typical of my Lady's correspondence, full of passion and detail. "Why have you brought this to me?" I asked.

"I'm sure that this letter, written with such conviction and out of true concern for the Egyptian people, will create a furor in England," Omar replied, his voice low, "when the *Frangi* are told what is really taking place in my country."

"Perhaps," I said. "But why have you brought it to me?"

"I wanted you to see," he replied. "*Sitti* Duff Gordon cares about Egypt. She has earned my loyalty."

I looked at Omar. What did he mean? Was he saying that his loyalty to my Lady was greater than his loyalty to me?

"You will see," he said, speaking quickly now, "this letter will show the *Frangi* the truth about my country. She sees through the layers of myth and conjecture that make up their version of my country's history. She does not look at Egypt and find the modern Egyptian people lacking. She does not look at Egypt and see only the colossal achievements of our ancestors, the ruins we live among. She looks at us and sees all manner of true things, and what she sees pleases her."

"She loves Egypt," I said. But the truth was that my Lady wrote many letters like this to her family and her friends, and the only furor they created was here in Egypt, when her opinions were brought to the attention of the Khedive himself, who was not, after all, pleased to hear the sound of Lady Duff Gordon raising her voice. Omar knew this as well as I did.

My Lady was well known to the authorities in Egypt, of course;

it was very unusual for a *Frangi* to winter in Upper Egypt, let alone a woman; even the men most interested in what was hidden in the sand came and went but did not stay. Of course she'd be watched, spied upon even; it went without saying. That winter my Lady had begun to get news that her letters were going missing and not arriving at their destinations. "Henceforth," she declared, "I'll send my letters by hand with travelers and people I trust."

And through all this, Omar was at her side. He was not among the men indentured to the Pasha's vast construction project in the desert; his wages were not purloined. His position in the household of Lady Duff Gordon sheltered and protected him. "I am safe," he said to me, and I saw that he despised himself for it and despised himself even more deeply as it became clear that while his own position remained sure, he could not protect me, the mother of his child.

14

MY ANGER HAS HARDENED A LITTLE NOW—CRYSTALLIZED—
and sometimes I can't help but show this anger to Omar
when he brings me my meal, when he pops in to see how Abdullah is doing. At these times I struggle to control my tongue; I want
to shout at him, argue with him, provoke him to do something,
anything, to save me. And I do control myself, most of the time, by
remaining silent. I turn away from him, I stare out the window and
will not allow myself to look at him. On these days he visits us less
frequently, sending Ahmed to deliver my meal.

And yet, at night Omar comes to me; he can't keep away, despite the fact that the door to my Lady's bedroom across the house
remains open and his sleeping mat is now permanently positioned
outside. Though the hour is late, and Abdullah and I are sleeping,
he enters our room and sits for a while, watching us both in the
moonlight. He removes his tunic—the night air smooth against his
skin—and lies down beside me; I wake up and reach out for him.
Our love is fraught and anxious now, but neither of us holds back,
whatever the daylight has revealed; we have no anger towards one
another. In the dark, he does not hesitate to show himself to me,
his urgency plain. The room is full of unasked questions, as well as
desire: I do not ask him, "When will I have to leave?"; Omar does
not ask me, "How will I live, once you have gone away?"

One night Omar stays on in my bed a little longer than usual and falls asleep. I curl against him and am soon asleep myself. In her room on the other side of the French House, my Lady stirs. Her lungs are heavy once again, and the pain in her side is worsening; she knows the signs all too well. She calls out for Omar. She needs a drink, hot tea laced with herbs and honey to soothe the pain. There is no reply. She calls out again, more loudly this time, "Omar." Still no reply. She sits up in her bed and reaches for her shawl, wraps it around her shoulders. Outside her room the sleeping mat is bare, as she knew it would be. She walks slowly towards the kitchen; though it is still dark, Omar could well have risen to begin work already, but the room is empty, the oven cold. She makes her way to the salon, where she opens the shutters to let in more light; since first waking she has known where Omar is, but she goes through the motions of looking for him, of allowing him to be anywhere apart from where she knows he will be. Down the corridor, to the other room, the room she now thinks of as belonging to "that woman and her child." She stands outside for a few minutes, listening. There is nothing to hear but she knows the house is full of the breath of lovers, lovers' breath all mixed up with that of our baby. She pushes the door open slowly: now she wants to see us together, wants to witness, once again, this travesty of a marriage. The door swings back, and there we are, laid out before her in the moonlight like a tableau, like a painting of a Bible scene, man, woman, child. What my Lady sees is this: Englishwoman, Egyptian man, and between them, their little half-breed.

She makes a low noise, she doesn't know where it comes from, it's a growl, the beginning of a roar, a howl. She moves forward and, before she knows what is happening, she is on us, scratching, screeching, pulling off the cover, revealing the tangle of limbs, my long hair loose and splayed, both of us entirely naked. Omar wakes and shouts with alarm, and I cry out with fear, and we scramble for our clothes, our dignity, and Abdullah himself wakes and begins to cry. My Lady, as though driven mad by what she sees, screams at me, "What have you done to him? Why have you brought all this into my house? Why have you destroyed our peace?" before pulling back suddenly, shocked into silence by her own behavior. She falls into incoherent sobbing, ashamed and righteous and vindicated all at the same time, blustering, gesticulating, choking. She gives me a look of such pure hatred that I gasp and turn away.

I look at Omar, unable to speak. He throws on his tunic and reaches for my Lady, his arm around her shoulders, as much to restrain as to support her. "Hush, my Lady," he says, his voice low, "hush. I'm sorry. It won't happen again. I'm with you. I'm sorry. I'll take you back to your room." She is shaking with anger in his embrace.

What have we done? What has taken place? Have we pushed her too far this time? I can see that Omar is frightened now, for his own position, as well as for me. He glances back over his shoulder at me, as though to apologize for taking my Lady in his arms, not me. I am weeping; I gather up Abdullah and hold him as closely as I myself long to be held. The baby quietens quickly, as though he has had a bad dream and forgotten it already. Omar leads his mistress away.

I spend the rest of the night and the next few days in a state of extreme agitation, unsettling Abdullah. I don't know what to do with myself. Omar does not come to my room; Ahmed delivers all my meals. He is, strangely, oblivious to what is happening, Ahmed who normally knows all the gossip in the village before it even takes place. He tells me all is well, *Sitti* is resting more than usual, there have been no visitors, Omar is busy in the kitchen, as always. I pace and worry and am convinced that my Lady will expel me and my child from her house any minute now.

But she does not and, slowly, I begin to breathe. And eventually Omar shows up at my door once again.

A FEW DAYS LATER, WHILE OMAR WAS DOWN AT THE RIVERSIDE NE-gotiating the price of a sack of flour, a man stepped in front of him. "Omar Abu Halaweh," the man said; Omar told me he was startled to be addressed by name by a stranger. "Please join me on my *daha-bieh for coffee.*" From his dress, Omar could see the man was some kind of government official, and this was alarming in itself, but he agreed to go to the boat, as much out of cautious obedience as curiosity. He knew that there could be little evidence of his opinions of the Pasha and his policies, but others had been convicted and sent to Fazoghou for less.

But it was not Omar himself in whom the envoy was interested. They sat together under a low canopy in the stern of the boat and, once the coffee was poured, the man dismissed his serving staff. He turned to point at the French House, which sat above them in Luxor temple. "Lady Duff Gordon," he said, smiling.

"Yes," Omar said, and he bowed his head to show his estimation of his mistress. "My employer."

"Her book," said the man, "her letters. Annoying. Worse than that—embarrassing. The Khedive would prefer it if she did not write any more letters home to England."

Omar did not know how to reply. "I cannot dictate what Lady Duff Gordon does or does not—"

"The Pasha will make arrangements for you. One hundred *fed-dan*s of delta land? Or another payment of some kind?"

Omar was silenced. Did he understand the official correctly?

The man mistook this silence for bargaining. "Next time you make a trip on the Nile. You are close by her all the time, we know this. We have been watching. It would be simple. Good land, in the delta."

Omar convulsed within and struggled to remain impassive outwardly.

The man continued, "You will be rewarded: the Khedive expects your loyalty."

Omar knew he must make some kind of reply. "Yes, sir," he said. "Thank you."

The man waved his hand as though to say, it is nothing. "Ismail Pasha will reward you," he said once again.

Omar stood and bowed and thanked the man for the coffee; he held his hands behind his back to stop them from shaking. As he made his way off the boat and along the embankment, he tried not to scurry; he knew the envoy would be watching. He forced himself to walk over to pick up the sack of flour he had purchased earlier. He did not allow Ahmed to load the sack onto the donkey but lifted it onto his own shoulder: he said it felt good to carry a load that was real, tangible. He walked up to the French House, through the ramshackle village, and greeted his neighbors in his usual fashion.

The French House was still cool; the heat of the day had not yet begun to accumulate beneath the high ceilings. My Lady was resting in her room, her door ajar to catch the breeze. Omar looked in on Abdullah and me: we were both sleeping; he had heard Abdullah crying in the night and me attempting to comfort and quiet him. He went into the kitchen and got out his pots and pans. He wanted to lose himself in his chores, he said, in cooking, to not think about what had taken place. I will feed and care for my Lady and Sally and Abdullah, he thought; that's why I am in Luxor. I will make the French House a gracious place, full of ease and refinement for my Lady. I am not in Luxor to watch over the *fellahin*, to worry about the fate of my fellow Egyptians, to speculate about better, more able, fairer forms of government. I am not in Luxor to do the bidding of the Khedive, to drown Lady Duff Gordon in the Nile and thus eliminate one of the Pasha's few *Frangi* critics. He picked up a pan and slammed it down hard on the work surface.

The noise Omar was making woke me, and I stole through the house, pausing to peer into my Lady's room to make sure she was asleep. When I got to the kitchen, Omar, in his agitated state, told me what had taken place.

"What kind of a man do they think I am?" he said. "That the Pasha would make me into one of his murderers." He picked up the pan and slammed it down hard once again.

I took his hand and tried to still him. "You'll wake her."

"I am here as dragoman to Lady Duff Gordon," he said. "I am, as you used to say of yourself so proudly, in service to my Lady. What can I do? Nothing. I can do nothing to help you, my wife. And now this."

One hundred *feddans* of land, I thought. I couldn't help but think.

"I will do nothing," he said. "I will continue to do nothing."

THE COOL AND CHANGEABLE WEATHER OF JANUARY AND FEBRUARY gave way to the growing heat of March, and then Ramadan arrived once again. Omar told my Lady he would not attempt to fast this year. "I need my strength, now that Sally is unable—" He paused. "Now that I am on my own." She nodded and waved her hand to show she trusted her dragoman to make his own decisions regarding his faith, and that she was not to be swayed by reminders of me.

"I'd like to make the fast myself," I said to Omar one night. "Not this year," I added, "I know. The baby. But another year, perhaps?"

Omar nodded. "Another year." And he looked at me then, and I could see him wonder at my ability to make assumptions regarding the future.

But the truth was I would have liked to make the fast for Ramadan; the ritual of fasting from dawn until dusk had a purity about it that I found appealing: let nothing pass your lips till night falls. Four weeks was a long time to endure such a thing and I couldn't imagine quite how the devout coped when the fast took place in the summer months; how did they survive in

the heat without drinking? Even so, I told myself, I would like
to participate one year. And besides, making assumptions about
the future was how I survived these weeks, hidden away in the
French House; I planned for calmer times, for an imagined future
when Omar, Abdullah, and I would be settled together, happy.
Cairo, I thought vaguely, a courtyard dense and cool with bright
red bougainvillea, Omar's father's house. One hundred *feddan*s
of land.

The festival brought with it a new outbreak of the gastric condition my Lady and I had battled against the year before, though
early signs showed it would not be as severe. However, when a
party of Bedouin pitched camp outside the French House, waiting
to be seen by the *hakima* they had heard could cure them, my Lady
struggled to cope. She attempted to train Ahmed as her helper, but
the little boy, though clever and keen to learn, was no replacement
for me, and Ahmed himself told me this made my Lady short-
tempered at times. "It's hard for me to remember everything," he
complained. But my Lady was stubborn: she kept on with the
makeshift clinic; she and Ahmed got by.

My Lady knew that she was being watched; Mustafa Agha had
told her as much one afternoon when he mentioned a government envoy had been seen talking to Omar. After he had departed
she called Omar into her room and asked him about the gossip:
was it true he'd been visited by an agent of the Pasha?

Omar did not want to tell her what the official had said. "Yes,
my Lady . . . they don't like your letters. You know this already.
They don't like the book."

Omar told me my Lady laughed and said, "They don't like me."

But she told Omar she didn't much care, and she wasn't worried. "I am resigned to my fate; Egypt is my fate. I am not afraid of
the Khedive." And despite the situation with me, it was clear she
trusted Omar absolutely.

One evening, after Ahmed had fallen asleep on the kitchen

floor, exhausted from his efforts in the clinic, Omar took my Lady her meal in the salon.

"Sit with me, Omar, please," she said. "Eat with me." They had not shared an evening meal since returning to the French House, since all our positions in the household had been so dramatically altered by Abdullah's birth. Omar gathered a few cushions and sat and ate a little of the lamb stew he had prepared for her, feeling, he said later, a strong mixture of relief and anxiety.

My Lady had some news for Omar. "We will travel to Europe this summer," she said.

Omar smiled and nodded.

"We'll travel with Janet from Alexandria onward. She is making all the arrangements. Janet is very good at making arrangements."

"I'm sure she is, my Lady."

"We'll travel by ship to Marseilles and take the train to Paris, where we will join the rest of the family."

"Paris," said Omar, and he sighed. "It will be like traveling to the moon and back again."

My Lady laughed. "Paris is lovely, much nicer than the moon, I'm sure. We'll stay a few days and we'll see the sights. The River Seine. Notre Dame."

"What's that?"

"It's a great cathedral in the center of the city, but we'll only stay a few days. Then we'll travel to a spa town in Germany for the family holiday."

"Germany," said Omar.

"You've always wanted to go to Germany, Omar, you just don't know it yet."

"I'm happy to travel anywhere, my Lady."

"We won't go to England—too far, too expensive, nowhere for us all to stay. Janet has everything arranged. I will see my family once again, Omar! I can't wait. We will have a wonderful time."

She beamed at him and he smiled back. "Have you seen all the villagers who want your help yet?" he asked.

"There's a few remaining. And, of course, there are still those who will need to return if the treatment has not been effective."

"This work is taking a toll on your health."

"It needs to be done. And while I am well enough, I shall continue."

"It would be easier if your helper was a little more . . ."—Omar paused—"skilled than Ahmed." Omar couldn't help himself; my Lady's mood was so buoyant and free.

"The boy does his best," she said. "And he is learning quickly. He is useful when I can't make out what the Bedouin are saying."

"You would see more people, more quickly, if you would allow Sally to help you—"

My Lady interrupted. "I know what you are going to say. Don't think you can use my good mood to help you argue your case."

Omar rose and carried the meal tray into the kitchen. He wanted to slam it down onto the bench; he wanted to punish himself for daring to argue with my Lady and at the same time he wanted to rush back into the salon to shout out his frustration. "But your life is in my hands, my Lady," he told me he wanted to say. "You might think there's no danger, that you can simply wave it away, but it's real. You know what the agent asked of me?"

"You must make her understand what she owes you, Omar," I said. "The Pasha is watching. If she trusts you with her life, how can she not trust you to know what is best for your own wife and child?" But it was no use. My Lady would not listen to him. Her resolve against me would not weaken. It was only a matter of time now until I was sent away.

LADY DUFF GORDON'S PRACTICE AS VILLAGE *HAKIMA* WAS FORCED TO end when she came down with a serious bout of her own illness.

Once again she was reduced to lying propped up in bed all day, unable to sleep from the coughing and blood spitting and fever, unable to lie flat, unable to sit. It was apparent that between bouts she was no longer recovering as well as she had done in the past. The disease seemed to grip her more fully now, her recovery less complete each time. At night Omar lifted her light body—what little weight he managed to put on her through the sumptuousness of his cooking almost always fell away, taking more with it, as soon as she became ill—and carried her out onto the terrace that overlooked the garden. He made her comfortable with mats and cushions and pillows and blankets, hoping the light breeze would make it easier for her to breathe; she stared into the distance at the dark outline of the desert hills, watching the stars, telling Omar that she sometimes felt as though she might drown in the fluid that filled her lungs. Omar did his best to treat her, making frequent forays down the corridor to my room to ask for advice and guidance, which I gave freely. At my suggestion, he moved his sleeping mat next to the door of the terrace, where he lay awake at night, listening to my Lady as she struggled to breathe.

One night Omar woke with a shudder, convinced my Lady had stopped breathing altogether. He rushed out onto the terrace, where he found her slumped, her breath reduced to a tiny rattle deep in her chest. He ran to wake me, and I did not hesitate. I went to fetch the implements, while Omar carried my Lady into the kitchen. He laid her on the table and we prepared to treat her. I asked Omar to heat the knife in the fire and when he gave it to me, its blade glowing in the lamplight, I stared down at her. How many times had I nursed her back to health when it looked as though her life had almost ebbed away? How many sacrifices had I made for her before discovering she was not prepared to sacrifice anything for me? Omar was heating the water and gathering cushions and trying to make my Lady's rudimentary gurney more comfortable; he could not read my mind and I knew he thought I was poised and ready, waiting for him to finish. Would he notice if I made the cut too deep, in the wrong place?

I gave myself a shake. "Watch carefully," I said, "you may have to do this by yourself next time." I made the incision in my Lady's breast confidently, as the doctor had shown me, as I had done before. I placed the heated glass cup over the wound and waited as the cup filled with blood. Omar looked at me from the other side of the kitchen table, across the body of my Lady, who lay insensible throughout. We were like make-believe physicians in a diabolically crude surgery.

"It will help," I said. "It always does."

My Lady recovered a little over the following week; I asked Omar if he told her it was me who had treated her that night, but he said no. He said he was unwilling to risk her anger and weaken her once again.

He was right not to tell her, I think. Though I wondered sometimes, had Omar given up on me?

A LETTER ARRIVED—OPENED AND CRUDELY RESEALED, LIKE ALL OF my Lady's post now—from the Prince and Princess of Wales. They had read Lady Duff Gordon's book and were in Egypt and would like to meet her; they were traveling up the Nile and would like her to visit them on their *dahabieh* when they were at Aswan in a week's time.

My Lady read the letter aloud to Omar and smiled and closed her eyes. "See, I told you: I've become a fixture on the Nile itinerary."

Omar was a little shocked that she could make a joke about her own monarchy. "You must be feeling better today," he said.

"You know," she replied, "I just might be."

That same afternoon, the man from the government who had invited Omar onto his boat for coffee appeared at the door of the

French House. Ahmed ran up the stairs to announce the unknown visitor. When Omar saw who it was, he told me later, he faltered and leaned into the wall involuntarily. The man smiled. "I have come to speak with Lady Duff Gordon."

"You must not . . . ," Omar began.

"Please tell her I am here."

"Your name?"

"Tell her I've come on orders from the Khedive."

My Lady insisted on seeing the man alone. The house buzzed—a royal missive, and now this, a government agent; Ahmed sneaked into my room to tell me everything, his voice squeaking with excitement. Omar made the envoy wait outside the house while he helped my Lady into the salon and settled her on the divan. Then he hovered in the kitchen; my Lady had asked him to prepare tea and pastries, as she would for any guest, but he positioned himself so he could hear every word of their conversation.

"Lady Duff Gordon," the man began, his tone even, well-mannered, "you have received an invitation from the Prince of Wales?"

"Yes," replied my Lady, and Omar heard no trace of fear in her voice. "They will be at Aswan, next week."

"The Khedive respectfully requests that you do not accept their invitation."

"Why should the Khedive care whether I accept an invitation from the Prince and Princess of Wales?"

Omar could hear my Lady was amused and he worried for one long moment that my Lady would laugh at the Pasha's envoy.

"If you hire a boat to take you to Aswan, the boatmen will be arrested."

"If I hire a boat . . ." My Lady stopped speaking.

Omar waited in the kitchen. He tried to force himself to get on with making the tea, with placing sweetmeats on the tray.

"You are threatening me," my Lady said calmly. "Whatever for? I'm a sick old woman, can't you see?"

The man cleared his throat but remained silent.

"What does the Khedive fear?" my Lady asked. "That I'll tell the Prince and Princess what I see outside my window every day?"

"I've given you the Pasha's message, Lady Duff Gordon. Now please, excuse me. *Ma esalaameh.* The Khedive sends his greetings."

"Will you not stay for tea?" my Lady asked blandly.

The man bowed. "No, thank you."

After the agent was gone, Omar took the tea tray through to the salon. He could not pretend he had not overheard. "That man," he said, "came to see me. He offered to bribe me to have you drowned."

At that, my Lady did laugh, out loud, but now there was no amusement in her voice. "How much was I worth to the Khedive?"

Omar did not reply to her question. "These threats, my Lady, they are not made in jest, they are not made in idleness. The Khedive—"

"Don't you think I've seen enough of his brutality to know that if it suited him I would disappear the next day?"

Omar nodded abruptly.

"Please pour me some tea." My Lady began to cough, clutching her side, and Omar could see she was in pain. He propped her up and tried to ease her by rubbing her back; before I had Abdullah, Omar would never have touched her. But now, he said, he'd grown accustomed to touching her almost as quickly as he'd adapted to doing my job as well as his own.

When my Lady could speak again she said, "I was planning to decline the invitation anyway. I'm too ill to make the journey. The thought of traveling to Aswan makes me feel even more unwell; I doubt I could travel to the end of the village. I'll write to the Prince later today."

Omar was surprised by this decision, though he did not show it. But late that night, my Lady took a turn for the worse. She railed against it, but no one can live on will alone, and each cough, each bout of blood spitting, brought her closer to death. And she knew it. He could see she knew it. Nothing could be as frightening, not even the Khedive and his men.

I found myself wondering what would happen if my Lady did die. Omar would have to find a new position immediately if we were to survive, and there was no guarantee that another *Frangi* employer would look on our situation more benevolently. The fact was that having a European wife and child might make finding work difficult for Omar. It was likely we would have to live separately. But no one could insist that I leave the country; I'd be free to stay. Perhaps Omar's family would welcome me into their household, as Mustafa Agha had suggested the day we were married. Perhaps . . . But this was not a useful train of thought; it was not seemly to speculate in this way. My Lady would pull through; she always did; she was indestructible.

When she had the strength, Lady Duff Gordon continued to write her letters home, sometimes only a few lines per day. She gave no thought to the government envoy and his warning and sent her letters via trusted travelers only. She stayed in her room during the day and slept outside at night. She alternated between the garden balcony and the terrace overlooking the Nile. "The changing views," she told Omar, "heal me." Her ongoing incapacity gave me a little freedom and I was able to spend part of my day in the kitchen with Omar, though the other household members were sworn to secrecy, Ahmed sworn doubly. They didn't mind, for the pleasure of holding the baby. Abdullah's skin had become paler since he was born, and his whiteness was much admired. He slept most of the time and, when he wasn't asleep, he was being fed or played with or cosseted or bathed by one of his admirers.

My Lady was not herself, but even so, she knew what was going on, behind her back, though she heard not a whisper or peep. "Another few weeks," she mumbled to Omar one afternoon as he wiped her face with a cool cloth. "Another few weeks and I'll send the baby to Cairo and Sally can be on her way. Beginning of May."

She opened her eyes and looked at Omar, but he looked away.

NEWS CAME OF A SUDDEN UPRISING IN THE VILLAGE OF QENA, JUST south of Luxor. The rumors began filtering through the village in the morning: a Prussian boat had been attacked the day before with all aboard murdered and the boat burned; ten villages were in open revolt against the Pasha's policies. Omar shook his head at the villager who gave him this news, and wanted to hear the truth, the real story, not just the rumors, which got wilder and larger each time Omar and Ahmed ventured from the French House. That evening, Mustafa Agha brought news to the house himself; my Lady was not well enough to receive him, so he sat in the kitchen with Omar and conveyed all that he had heard.

"A dervish from the desert has proclaimed himself the Mahdi," he said. "May I have another pastry?"

"Of course," said Omar, and he pushed the tray closer to Mustafa Agha. The Mahdi is the messiah who will come to slay the Antichrist and convert all of humankind to Islam at the end of the world.

"These are delicious, Omar; you are the best pastry cook in all of Luxor. When you need a new employer—" Mustafa stopped himself, and both men were embarrassed by this unintended reference to the graveness of my Lady's illness. "The *fellahin* in a village south of Qena have proclaimed him their savior and have risen up against the Khedive. These people are starving; they have lost their land and their livelihoods. It's no wonder they have had enough."

"It's not like you, Agha Bey, to defend the rights of the *fellahin*."

"Ach, I know, but the Khedive has gone too far. He has made the people desperate, and all they have left is their own violence."

"What about the Prussian ship?"

"All rumors and lies. There was a merchant boat—Greek, I think—that was robbed by a mob, but no one was hurt. The troops are massing with their boats at Qena. Ismail Pasha himself is there, they say, in his steamer."

"And the dervish?"

"He's a trickster. He repeated the names of Allah three thousand times every night for three years, which rendered him invulnerable. He made friends with a djinn, who taught him more tricks. Then he proclaimed himself El-Mahdi."

"What will happen?" Omar thought of the villagers. Revolt on this scale had been a long time coming; it took a madman and fanatic to tip the balance.

"The Khedive will prevent this unrest from spreading. It will not reach Luxor, I guarantee you."

"But they are miles away." It hadn't occurred to Omar that the unrest could travel this far.

"The *fellahin* are starving, Omar. Anything can happen. But don't worry. We will be prepared, I assure you."

When Mustafa Agha left, Omar grabbed hold of Ahmed and made him swear not to tell my Lady what was happening. I know he meant to include me in his pact with the boy, but he forgot, so Ahmed made it his business to keep me informed. In return, I paid him with sweets, and when those ran out, I let him hold Abdullah.

That night, my Lady was gripped by a burning fever, which Omar struggled for hours to bring down. Though she was insensible, he bathed her gently in cool water. Once again, I ventured out of my room to assist him. I went into my Lady's traveling trunk and brought out the inlaid box that contained the laudanum. "This will help," I said, as I dosed my Lady.

"I will tell her this time, Sally; I will tell her that without you I would not have been able to cope."

I shook my head. "You can cope, Omar; you know how to treat her yourself. You're as much of a *hakima* now as my Lady."

The laudanum took effect quickly and my Lady rested more easily. We went back to the kitchen for something cool to drink. Omar could not sit but continued to pace. When I asked him what was troubling him, he said it was nothing.

"I know what is going on at Qena," I said.

He looked at me, annoyed and amazed.

"Ahmed told me. He's my own little agent."

"That boy," Omar said, shaking his head.

I couldn't help but smile. "I know," I said, "he's so serious, he lowers the tone of his voice and puffs out his chest and speaks to me like a man and I try not to laugh—"

Omar interrupted me. "But it is serious, Sally! The violence is spreading. Every moment of every day, it's getting worse. There are people dying."

"I know," I said, "but I find it hard to separate rumors and tall tales from the truth, especially under Ahmed's supervision."

"I've made a plan," Omar said, "in case the violence reaches Luxor."

Ahmed had not mentioned the possibility of the unrest coming as far as Luxor.

"The French House is like a kind of fortress," Omar said, "up high on top of the temple. Its walls are twice as thick and more sound than any other building in Luxor. There is room for a lot of people," he continued. "The women and children can take shelter on the ground level; the men and boys can keep lookout from the terraces and the roof and watch for movement in the desert as well as boats from either direction on the Nile. I've got Sir Duff Gordon's old pistols and I'm sure other men in the village will have weapons; Mustafa Agha will have his hunting guns."

He had clearly given it a lot of thought. "Have you told anyone else this plan? Have you told my Lady?" I asked.

"Not yet. There is no way of predicting what will happen: will the *fellahin* in the grip of the Mahdi attack Luxor, or will the

villagers, themselves angry and tired, want to join in the uprising?
If it comes to it I shall have to force my Lady to shelter with you
and Abdullah—"

"She won't agree to that. She'll want to grab Sir Alick's pistols
and take a stand herself."

"I will force her. No one would harm an infant and two
women. You will be safest of all."

"Surely the Khedive's troops will arrive in time to protect us?"
I said. Omar and I looked at each other then and shuddered to find
ourselves hoping for protection from the same Khedive who had
threatened my Lady.

MUSTAFA AGHA RETURNED TO THE HOUSE IN THE MORNING WITH
the news that the uprising had spread to several other villages and
that hundreds of *fellahin* were now in open revolt. "It could spread
further," he said, "if the troops don't act. We must be ready."

Omar told him of his idea to use the French House as a bas-
tion and Mustafa Agha agreed that, as a last resort, this is what they
would do.

In Luxor there was no sign of what was happening in the villages up the river; the occasional tourist boat continued to dawdle
on the Nile, the call to prayer rang out from the mosque, the villagers went about their business as before. But there was a stillness
in the air, a feeling of anticipation, and tempers were short in the
market and in the narrow alleyways.

Omar continued to keep the news of the insurgency from my
Lady and she mistook his increasing agitation for something else.
Each time she woke from her heavy, drug-induced sleep, her first
thought was to call out for him—to call out in panic, as though
convinced he had left her. "He's gone!" I heard her cry out, and
I knew then that she was afraid that Omar would leave with me,
that I had somehow convinced him to take me and the child and

abandon my Lady, to travel somewhere she couldn't find him, to abandon her here in Luxor, on her own, far away from her friends, far away from her family. I heard it in her voice; she thought he had left her, and that there was no one here for her, no one to care for her. And she'd call out, as loudly as she could, and if Omar didn't reply immediately, she'd call out again, and attempt to sit up, try to get up out of bed, her lungs aching, her heart pounding, blood rushing to her head and . . .

Someone always came, someone always answered, if not Omar, then Ahmed or Mohammed; she was never left on her own in the house, never left without someone nearby. And she would lie back on her cushions, able to rest once again, to forget her panic and say to herself, of course he's here, how foolish of me. Of course he's here; he is loyal and obedient.

OMAR REGRETTED THAT AHMED HAD TOLD ME WHAT WAS HAPPENING in the villages. But for me it was a relief to have something so much more concrete and pressing to fear after weeks and weeks of hiding away in my room, waiting, hoping, speculating over my own fate. I kept thinking I could hear men shouting in the distance and that shouting moving closer, but then I'd realize it was only villagers chatting beneath my window, or the breeze rattling through the palm trees. My skin crept, and I was easily startled, poor Abdullah clasped tightly in my arms—too tightly—on more than one occasion.

After lunch one day, Omar went into the village to try to get more news, leaving Ahmed to stay behind to watch over my Lady. As soon as he was gone, however, Ahmed, the naughty boy, set out to follow him, determined to find out for himself what was happening, not wanting to miss anything. I paced in my room and contemplated moving out into the salon where I would have a better view of the village from the balcony—might be able to track Omar's progress even—when I heard my Lady call out. Of course, this time there was no reply; Mohammed was away from the house as well; there was no one there to reply. My Lady called out once again and I could hear the panic in her voice. She's become a tyrant, I thought, she was never a tyrant before I had my baby, it's my fault, and I felt a fresh flush of guilt and shame. But that guilt and shame led me on into anger when I remembered my fate, and the extremity of the current situation—the countryside in open rebellion—spurred me further still. I laid the sleeping Abdullah in his fine basket and marched into my Lady's room.

She was sitting up; she'd swung her feet to the floor and was about to attempt to stand. It was a shock to see her: she was thin and drawn and had a green tinge to her skin, and her shorn hair was now almost completely white. "What are you doing here?" she said, her voice shrill. "Where's Omar?" and I could see that she was panicked. For a moment I felt a strong impulse towards cruelty; I would tell her Omar had left us, left us both here to die at the hands of the villagers who had joined the uprising.

"Omar has gone to the village," I said, and I stopped myself from adding the familiar, the familial "my Lady." "I can help you. What do you need?"

"I don't want your help," she said. "Omar will tend to me when he returns." She turned away to look at the wall, dismissing me like a child.

But I could not leave. "Please," I began, and the words felt like chalk in my mouth as I realized what I was about to say. "Lady Duff Gordon, please," I said. "I beg you. Please—do not send me away." I allowed myself a breath. She was not looking at me and this enabled me to continue. "Do not force me to leave my child and return to England. Think of your own children—think of Miss Rainey—do not force this separation on me. Omar and I are married now, we will find a way—"

"Get out." My Lady did not—would not—look at me. Her

voice was low and even. "Get out of my room immediately or I will make you leave the house today."

I was desperate now. "He loves me. You know this is true. Why do you hate me so, after all I have done for you, all the years I have given to you? You would deny me my child? You would deny me any happiness of my own? You would—"

My Lady picked up a book off the table next to her bed as though she was about to begin to read. As I continued to plead, my words accelerating, she turned towards me abruptly and threw the book with all that remained of her strength, striking me in the face.

I staggered backwards, clutching my nose, which I could feel had begun to bleed. Then I ran from the room, back to my baby.

SEVERAL HOURS LATER OMAR RETURNED AND THE HOUSE FILLED UP once again with people and activity. When Omar checked on me he noticed my injury; my cheek was swollen and the skin beneath my eye was beginning to bruise. I told him I had slipped and fallen and struck myself on the edge of the table. He could tell there was something not quite right about my story, but he was too preoccupied, there was too much going on, and I assured him I was fine. He had been unable to gain much in the way of actual information on the events south of Qena, and the village was in a state of high tension, as though ready to shift its allegiance either way, to the uprising or to the Khedive.

"Perhaps now it is time to tell my Lady my plan," Omar said.

I did not reply.

"Perhaps I should send for Mustafa Agha and get out the pistols."

I did not reply. I had no idea what to do; I had no idea about anything.

Just then Ahmed came clattering up the stairs. "They are

coming!" he shouted. "They are here! They are making their way through the village!"

Omar rushed to fetch Sir Alick's hunting pistols, which he kept hidden in his room. I ran to the windows at the front of the house, and what I saw brought me to a halt.

It was not the villagers responding to the uprising, en route to storm the French House, but something equally extraordinary: a splendid procession, borne by horse and donkey, was moving through the village, making its way towards the French House from two vast and luxurious *dahabiehs* moored at the riverside. I wondered who on earth it could possibly be, when it came to me: it was the Prince and Princess of Wales.

MY LADY RECEIVED HER ROYAL VISITORS IN THE SALON AT THE French House; the royal entourage took up residence in the kitchen, and Omar and Ahmed rushed from room to room madly, attending to the needs of the venerable guests, Ahmed flying down the corridor to bring me minute-by-minute updates.

After they were gone—they stayed for less than an hour, but it felt like several days—I could not contain myself. There was too much happening, a royal visit in the midst of the threat of an up-rising. I needed to see Omar, I needed to get out onto the terrace of the house myself, to see the visitors departing, to see whether or not a mob of angry villagers was about to rise up in their wake. But Omar was not in the kitchen; he was with my Lady. I did something then I had never done before, not in all my years as a domestic servant: I stood outside my Lady's door in order to listen to their conversation.

"The Khedive would be proud of me," my Lady said. "I spoke not a word against him. The Waleses are, after all, his guests in Egypt. They would not have wanted to discuss politics with me."

I could hear she was fatigued by the visit and shivering. Omar moved to place a shawl at her knees and another around her shoulders. "Omar," she said, "stop fussing. Listen to me."

She had become very serious now. "Give me your hand."

"Yes, my Lady?"

"I asked the Prince of Wales for a favor. If you stay with me—" She interrupted herself. "Omar, are you listening?"

"Yes, my Lady."

"If you stay with me and do not leave me and care for me until I die—"

Omar began to object but she silenced him.

"Because I will die, there is no escaping that fact—" She paused again. I held my breath. "If you stay until then, the Prince of Wales has promised me that there will be a place for you in his household."

Omar said nothing.

I stifled my own gasp with my hand. A place in the household of the Prince of Wales.

"You will be given the position of dragoman to the Prince of Wales."

Omar did not reply. It was as though he was unable to speak.

"Do you understand what I am saying?"

Another long pause, then at last he found his voice again. "Yes, my Lady."

"If you stay with me, your future, and the future of your family in Cairo, will be secure."

Omar took a breath. He had no choice. We would never be together: it was not an option, had never been a real possibility. He was beholden to too many people—his parents, Mabrouka, my Lady, now the Prince and Princess of Wales. Too many people relied upon his choosing the right path through life.

"I will stay with you, my Lady," he said. "I will stay by your side, always."

There was no choice. I would have to leave.

I WAITED FOR OMAR OUTSIDE MY LADY'S ROOM; I FELT COMPELLED to see him, to show him I knew what had gone on behind that door, where my life's balance had been weighed and determined. I stood outside that door, silent, waiting.

Why did my Lady act as she did? Why did the news of my love affair cause her to despise me? In another household, this event— two devoted servants bound together by marriage, thus diminishing the possibility of losing either to another employer—might have been a happy thing. As I stood outside that door I wondered if my Lady had always wanted Omar to herself and had looked on my downfall as her excuse to get rid of me. I wondered if my Lady was in love with Omar herself. But I knew that was preposterous. She would no more fall in love with a servant than she would with a donkey.

Omar emerged from her room. I looked into his face and I knew that I was truly lost, that I had lost Omar to my Lady, and that if I was not very, very careful, I would lose my child as well, and then I would have lost everything.

I WROTE TO MY SISTER ELLEN IN ALEXANDRIA THEN. I HAD NOT MAN-aged to write to her yet, though I had tried many times. I told her what had happened, giving her my point of view as plainly and simply as I could; I said I hoped she wasn't angry with me. Of course, what I really hoped was that she would come up with some kind of solution; we had always helped each other in the past. I'd helped her gain her post in the Duff Gordon family and I remember well the day she became Miss Janet's maid, both of them, two little girls, equally pleased with themselves and each other.

Ellen wrote back to me; of course she knew all about the situation already. She wrote that both Miss Janet and Mrs. Austen, my Lady's mother, and even Sir Alick himself had said in no uncertain terms that they felt my Lady had dealt with me too harshly. For a moment, as I read her response, I felt hope wash over me. But Ellen had no solution to offer me—no plan for the Ross household to take in me and my child (I berated myself for ever imagining such a thing), only kind words and sympathy colored by amazement, chastisement, and sorrow that I could find myself in such a place. I knew well enough that feeling of tension and relief that grips the hearts of all unmarried female domestic servants. "There but for the grace . . ." was what my sister was feeling, even if she did not express it that way.

THAT NIGHT, OMAR WAS ASLEEP ON HIS MAT OUTSIDE MY LADY'S room when he was woken by the eldest son of Mustafa Agha, the one who had proposed to me what seemed a lifetime ago. He bore news: Ismail Pasha's troops had shot one hundred men involved in the Qena uprising and burnt the villages and devastated the fields all around, crushing the rebellion before it had a chance to spread as far as Luxor.

"The dervish has fled into the hills," the young man said. "We are safe."

15

I AM PACKED AND READY. I HAVE FEW POSSESSIONS—ONE TRAVELING
trunk, and Abdullah; much of my life was furnished by my Lady
and must remain with my Lady. The baby is asleep in his basket, unaware of the turmoil around him. The government steamer
docked at Luxor this morning and will leave again this afternoon,
taking me and Abdullah with it. I am leaving. After months of
waiting, I am leaving Luxor.

I undress slowly. I fold my Egyptian clothes carefully—the
clothes that my Lady ordered for me specially just last year. I
have spent the past week mending and readying my English
clothes—the heavy undergarments and cumbersome petticoat.
I take the stays out from the bottom of my trunk and unwrap
them. They are like an extra set of ribs, a compact external cage.
I put them on and lace them tightly; my fingers have not forgotten what to do. Then I pull on the brown high-necked muslin
dress. I find my button hook and button myself into it, prickly
with heat already. My leather boots are heavy, as though caked
in English mud. I pin my hair up and place the white bonnet
on my head; I can't remember the last time I wore it. Gloves. I
am completely encased. I am ready.

My Lady stays in her room. There has been no farewell. She
has refused to give me a letter of reference for future employers,

nor would she agree to give me letters for the consular agents, to ease my passage down the Nile. Through Omar, she has passed on my final wages and a sum of money sufficient to buy passage to England, nothing more.

I don't want Lady Duff Gordon's money, though I take it, I must. what I want is for my Lady to change her mind, at this, the very last moment. What does she expect me to do when I get to England? I find myself wondering. But I am calm, I have no rage left today. I have no references, no money of my own, and no reputation either; everyone in London has heard what has happened to me. How does she think I will survive?

Omar's wife Mabrouka and his parents are expecting me in Cairo; Omar has sent messages on ahead of me. My Lady has arranged for me to deliver Abdullah to them before continuing on my journey. But I have other plans, plans I have told no one, not even my husband. I am leaving Luxor, yes, but I will not be leaving Egypt.

OMAR AND AHMED ENTER MY ROOM. TOGETHER, THEY LIFT THE traveling trunk and Abdullah's basket, taking them down to load onto the donkey. The boy does as he is told, but he can't stop crying. "Ahmed," I say, "you've proved your usefulness today: you are doing my crying for me." I mean this as a joke, but no one laughs. I have Abdullah in my arms; he has woken up and he pats my cheek happily. I carry him down the stairs, and out of the door, and that's it, we have left the French House, we are on our way through the village. The neighbors emerge, and they present me with gifts—dates, pastries, honey—for my journey and it is all I can do not to weep at their generosity. When we reach the steamer, Mustafa Agha rides up on his horse, dismounts, and bows to me. He gives me a large blue scarab, one I had admired once in his house, and he tells me he is desperately sad that I am leaving.

I AM IN THE TINY CABIN OF THE STEAMER AND OMAR HAS BROUGHT up my trunk—he has been to see the *reis* and given him money to ensure my safe passage—and the whistle blows, the boatmen call out, and Omar embraces me. He is trembling, I can see he can't find the right words, can't think what to say. But the whistle is blowing steadily and it is time for him to leave. "Take good care of my son," he says finally.

I bow my head. "*Insha allah*," I say.

And then my lover runs down the ramp towards the weeping Ahmed. I look across the village at the French House, where it sits up on the temple; there is a figure on the balcony. I strain to see through the glare of the afternoon, hoping it is my Lady. But it is Mohammed, and he is waving madly. I wave back at him and find myself smiling, in spite of everything. The steamer pulls away, and I have left Luxor already.

PART
3

AFTERLIFE

16

O NCE I LEFT MY LADY'S HOUSEHOLD, EVERYTHING WAS DIFFER-
ent. I felt as though my shame was written across my face
in indelible ink. I was entering the world alone, as I had years ago,
when I left my aunt's household and went into service for the first
time. I had lost the status and position that traveling with Lady
Duff Gordon conferred: the government envoy in every port, the
contacts both Egyptian and European, the friends of friends of
friends of my Lady's dotted here and there along the route; I was
left to fend for myself and my child. I had never traveled alone before, apart from taking the train up to London on my day off, and
I felt a million miles, and a million years, away from those days. I
had never traveled by government steamer and I was unused to the
crowded conditions; though it looked quite grand when it docked
at Luxor, towering above the feluccas, once on board I saw the
ship was battered and filthy and crawling with vermin. It had no
modern facilities to speak of; neither had many of the *dahabiehs* on
which we had traveled, but when you are two women with a crew
of twelve at your disposal, life is rather simpler than when you are
a woman and baby on your own, surrounded by strangers.

I passed the first night in a state of near panic, unable to leave
my cabin, certain I was surrounded by thieves and scoundrels
who would like nothing better than to snatch my baby from

me and throw him into the Nile. The door had no lock and its frame was so warped and crooked it took a great effort to shut it; I was unable to sleep and spent the night attempting to clean the cabin so that it would be habitable during the journey, but the windowless bunker—big enough for a camp bed and my traveling trunk, Abdullah's basket occupying what remained of the floor, though I kept him in the bed with me, afraid to let go of him—was too dark and airless for me to make much progress in that regard.

The next morning I was forced to leave the cabin to find water with which to bathe Abdullah. I emerged, clutching the baby in my arms, broiling hot in the high-necked muslin dress despite the early hour. The moment I came out on deck, a group of peasant women gathered around me, and I wanted to rush back into the dreary cabin and push the trunk against the door. They stared at me, in silence, and I stared back at them, unable to move. I would say I have never been so frightened in my life, except since Abdullah's birth I have been afraid for myself and my child over and over again.

But then one of the ladies smiled at me.

And I remembered. I remembered where I was, and I remembered by whom I was surrounded: Egyptians. Could there be a kinder, more hospitable race on this earth? I took a deep breath, returned the smile, and greeted the women respectfully: "*Es salaam ahlaykum.*" They began to talk at me all at once, happy and cheerful and friendly and curious; they whisked the baby out of my arms to fuss over and pamper him, and they shared their water and food with me, giving me the best, the most sweet, the most delicious of everything, and would not allow me to return the favor, and they made me sit in the shade on deck at the stern of the steamer and rest while they entertained Abdullah, and they asked me dozens and dozens of questions, and were amazed by my Arabic, even more amazed to hear I had married an Egyptian, though they disapproved of the fact that he had allowed me to travel down the Nile by myself. It was unheard of for *Frangi* to travel by government steamer, and they swore I was the first-ever *Frangi* woman to do so, and they brought word from the *reis* himself that I was the first he had ever seen.

And so it happened: I left the world of Lady Duff Gordon, surrounded by men, with men as our companions, our servants, our teachers, our friends, and I entered the realm of women for that journey, where men, except our children, those much-loved boys, scarcely existed. The boat steamed down the Nile at a steady, even pace, not subject to wind or calm as a *dahabieh* would have been, and my days aboard were a kind of blessed reprieve, though I did not realize this at the time.

I SPENT MY DAYS ON THE STEAMER PLANNING. IT TOOK ME A WHILE to realize it, but if there was no one to take care of me, there was also no one telling me what to do. I fobbed off the women's inquiries about where I was going, what I was doing, as best I could: of course my husband's family was meeting me in Cairo, of course I knew where to go, what to do. The women around me and the white lies I told them helped me see the truth. I was not going to give Abdullah to Omar's first wife and return to England. Why on earth would I do such a thing? Lady Duff Gordon had thrown me out, it was true, and in doing so, she had released me from my burden of loyalty. I was not going to do what Lady Duff Gordon demanded of me.

There was my husband to be considered, of course, and if Omar had been there, I would have asked his permission, and I would have obeyed him; I was a good wife. But he was not there. I was not going to give up everything I had ever loved and meekly go away so that my Lady would never have to face me again. I was not going to do such a thing, no matter how far Lady Duff

Gordon's influence reached. I would find a way to stay in Cairo, and to keep Abdullah with me.

My resolve gave me courage; courage stiffened my resolve. Omar would forgive me. I felt as sure of that as I was of anything.

AT THE PORT OF BOULAK IN CAIRO THE TRUE NATURE OF MY PRE-dicament presented itself to me yet again. On the steamer I had been occupied, entertained, and cosseted by my traveling companions. Even a small dose of dysentery did not have too great an ill effect on my journey. But Cairo: once we were docked, the women who had accompanied me said farewell, *Insha allah, Al-hamdulillah,* and disappeared into the crowds like water sluicing off the ship's deck. As I walked down the gangway I felt the scrutiny of all those present on the dock and regretted my decision to wear European dress that day. Egyptians may be kind, but they have no compunction regarding staring and do not seem to consider it rude or intrusive in any way. And I was an unlikely figure, loaded down with trunk and baby, on my own. I had not allowed Omar to arrange for anyone to meet me at Boulak; as far as he was concerned, I was to travel straight to his parents' house to hand over Abdullah, and from there to Alexandria to await my passage across the Mediterranean Sea. This was the point I had planned to melt into the crowd myself. Only I was far too conspicuous for melting.

WITH THE MONEY THAT MY LADY HAD INTENDED FOR MY PASSAGE TO England, I installed myself in a pension in the center of the city. I paid Umm Mahmoud, the elderly wife of the pension owner, a small amount to care for Abdullah for a few hours every day. She was a tall woman with a broad lap and a rich smile; she smelled of rosewater and anise and told me she loved Abdullah already. I began to look for work. I started at Shepheard's Hotel, familiar territory, where I knew I would find other English people, other English ladies' maids.

In the foyer of the hotel all conversation stopped the moment I entered. I saw myself through English eyes for the first time in a long time: my face and hands were tanned a warm peasant brown and my dress was suddenly unbearably shabby, my bonnet scuffed and shrunken, my gloves in need of replacing. I held myself very upright and approached the first English servant I spotted.

"Are you a lady's maid?" I asked, my voice strained with the unfamiliar English; I could hear how peculiar my accent had become.

The woman—no more than nineteen or twenty years of age—was wearing a version of what I wore, only cleaner, fresher, brighter, unstained. She looked at me and recoiled. "Why do you ask?" she said in a little mouse shriek.

"Do you work here in Cairo?"

"We leave for Alexandria tomorrow; we are returning to England." The young woman pulled herself together. "Why are you asking?"

I could see the attention of the people in the foyer, small clusters of women drinking tea, pairs of men smoking, remained focused on me. And I understood my mistake: Shepheard's Hotel was not a good place to look for English people who live in Cairo; Shepheard's Hotel was full of people who were just arriving and people who were ready to leave. At that moment, a member of the hotel staff approached. He put his hand on my arm and I was so shocked at being touched by a strange man that I told him off, sharply, in Arabic. The little maid I had been addressing ran away.

The hotel steward scowled. "You are not welcome here."

He thought I was a prostitute. Mortified, I fled.

AFTER THAT I WAS SUNK INTO SUCH DESPONDENCY THAT I WAS scarcely able to leave the pension. I spent my days in my room with

Abdullah and fell into the rhythm I had grown to know well in the French House, hiding away, waiting. My room, though spartan, was dark and cool and had a wind catcher, one of the wooden latticed window bays so typical of Cairo, jutting out over the narrow street. I sat there, like a good Egyptian daughter, and watched the world pass by.

After a few days I pulled myself together and, with Umm Mahmoud as my adviser, found a tailor in the market and used a good portion of my Lady's money to pay him to make a copy of my high-necked dress, only this time in lightweight Egyptian cotton, covered in tiny floral sprigs. I knew the truth now: no English person would employ me. My time in Egypt had transformed me; I was no longer the ideal servant I had once been. But I had a new idea: the Egyptian elite might be amused by the idea of a proper English lady's maid in their household, even one with a damaged reputation. But who on earth could provide me with the necessary introductions to these people? Lady Duff Gordon moved in a world of introductions; it seemed that whatever she needed, whatever we needed, was only an introduction or two away. But here in Cairo there was no one to ease my way in society. The thought of what I needed to do in order to survive made me quite breathless at times; I'd have to sit down and put my head between my knees, like a grand lady overtaken by a spell of the vapors, like my Lady herself on one of her bad days. I had no time for such weakness. Time and again, I forced myself back onto my feet.

THE CITY WAS CHANGING RAPIDLY; THE BANKS OF THE NILE HAD been made secure and the flood plain had given way to a vast building site as Ismail Pasha set out to fulfill his grand plan of turning Cairo into the Paris of Africa. In the almost two years since my first visit to the city with my Lady, I had seen great changes take place, yet more palaces finished, great wide boulevards crisscrossing the medieval city, roads tarmacked, gardens planted, pavements laid. The pace of change increased as work progressed on the canal at Suez, while the great and good of Cairo looked to Europe for inspiration. The *Frangi* quarter flourished to the west of the Old City, but I was still smarting from my visit to Shepheard's Hotel and had decided to avoid Europeans. My cash was dwindling, despite the generosity of my landlady, and I needed to find work. I had not written to my sister Ellen to tell her where I was, and I hoped that the news that I had not handed over the baby had not yet reached Omar in Luxor. Cairo was quiet for only a few hours each day, just before dawn, and again at the hot hours of midafternoon, when there was silence, broken only by the cool tinkle of the water seller with his brass cups and his call for custom, offering liquorice water and carob and raisin sorbet as well; it was during these quiet hours, kept awake by my worries, that I decided what I must do.

In the early morning light I put on my Egyptian clothes, including the headscarf and veil, which I never felt the need of in Luxor but wore often here in Cairo, where I had rapidly grown weary of the curiosity my presence provoked. I left Abdullah with Umm Mahmoud yet again, and he settled into the lap of the old woman without complaint. I made my way through the streets of Cairo; like all other pedestrians, I was forced to pause frequently to flatten myself against the stone walls of the buildings that line the streets to enable the camel and donkey traffic to pass by. Finally, I reached the boundary of the city, where I struck out into the countryside. I had visited my Lady's friend Hekekyan Bey in his country residence several times by carriage, and I remembered the way. It was a long walk, through cotton fields; the heat bore down on me beneath my veil and I had to stop and drink water from the irrigation ditch that ran beside the road. After several hours I began to fear that I had taken a wrong turn and was lost, when I saw Hekekyan Bey's house in the distance, surrounded by tall palms, shimmering like an oasis.

The house lies within a walled compound and I pulled on a bell rope at the gate. It was midmorning now, and the early June temperature rose relentlessly. A servant came to the door and frowned to see a strange veiled woman standing there, but I addressed him in Arabic and, remembering myself, pulled my headscarf down onto my shoulders and removed my veil. The servant's eyes almost popped out of his head at this spectacle of an Englishwoman revealed, and I smiled in spite of everything. Hekekyan Bey was not at home, the servant informed me; he went to fetch Hekekyan Bey's wife, whom I had also met several times.

I knew I was taking a risk in going to Hekekyan Bey for help; news of my visit would almost certainly find its way back to my Lady. But news travels slowly in Egypt and I hoped that by the time she discovered my ruse I'd be well established in a new position, beyond her reach.

Hekekyan Bey's wife received me in the formal salon of the house, among the antiquities that her husband buys and exports from the country. While I waited for her to appear, I rested on a divan beside a black granite sphinx, seated on its haunches like a large, alert dog. Across the room, a green marble cat watched me. And in the shadows on the far side of the room I could see a mummy in its painted wooden box leaning against the wall. After long minutes during which I adjusted and readjusted my clothes, wishing that I had worn my English dress after all—Egyptian dress for the journey, *Frangi* once I arrived—Hekekyan Bey's wife appeared, followed by a servant bearing lemonade and pastries. She welcomed me to her house with a good deal of grace and we made an elaborate exchange of greetings and blessings.

"We heard that you had left the service of Lady Duff Gordon."

I bowed my head and did not speak.

"Mrs. Henry Ross wrote to the father of my children; she wants to convince Lady Duff Gordon to hire a new maid. She should not be in Egypt without the service of an English maid, don't you agree?"

I looked up at Hekekyan Bey's wife and then bowed my head once again. "No," I concurred, "she should not be without a maid. But Omar Abu Halaweh"—I paused—"the father of my son, cares for her ably."

"Yes. He was a good find."

We looked at each other then but said nothing.

"Where is your child? I would have liked to have seen him."

"I have left him with a—friend—in Cairo today," I said. "I wanted to ask Hekekyan Bey for advice."

She smiled. "The father of my children is expert at giving advice."

"But he is not here."

"No. Tell me why you have come, and I will speak to him for you on his return."

"I need to find a new position," I said.

She frowned.

"Not with the *Frangi*, but I thought, perhaps, an Egyptian family? A family with daughters, perhaps, who would like to learn to speak English, who have need of all the services that an English servant could provide. I'm very skilled—"

"I don't doubt it," Hekekyan Bey's wife interrupted, as though she had suddenly grown weary of me. "It's an interesting idea. The father of my children is away on business; he'll return at the end of the month."

"The end of the month?" I said, and I struggled to hide my dismay; that was weeks away.

"I'll speak to him about you. He will doubtless have some idea of how to help."

"Thank you. I would be most grateful."

"Tell me where you are staying."

I gave the wife of Hekekyan Bey the name of the pension; I knew I was taking a risk giving her this information, but there was no choice, it was the same risk I took coming here in the first place. I got up to leave, refusing lunch so that I could get back to

Abdullah. At the gate, Hekekyan Bey's wife said, "You have not hired a carriage?" and I could hear the surprise in her voice and, with it, her reappraisal of my situation. A donkey was summoned, along with a boy to lead it along the track. As we trotted back to Cairo I felt my confidence in Hekekyan Bey slip away: too much time would elapse before his return to Egypt and any introductions he might consent to give me. I would need to do something else in the meantime.

At the suggestion of Umm Mahmoud, the next day I made my way to one of the new hotels that had opened; every season Cairo saw a bigger influx of tourists from a greater range of society, and new hotels had begun to open all over the city. Not all were as venerable as Shepheard's, and the hotel in which I found myself employment was not venerable at all, only a few shallow steps in status above Umm Mahmoud's humble pension. I was hired by the Italian owner, Roberto Magni, a carpetbagger who had struck on the excellent idea of separating tourists and their money by providing them with not-very-clean rooms. He was pleased to find himself an English-speaking employee, and from the first day onward I was engaged to do all manner of tasks, from scrubbing floors to dealing with the English-speaking clientele. Mr. Magni wanted me to board at the hotel so I would be able to work longer hours; I had no intention of telling him about Abdullah and so refused. But I was a rare enough beast, with my English and my Arabic, that he decided to hang on to me anyway.

The wages were low, and after paying Umm Mahmoud to care for Abdullah as well as paying for our room and meals, I earned nothing extra, although the work meant that I no longer had to continue spending the money Lady Duff Gordon had given me for my passage to England. I was unused to managing money— my Lady had always paid all my expenses—but I learned quickly.

Though the work was lowly, I was immeasurably relieved to discover that, in some quarters, I was considered employable; I slept better at night now, kept awake only by Abdullah, and waking with him was sweet.

After a few days at the hotel I realized that the new breed of tourist was nothing like I had ever met before, not even in Luxor, where, it seemed, a great chunk of humanity had floated past on the Nile tour. News of Egypt's belle époque had spread throughout Europe and tourists came anticipating access to dancing girls and exotic harems full of naked houris and found themselves instead in a medieval city where the layer of European-style sophistication was wafer thin, where only peasant women were not kept secluded, out of sight. The hotel had its own bar and it was peopled with adventurers, men who already were, or were about to be, disappointed. Missing the female companionship I had found aboard the steamer, I did my best to steer clear of them, though I was not entirely successful, given my role as chief English-speaker.

One night one of the men followed me back to Umm Mahmoud's pension. As I made my way through the streets, I felt him behind me, and all the warnings I had ever had about being alone in a city at night rushed up to overtake me. At the entrance to the pension I opened the door with the intention of slipping through and locking it behind me, but to my horror he caught the door before I could close it and strong-armed his way in, trying but failing to grab me. I ran past him up the stairs to get to my room, where I knew that Umm Mahmoud would have put Abdullah down to sleep for the night: if I can just get to my room, I thought, and bolt the door. But the man caught up with me as I reached the landing and, though I regretted it deeply a moment later, I did not shout out for fear of waking and scandalizing the old woman and her husband. The man bundled me into my room and shut the door.

I thought I would die. I thought he would kill me. In the darkness of the room I could hear him breathing, I could smell his rancid breath, his clothes stinking of alcohol and cheap tobacco. I held my ground as he came towards me. His hands were at my throat.

And then, I fought. In silence. Without waking the baby, without making any noise at all apart from the scuffling of feet, the tearing of fabric, the *whump-whump* as I used my fists. I was furious, absolutely stone-cold furious, not just with this man, but with everything and everyone—with Lady Duff Gordon for expelling me from her household, with Omar for allowing me to leave, with Hekekyan Bey for not being there when I went to see him, with Roberto Magni and his ghastly hotel—and I let all my anger out as I pushed and hit and scratched and tore, until I shoved the surprised and bloodied man out the door.

I woke up Abdullah and held him to my breast as though I hoped he would protect me, not the other way around.

THE MORNING AFTER THE MAN FROM ROBERTO MAGNI'S HOTEL ATtacked me, I rose from where I had lain all night in my new dress, now soiled with blood, torn and beyond repair, and went about my business as though nothing had happened, as though my baby and I had passed the night in equal peace. I washed and dressed myself gingerly, grateful for once for the high collar of my brown muslin as it served to hide the bruises on my neck. As I dressed, I examined my life coldly. I knew that until I could speak to Hekekyan Bey about a new position, I would have to keep working for Mr. Roberto Magni, whether the man from last night was still staying at the hotel or not. I knew that I could not rely on Umm Mahmoud to care for Abdullah indefinitely, no matter how much the kind old lady professed to adore him. I knew I had to hang on to the small sum of money I had left, in case of emergencies, of which, all things considered, there were bound to be a few. I knew that if anything untoward happened to Abdullah, I would die.

And so, as I dressed that morning, I made my decision.

It was all very well making plans; it was all very well finding employment and making my way through the city. But it was not enough. Lady Duff Gordon would have laughed if she could see me: begging at the door of Hekekyan Bey; preyed upon by the kind of man I had spent my life avoiding; placing myself and worse, much worse, placing my baby in harm's way.

I looked at myself in the stained and cracked little mirror that hung above my bed. I had nothing left. I had no choice. I would give up my child to my husband's other wife.

17

Mabrouka was different from what I expected; she was taller and stronger-looking somehow. She was much younger than I had anticipated, at least a decade younger than me, if not more, though she had been Omar's wife for over three years already. When he described to me how she lived—brought up cloistered in her father's house, betrothed to Omar before they had ever met, and now living in his father's house with as little as possible to do with the outside world, the society of men—I imagined she would be tiny and timid, with a voice so quiet everyone would have to strain to hear it. But she was not like that at all.

Omar's parents welcomed me fulsomely, calling me "daughter" as soon as they realized who I was. I had gone with what I thought was great resolve; I knew what I had to do, and I had to do it for Abdullah. But to be called "daughter" because I was Omar's wife, to see Abdullah taken up and celebrated as a beloved grandchild by both Omar's mother and father, made me understand, yet again, the harshness of my situation. From the moment I arrived I had difficulty controlling myself. I was there to give up my son to these people, and they were treating me with such kindness. It could not have been anything other than very strange for them—a woman whom they had never met, to whom they had no connection, not a Muslim, not an Egyptian, turning up on their doorstep with their son's baby—but they treated me as if it was all perfectly natural, as though they'd always known Omar would take a second wife and that it would be someone as old, odd, and alien as me.

"When are you leaving Egypt?" Omar's mother asked.

"Oh," I said, at a loss.

"Omar's message was that you must return to England."

"Yes, but I—" I hesitated. "I no longer need to go."

"You are staying in Cairo?" Omar's father asked.

"Yes," I said, "I have a new position."

"This is good!" he declared, smiling broadly. Then the servant interrupted us with tea.

Omar's father's house was cool and fragrant and well ordered; the rooms I was shown into were comfortable and very clean, with low divans and large cushions lining the walls, well-beaten carpets on the floors, mirrors and candles and incense and flowers, the worn old walls painted warm oranges and yellows, windows shuttered against the sun, the central courtyard cool with its blue-tiled well and its little fountain. It took a while for Mabrouka to appear, and the pleasure of watching Omar's mother and father—who kept insisting that I call them "mother," *umm*, and "father," *ab*—play with Abdullah almost made me forget about her. She entered the room quietly, and Omar's mother rose to introduce us, and Mabrouka said, "Welcome." She was carrying her little girl, Yasmina, and I could not look away from the child, she was so like Abdullah, so like my son, Abdullah, and their father, Omar. The child came as a shock to me, in fact the whole family was a shock to me; all thoughts of them had been crowded out of my head by my circumstances since Abdullah's birth. But here they were, here we were, and I was giving Abdullah to them just as Lady Duff Gordon had decreed.

Mabrouka did not speak beyond greeting me; in that she conformed to my expectations, but the look she gave me was so direct, and so piercing, that I was taken aback, though I had no idea whatsoever what that look might mean. How did she view me? Was I her rival? Second wives are less and less common in Egypt now, though still permitted by law, but so far I had failed to comply with virtually every social custom to do with marriage. I could not afford to dwell on these thoughts, so I began to talk about Abdullah—his routines, his needs, what kind of tricks I used to keep him happy—and with that my resolve collapsed even further as I felt the time to hand over my baby approaching. I stood, unable to recall the niceties of Egyptian leave-taking.

"I must go," I said, bluntly.

Omar's family looked at me, but again, I had no idea what they were thinking. "Please," said Omar's mother, "stay a little longer. You must eat."

I shook my head quickly and knew I was being impolite but before I could stop them, tears began to spill from my eyes. "May I come to visit him, from time to time?" I asked.

"Yes, of course," said Omar's father, and he looked as bewildered and dismayed as I felt. "You are our daughter now. This is your home."

I looked at him, and I looked once more at Abdullah, who was mesmerized by a trinket his grandmother had given him. How I longed to stay in that house, to reside with Omar's family like a good Egyptian wife, to find a way to make our strange situation benefit us all. But I had already disobeyed Lady Duff Gordon and misled my husband by not leaving for England, and I knew the repercussions for Omar once my Lady discovered the truth could be harsh. So I gave Abdullah another kiss and a cuddle, and I handed him to Mabrouka, my husband's other wife. And I walked away.

I went back to work for Roberto Magni that day, and he was pleased when I agreed to do the extra hours he asked of me. There was no sign of the man from the night before. When I returned to the pension late that evening, Umm Mahmoud had already retired; she had been very upset that morning when I told her that

Abdullah was going. And now I'd have to tell her that I'd be leaving myself; money was too tight to continue living in one cheap hotel while working in another. I went into my room and lay down on my bed and my battered body ached, not from the bruises I had sustained, but from losing my child. "He is safe," I whispered, "he is safe and well cared for, with his family who will show him their love. He is safe. He is safe." But these words did not reassure me. These words did nothing to assuage my grief.

I USED TO GO AND STAND OUTSIDE OMAR'S FATHER'S HOUSE, AT ODD times, when I could slip out from beneath the gaze of Roberto Magni. I'd stand by the corner where I was sure no one inside that house could see me, and I'd listen and watch and wait. What I was listening and watching and waiting for, I had no idea—a sign of some kind, of my baby and his welfare. Once I saw the servant emerge with an empty bag, on her way to market. Once I saw Omar's father come out: I froze with panic—I didn't want to be seen; I longed for him to see me—but he went in the other direction. I noticed he walked with a stoop, as though his back was tired and sore, and this, of itself, made me cry. I was always crying, all day and all night; my eyes leaked tears, my breasts leaked Abdullah's milk, I was damp with sorrow and self-pity. I knew it was the best I could do: I needed to work; Abdullah needed a family.

IT WASN'T DIFFICULT TO HATE LADY DUFF GORDON. IT WASN'T DIF-ficult to blame her for what had happened to me. I hated her beautifully: my hatred was polished and hard and shiny and, truth be told, at times it sustained me. I sometimes wondered where she was: had she left Luxor yet, to travel to Cairo and on to Europe as planned? How was her health? Travel always made her weak, prone to infection and illness. Was Omar caring for her properly?

And Omar, where was he? Late at night I tested my love for him, as if I was testing a wound; I probed it in order to feel it sting. It was still there, as painful as ever, no sign of it healing. I comforted myself with a series of unlikely scenarios: Omar, Abdullah, and me happily ensconced in our own rooms in the Abu Halaweh Cairo household; Omar, Abdullah, and me with one hundred *feddan*s of land in the rich and fertile delta of the Nile; Omar, Abdullah, and me on a grand *dahabieh* floating gently upstream. These scenes, bright and clear for a few moments, crumbled to dust on the floor of my room in Roberto Magni's hotel. It was an effort to conjure them, keep them vivid. And Lady Duff Gordon never featured in these stories.

Instead, she stalked my dreams. Night after night, always the same dream: my Lady and me sitting together in the French House, the warm spring sun streaming in through the shutters, me reclining half-asleep on the floor cushions, my Lady laughing and gossiping while she brushes my hair, Omar smiling at us both as he pours our mint tea. The little owl sits on the windowsill, blinking.

Then I wake up and I mourn the loss of languor and ease. I mourn the loss of that life, itself a distant dream. But most of all, I mourn the loss of my child, who is, I can't help but believe, the natural result of that scene.

I WAITED FOUR WEEKS BEFORE I RETURNED TO OMAR'S FATHER'S house to visit my baby. Four long and awful weeks. I resisted the strongest urge I have ever felt—stronger even than that which pulled me towards Omar in the first place—and I did not visit Abdullah at all during that time. I wanted him to settle into his new home, and I wanted to allow Mabrouka and Omar's parents time to get to know him in their own way. I wanted my bodily connection to him, my desire to feed my baby, to have gone away. I wanted Abdullah to be loved, to be happy.

218 # KATE PULLINGER

After four weeks had passed I allowed myself to make that journey through the streets to Omar's father's house. I went first thing in the morning, as I wanted to look fresh and to appear in control of my situation. I did not have long—Roberto Magni and his hotel continued to dominate my waking hours—but I hoped, at least, to see Abdullah for a few moments. I pulled the bell rope and the servant who opened the door recognized me immediately.

This time it was Omar's mother who greeted me. She took both my hands into hers and smiled and welcomed me.

"Please," I said, "I know you'll think me very rude, but may I see Abdullah? Please?"

"Yes, of course," she said, "you must have missed him terribly. We have been waiting for you to return."

"I wanted to give him, and you, enough time—"

"I know," she interrupted, "you did the right thing."

She took me straight to Mabrouka's private quarters and knocked lightly on the the open door.

"Come in," Mabrouka said.

We walked into the room. On the floor, taking breakfast around a low table, sat Omar's wife Mabrouka, Yasmina on one side, my baby Abdullah on the other. He was sitting up on his own—I couldn't believe my eyes—supported by two cushions, his hands gluey with mashed fruit. He gave his grandmother a broad smile, and then he looked at me.

I couldn't move. I did not know what I should do.

"Peace be with you," Mabrouka said.

"*Alhamdulillah,*" I replied.

"Please, come and sit with your child. Let me pour you some coffee. Mother," she said, her voice light but formal, "will you join us?"

And so I sat with them, and I drank coffee, and after a few minutes I took Abdullah onto my lap and he twisted around to look up at me and smiled and reached up and patted my cheek, and I have scarcely felt such bliss before; it was as though I had been in jail and this was my day of release.

"Where are you living?" Omar's mother asked. "You did not tell us last time you came. We had no way of sending you news."

I told them where I was living and working.

"I will give Omar your address when we see him," Omar's mother said.

"Omar is in Cairo?" I said, and I'm sure my face displayed my shock.

Omar's mother and Mabrouka exchanged a look. "Yes, he is," Omar's mother replied. "At Boulak. He sent a message, but he has not been to see us yet; Lady Duff Gordon has been very unwell. The doctor visits twice a day."

Omar in Cairo. Omar in Cairo. Hope rose up inside me and I forced it back down again. I couldn't afford to think about Omar and what his presence in the city might mean for me. I had to focus on Abdullah, on these few moments I could spend with my baby. "Tell me about him," I said, looking down at my baby. "How does he sleep?"

"He is fine," Mabrouka said. "He is a most happy and cheerful baby," and she gave me a warm and open smile.

The time sped by. Before it ended, Mabrouka said, "You must come to see him as often as you like."

"I will," I said, "if you will allow me."

"Of course," said Omar's mother, "you must come every day. You are welcome at any time."

I had no idea if they were simply being polite, but I intended to take up their offer. I would see my child, sometimes only for a few minutes, but I would see Abdullah every day.

A WEEK LATER, I WAS ON MY HANDS AND KNEES, SCRUBBING THE staircase of Roberto Magni's hotel, when I heard Omar's voice.

"Sally?"

I heard him say my name. And again. "Sally."

I sat back in a pool of water and looked up. I was not hallucinating. My husband was standing in front of me.

"You are working here?" Omar asked, his voice hard with anger.

"Omar," I replied. "Omar!" I stood; my skirt was dripping. "You found me." I couldn't believe it. Look at me, I wanted to say: everything has changed since I left Luxor. Do you still love me?

"Why did you stay in Cairo?" Omar asked. His voice was thick; he cleared his throat. "My Lady gave you money to leave."

I stood in the dim light of the stairwell, brushing down my dress; I could see he was shocked by my appearance. The past weeks had aged me; my face was drawn and lined with fatigue. I was thin and toughened, like a leather strap. "I went to see Hekekyan Bey," I said, as though this was a proper explanation. "I'm hoping he'll be able to help me find a more suitable position. Have you heard—has he returned to Egypt?"

Omar shook his head. "You should know better, Sally. Hekekyan Bey will not offer you his influence."

I frowned. Then I read Omar's expression, and closed my eyes. "I couldn't leave," I said. "Even though I was alone. How could I leave our child? It is bad enough not being able to care for him myself; how could you even think I would leave? I don't want to work in a place like this, but how else can I survive? Omar," I said, "I have to stay close to our child."

"Sally," Omar said, and I saw all the regret he had ever felt come rushing into his face. "Take this," he said, and he emptied his purse of money, a small sum, all he was carrying. And before either of us could say another word, he took me into his arms and held me, and our long nights together in Luxor and Cairo came back to us and he pulled me closer and closer into his embrace.

I wanted to live—sleep, dream, wake—in his arms and it was as though I could feel myself growing soft and warm and generous once again, even as we stood together in that mean foyer, our feet in a puddle of filthy water.

Roberto Magni rounded a corner and saw me—his brittle and unfriendly employee—caught up in a luxurious embrace. He coughed loudly, and Omar and I fell apart, and he saw the money I was holding in one hand. "Sally," he said, in his poor English, "who this?" When I did not reply, he continued, "There's room upstairs you need clean." Then he treated Omar to a knowing wink and spoke to him in equally poor Arabic, "Need a room, do you?"

Omar, angered by the man's insinuation, quickly turned to leave. "I'll be back," he said to me.

That night when I had finished my duties, Roberto Magni informed me he was docking my wages because I was using the hotel to earn extra money. "I saw you and Egyptian fellow," he said and he touched a dirty finger to the side of his dirty nose. "I surprised to see you go with Arab. I thought you'd stick with *Frangi*."

I did not reply. Roberto Magni could think whatever he liked. My child was safe. And I had seen my husband and I knew now that he still loved me.

18

AND SO MY LIFE CONTINUED LIKE THIS: EARLY EVERY MORNING, I made my way to the house of Omar's parents, to spend a few minutes with my baby. The household came to expect me; my arrival was no longer a surprise. The servant, Umm Yasin, who had been with the family for many years, opened the door to me and I walked through the internal courtyard, past the lovely ancient jasmine vine so carefully tended by Omar's mother, and into Mabrouka's rooms. A place was laid for me at the breakfast table, a cup of strong sweet coffee, a pastry fresh from the oven room, a ripe fig. I became part of their routine, and no routine has ever been as precious to me. Abdullah sat on my lap, happy, and we taught him to say "Mama" in English. When I entered the room he'd look up and say "Mama" and I thought I would burst from smiling.

Omar's mother passed Omar's news on to me. "Lady Duff Gordon's health is improving."

"That's good," I said.

"Omar thinks they'll be ready to travel to Europe soon."

I paused. "My Lady will be pleased to be reunited with her family."

"Omar is able to visit us most afternoons for the time being."

I looked at Mabrouka, and she looked at me, her gaze steady. "He must be pleased to see Abdullah and Yasmina every day," I said.

"He is," Mabrouka replied.

I could not read her; I could not begin to guess what she was thinking.

"Tell us about where you are working," she said.

"It's a hotel," I replied. "A pension."

"Is it very grand?"

"No, it's—well, it's rather small. Only a few rooms. It's not . . ." I wasn't sure what to say; I didn't know why she was asking me about Roberto Magni's. "It's a decent job," I said. "I need to work." I turned to Omar's mother, worried; had I misread the situation all this time? "I can contribute to Abdullah's upkeep, if you need me to. I'm sorry not to have spoken about this sooner; it did not occur to me."

Omar's mother looked as shocked as if I had turned and struck her face. "Daughter, no," she said, "that's not what Mabrouka is saying!"

"I'm sorry," I said, more embarrassed than ever, "what are you asking me?"

Mabrouka looked at me again with that unreadable expression. Then she began to laugh. "Sally!" she said. "I'm just curious! You work in a Cairo hotel. I want to know what it's like."

Omar's mother laughed as well, and so did I, with relief.

"Please," said Mabrouka, "tell me about what you do."

And so I told her, and from her response I realized that, although to me it was mundane drudgery, for Mabrouka I might as well be describing life in another century, it was so far removed from her experience. From then on during each of my morning visits I allowed myself to talk a little more; I made sure to bring along an anecdote or two, a story about a guest who could not pay his bill and how Roberto Magni made him give up his wedding ring, or a tale about the puzzling presence of mismatched boots left behind on the floor of a room. Mabrouka rewarded my talk with talk of her own, gossip about the neighbors who made too much noise at night, the scandal involving the daughter next door, the family's plans for the next holiday feast, and always, endlessly fascinating stories about Abdullah and his every new trick, his every sigh.

My visits never coincided with Omar's; when he could get away, he came during the afternoon, while my Lady was resting, crossing Cairo on foot at the hottest time of day. I was never told much about these visits, beyond the news he brought: my Lady's daughter, Mrs. Ross, had been to visit; she was leaving for Europe without my Lady. "Leaving for Europe without my Lady," Mabrouka said, "what kind of a daughter is she?"

"Mabrouka!" Omar's mother said.

"Well, it's true. Her mother is unwell, and still she cannot delay her departure a few weeks?" They looked to me for a reply.

"That's Miss Janet," I said. "Miss Janet never changes her mind, nor her plans."

They were baffled by this and I could not begin to explain.

"Tell me about where you live," Mabrouka asked another day.

"I live in Roberto Magni's hotel. I have a small room," I said. "There's a European-style bed. There's a shelf for my things." I did not say it's like a prison cell, there is no window, at night with the door locked it is stifling.

"Do you like living there?"

"I have no choice."

"Will you remain there, always?"

I was not sure what to say. Omar's mother scooped up Abdullah, who was crawling towards her across the cushions. "Look at him," she said, "look at how this delicious boy is growing." Mabrouka's questions dropped away.

When I left Omar's family's house that day I thought about Mabrouka and Omar's mother. Was I missing something? Were they waiting for me to ask if I could live in their house? Did they think my insistence on living in the place I worked was yet another unfathomable *Frangi* habit? Were they too polite to ask if I really did prefer it that way? How could I discover the truth? I would need to see Omar first. I would need Omar to sort out everything. I would, of course, continue to work for Roberto Magni; I would contribute to the household income, perhaps even enabling Omar's father to work less himself. I would not need my own room; I could sleep with Abdullah; it would give me such joy to sleep with Abdullah once again, the tiniest space would do. I could be the family servant, that would also suit me, though I wouldn't want to usurp the old family retainer, that would not be right, but I could make life easier for her in the oven room and the pantry. I could—

I put a stop to these thoughts, before I got carried away. I needed to speak to Omar about my situation. But how? There was no point trying to time my visit to Abdullah with his; I couldn't get away from the hotel in the afternoon, and besides, I wanted to see him alone. Going to Boulak ran too many risks. I did not want Lady Duff Gordon to discover I was still in Egypt; she'd learn soon enough, doubtless, but I was fairly sure that Omar would not have told her that I had not done as she ordered and returned to England. There was little time: soon Omar would be leaving for Europe with my Lady and I could not take it upon myself to move in without his permission. At night all this rushed around and around in my head.

But one morning when I sat down with Mabrouka for breakfast, I felt a change in the atmosphere: something had shifted. The air was hot and still; the night had not brought much relief from the heat of the previous day. Something had happened since my last visit, a conversation had taken place. Mabrouka looked at me, frowning. Abdullah began to fret; Omar's mother picked him up and carried him away, saying she was taking him to fetch a cool drink. I felt cold, despite the heat. Had I done something wrong? Were they going to stop my visits?

"I told him you love your child," said Mabrouka. "Any fool can see it."

I did not know what to say.

"I told him the life you are leading is too harsh, much too harsh for any woman, Egyptian or *Frangi*."

I could not reply.

"He says it is not my place to speak of such things, but I told him I'm ashamed that his wife, a daughter of this family, should have to live in this way."

I bowed my head and stared at my hands, engulfed by shame.

"And do you know what he said?"

I looked at Mabrouka. I felt no hope. I felt as though my head might burst into flames.

" 'Sally will not be coming to live here, in my father's house,' " she mimicked Omar's voice cleverly. " 'She will do no such thing.' And when I asked him why, he said it was his decision. Then he told me to stop talking about you, to stop asking questions, that your fate was none of my business. He told me to be silent."

I sat for a moment. Mabrouka put her hand on mine. "I'm sorry," she said, whispering. I closed my eyes and sat in that quiet, calm house in the midst of the family that would never be mine.

Then I got up and headed back out into the city. I walked directly to Boulak, crossing Cairo swiftly as though it was a journey I made every day. At the port I inquired as to the whereabouts of Lady Duff Gordon's *dahabieh*, and when I found it, I climbed on board without being seen and went straight to the galley. Omar was there, as I knew he would be, preparing lunch for my Lady.

"Seeing you in the hotel—," I said.

"I know," he replied, "but . . ."

"—made me realize how I have missed you." I watched him closely.

"As I have missed you, Sally, but if my Lady discovers you here . . ."

I held up my hand to silence him; we were both keeping our voices very low, well aware of the proximity of my Lady.

Omar took my hand and pulled me to him and began to kiss me. The months apart burned beneath my skin. We stumbled from the galley into Omar's cabin and, the door shut, pressed ourselves together with more urgency than before. I let my husband kiss me, I let my husband undress me.

Afterwards, we held each other, and I couldn't help but laugh and smile.

Omar was altogether more serious, worried. "Why have you come here?"

"I've come to ask for something," I said, still smiling.

He shifted a little, and a gap opened between our bodies. We were sticky with passion, aware of how completely airless the cabin had become. "Yes?" he said.

"Let me live with your parents and Mabrouka. They want me to, Mabrouka wants me there, and I can no longer remember why I do not live there with Abdullah. I need your permission to live with them. I will find a new job—"

"I can help you find a new job," he said quickly.

"I need to find somewhere decent I can live, and I want to be close to our child. Omar, I need to be able to see my baby for more than a few minutes every day. Please." I felt exhausted by having made the request I'd been storing up for so long.

Omar shifted again. He cleared his throat. "No," he said. "You can't do it. I won't allow it."

I sat up. My voice rose an octave, before I remembered to lower it once again. "No? You'd deny me, your wife, the security of your father's household?"

Omar cleared his throat again. He sat up and pulled his shirt back on. "It is not possible. You cannot live in my parents' house. That's final."

"That's final?" I looked at him, but he would not meet my

gaze. He turned away. The truth suddenly dawned on me. I put my hand on his back. "It's not your decision, is it?" I said, looking at the door, and beyond, through the *dahabieh* to where my Lady lay asleep. "She won't allow it, will she? And you cannot defy her."

Omar did not reply. His fists were clenched hard, I could see his nails biting into his skin.

I got up and dressed, as though I was going to leave. I could tell he was relieved.

"I'll find a job for you, a better position, I promise," he began, but I gave him a look of such ferocity that he stopped speaking. I could read his thoughts: she'll go now, she's angry now, but I'll find her a good post, and I'll find her somewhere better to live, and I'll be able to help her, and she can see Abdullah at my father's house whenever she pleases, and we can see each other as we've seen each other today.

I walked out of Omar's cabin, through the galley and the sitting room. I opened the door of Lady Duff Gordon's cabin and walked in.

She was lying on her divan, looking drowsy and comfortable; earlier, she had been drinking tea and smoking the *narguile*; I could see the familiar paraphernalia spread out on her table. She looked up now and saw me standing in front of her and, for a moment, it was as though we'd slipped back through time to a place where I was still her loyal and intrepid companion. But that moment did not last.

"I've come," I said, "to ask you for money."

"You've what?" she said, and she pushed herself up from her cushions into a sitting position, almost knocking over the little table next to her divan.

"Yes," I said. "I've given up Abdullah to Mabrouka, as you ordered. I've been working in Cairo."

"I gave you money," she said, "for your passage to England."

"That money was useful when I first arrived, when I was trying to find my way in the city. I tried to keep Abdullah with me, but you were right, he is better off in Omar's father's house. I have done as you asked. But I am not going to leave Cairo."

"Yes, you are," she hissed. "I'll book your passage myself this time."

"Lady Duff Gordon," I said, and I drew myself together, "I was your maid for many years. During that time I was at your side day and night. I worked for you in Esher when you ran a busy household. I helped you through your confinement with Miss Rainey. I nursed you as your illness grew more serious; once we left England I was your physician as well as your maid. I lived with you in Luxor, hundreds of miles up the Nile, where we were often the only Europeans. My wages were poor, sometimes you were unable to pay me anything at all, but that did not matter to me: my life in your household was secure—better than that, my life in your household was rewarding—and I never wanted for a thing."

Omar, having thought I had left, must have heard our voices. He entered the room behind me, but at first I did not notice him.

"When I left Luxor I had nothing. All those years—no savings. You threw me out, with no regard for my safety. I'm only asking for what I am owed."

There was a silence; the air felt heavy. It was hot, perhaps the hottest day of the summer so far.

I had been addressing my Lady in English; she replied in Arabic, to make sure that Omar understood every word. "Get off my boat. If you do not leave now, I will have you arrested. Omar?" she addressed her dragoman.

I turned quickly, to see Omar standing there. "I'm sorry," I said to him, my voice low.

He glared at me. "Yes, my Lady?" he said.

"Did you put her up to this?"

"No!" we spoke in unison.

"I thought I was rid of you. Get off my boat. You will not

have a penny from me." She kept her tone even, matter-of-fact, as though she turned away former intimates every day.

At that, I turned, stiffly. As I stepped past my husband, I said, "She'll forgive you. She always does." And I left the *dahabieh*.

In that moment, Omar stood in the door of my Lady's room unable to move, uncertain what to do next. I could see him in my mind's eye, I knew him so well. My request for money was doubly humiliating; could he not support his own wife? And yet, the plain truth was he could not; he did not earn enough to provide for both Mabrouka and me while we kept separate households, while I was not living, was not allowed to live, in his father's house.

"All right, Omar," I pictured my Lady saying, as though nothing untoward had taken place. "I'm ready for my lunch now. I'll eat on my own, thank you."

But instead of returning to the galley, Omar came after me.

I hadn't got far, and I was easy to spot, tall as I was among the throng of Egyptians. He caught up and grabbed me by the arm roughly.

"Omar! Let go of me."

"How could you go to my Lady behind my back like that?" he said. "How could you endanger everything I've worked for?"

"*I've* placed *you* in danger?"

"To go to her like some beggar off the street. How could you betray me like this, Sally?"

"Betray you?" I was shouting now. "Me, betray you? You have gone along with her every decree. You have failed on every count to stand by me. You have left me to struggle on my own in the city." My voice grew in volume, and I could feel hot tears pooling behind my eyes. "You have denied me a place in your family!"

"Everything depends on my retaining my position with Lady Duff Gordon—you know that! Do you expect me to lose everything as well, just because you have lost—" He stopped speaking.

"Say it—say it, Omar—just because I have lost everything." I couldn't stop myself from crying now. "No, that's not what I want. I'm punished, I'm punished enough for both of us, I know that. But you have gone along with everything she . . ."

"I married you! You are my wife!"

I stopped. I lowered my voice. "But it hasn't worked, has it? You are not able to be any sort of husband to me. What happened just now, between us, that means nothing. For as long as you work in her household"—Omar tried to interrupt, but I held up my hand to stop him from speaking—"and I know you must stay in her household, I know that only too well, but for as long as you work for her, you will not be husband to me." And with that, I turned and walked away.

19

I N THE END, OMAR DID NOT TRAVEL TO EUROPE WITH MY LADY. A week before they were due to sail, my Lady received a letter from Sir Alick, instructing her not to bring Omar with her to Europe. Mabrouka told me that Sir Alick felt it was not appropriate for my Lady to travel on her own with a male servant. Though she regretted this—she knew her family would love Omar's Egyptian manners, as well as his cakes—my Lady was so buoyed with anticipation over the reunion that she accepted her husband's demand without complaint. Mabrouka said that Omar would not admit to any disappointment, but she could tell that he felt it; however, he would stay in Cairo once my Lady departed from Alexandria and oversee the letting of the *dahabieh* for the summer. And he would move back into his father's house.

Move back into his father's house. I looked at Mabrouka, but she was fussing over Abdullah, who had spilled his drink. Move back into his father's house, I thought, and assume his role as husband, father, and son. Husband to Mabrouka. What could it be like to be married to a man with whom you had spent so little time? They had had a child, the sweet little Yasmina, to whom I was becoming almost as attached as I was to Abdullah. Perhaps, I thought, they would have another child.

IN EARLY JULY MY LADY AND OMAR TOOK THE TRAIN TO ALEXANdria, where they stayed with Henry Ross, who had not traveled to England with Miss Janet the month before. Booking passage on a ship to Europe proved to be difficult; although we had heard nothing of it in Cairo, a cholera epidemic was sweeping Alexandria and anyone who could afford it was clamoring to leave the city, Ismail Pasha having fled abroad already. Omar had no luck down at the docks and it was only when Henry Ross himself used his network of connections in the port that my Lady was able to find a berth aboard a steamer. Omar sent word to Mabrouka; he would be back in Cairo soon. My Lady had instructed Hekekyan Bey to find him a position while she was away.

"I've told Hekekyan Bey that this new post must be temporary. I don't want anyone stealing you away from me," my Lady said. He promised to be there to meet her ship when she returned.

On his return to Cairo, Omar moved back into his father's house. Mid-July, and Cairo hardly moved in the heat. The shutters were kept closed on all the windows, and at dawn every day, Omar's mother and her servant, Umm Yasin, hauled on ropes and pulleys to draw a great canvas tarpaulin across the gap in the roof above the courtyard. Everyone in the house moved slowly through the gloom. The sun bored through any chinks in the shutters like white-hot rods of iron from the blacksmith's across the street. The baby and his sister were lethargic, with hardly enough energy to eat or play.

I did not allow Omar's presence in the house to affect my morning visits to Abdullah. Most days, when I arrived, Omar had left the house already, so I could almost convince myself that nothing had changed. At breakfast we all picked at our food and took turns to fan each other. "He can't eat that," Mabrouka said of a piece of cake Yasmina was attempting to stuff in Abdullah's mouth. "Yes," the little girl insisted and, indeed, Abdullah took the cake from her and chewed on it with his single tooth for a considerable amount of time. Mabrouka seemed no different to me: she was as keen to gossip and hear the news of the previous day; she bore no signs of the simple fact that her husband was with her once again. It was helpful to me to be able to pretend everything was as it should be. Her direct charm and lack of guile enabled me to carry on with life.

In high summer the pastry shop opened for several hours in the early morning, and then again in the evening, and the kitchen there was an inferno. Omar was working for his father while he waited to hear from Hekekyan Bey. Omar's mother prepared the meals with Umm Yasin, and Mabrouka told me that after the sun went down they gathered together to eat. Their menu had become simpler; it took a special type of discipline to face going into the oven room more than once or twice each day, although the women still produced bread and beans and stews and salads and, of course, tea. After supper Omar climbed up onto the roof of the house, to lie in the hammock and survey the stars and look out at the city. I knew he had not spent a whole day without my Lady for a very long time and I imagined he felt an unexpected sense of freedom, in his own house, in his own city.

Mabrouka told me that Omar was relieved to be away from Luxor. The news that came down the Nile to Boulak from friends and other travelers was not good; this year the annual floods were much higher than usual and had already caused huge damage, washing away several small settlements in the region and leaving muddy devastation in their wake. As well as that, Ismail Pasha's forced labor recruitment had snatched more than a third of the male population of Luxor; many of these men, men Omar had come to know well, would never return but would die in service to the Pasha's schemes. Disease was rampant among the public works crews. Every day brought with it some kind of new tax: every beast, from camels to cows to sheep, drew a heavy tax on its head, and most *fellahin* were unable to pay. In Cairo, Omar was even more powerless to help than he had been in Luxor, where the daily acts of kindness that he carried out alongside my Lady had made a tiny difference to the lives of those who remained—acts of kindness that were returned to them, many times over. In the city the pace of change was so rapid, the Pasha's building schemes so advanced, that it was impossible to do anything apart from sit back and watch and wonder where it would all lead. To do anything else would be foolhardy. At least in Cairo Omar felt that Lady Duff Gordon had attracted less attention from the Pasha and his cronies, where she was just one of many *Frangi* passing through the hurly-burly of the city.

I imagined that Omar worried about me. I had become a problem to solve: what to do about Sally? He could help me find a better job, and hopefully that would pay for a better place for me to live. But the fact of me: there was no getting round how awkward my presence in Cairo was for him. If he'd been willing to defy Lady Duff Gordon and move me into his father's house, that would have solved many problems. He could have found a way to make it work. But that wasn't an option. Instead, he was trapped in this situation, a wife at home, another at large, as though I was his mistress, not the mother of his son. I knew he was ashamed of what had happened that day on the *dahabieh*: my confrontation with my Lady, of course, but as well as that, the way he'd abandoned himself, been seduced by the moment. Lowered his guard. He hadn't wanted two wives. He'd married Mabrouka. Then he'd fallen in love with me. But he was a dutiful man, dutiful to my Lady, to Mabrouka, to his family. He'd find a way. He had to find a way.

I pictured him lying on the roof in his hammock. The call to prayer woke him from his rooftop reverie and he went down to the courtyard to pray with his father, who had risen from his divan specially. Afterwards, he went into his private quarters. Abdullah and Yasmina were both asleep on their mats; Abdullah had outgrown his basket, to everyone's regret. In the next room, Mabrouka had drawn the curtain around the sleeping area. He slipped his head through a gap and tried to see through the darkness to where his wife lay; her even breathing suggested she was asleep, but Omar knew her well enough to understand that she was awake, waiting. He stripped off his clothes and put on his too-hot nightshirt. Then he got into bed with his wife.

As he had expected, she was not asleep, but she continued to lie absolutely still for some time. Omar lay on his back and tried hard not to think.

Mabrouka began to speak. "I was afraid you would divorce me. You would divorce me and keep Yasmina and make me leave your father's house, and have this other woman, the mother of Abdullah, as your wife."

"I would never have done that, Mabrouka." He turned onto his side to face her. "You should have known I would not divorce you."

"I know. Your mother and father assured me of that every day after we heard about—after we heard the news. But Sally, she is a *Frangi*."

Omar placed his hand on her stomach. Her nightclothes were damp with the heat, like his. "I will not divorce you. You are the mother of my child."

I knew about this conversation because Mabrouka told me about it. She didn't describe what else happened that night, but I was not naive. I saw it happen, in my mind's eye. Mabrouka moved towards Omar. He took a sharp breath and held it and moved towards her. It had been a long time since they had shared a bed, and longer still since Mabrouka had wanted him close to her. He stroked her black hair: how different from me she smelled, how different she felt, how different it was when she brought her face to his, her lips. He forced himself to stop making these comparisons; Oh yes, he thought, he made himself think, I remember this, I remember how this feels. "I am a lucky man," he said after a while, his voice throaty with desire. In the dark he felt Mabrouka smile.

I don't know if this is what happened between them. But I

know enough to understand that it probably did happen this way. They were, after all, husband and wife.

HEKEKYAN BEY DID, INDEED, FIND OMAR A POSITION, WITH AN ENglishman, Mr. Smith, who was in Cairo to work with Doctor Mariette in the Egyptian Antiquities Service and had decided, unusually, to stay in the city over the long summer. Mr. Smith lived in a new house in the Frankish Quarter on the Nile and wanted Omar to act as valet and factotum. He would be needed during the day most days, and in the evenings only when Mr. Smith entertained, which was not often. Mr. Smith—there was no Mrs.; Mabrouka told me she found it puzzling that so many *Frangi* did not marry— was happy for Omar to continue to live with his own family.

From the first day, Omar's duties for Mr. Smith included crisscrossing the city on foot to deliver messages; these excursions took him in and out of the new hotels that were opening across the city. Omar began to inquire after employment opportunities for me. I had continued to work for Roberto Magni, but my situation there was deteriorating. Roberto Magni's clientele seemed to get rougher with each passing month, and Roberto Magni himself was frequently incapacitated with drink. His overtures towards me were becoming more aggressive; he announced to me one night that we'd both be better off if we were married. He said, "It would be cheaper; I would no have to pay you." To tell the truth, I couldn't help but laugh at this most unromantic of proposals, and even Roberto Magni saw the humor in it. But I needed to leave. I'd been to visit Umm Mahmoud, who had offered to give me a room and take me on as her cleaner, in lieu of rent, but I knew this arrangement was not feasible as the old couple could ill afford the loss of income. When another paying guest arrived, I would have to move out and sleep on the floor in the small, hot kitchen, just like when I first went into service as a scullery maid in Esher.

I continued to visit Abdullah every morning and my visits never coincided with Omar's time at home. I didn't mind not seeing him, not now; there was no possibility of any privacy, not even for conversation, and besides, we no longer needed privacy. Seeing Abdullah every day was enough to keep me happy; I looked forward to visiting Mabrouka as well, who, it seemed, had taken it upon herself to give me a Cairene education.

"Omar says he'll be able to find a new position for you, Sally," she said one day. "He says the new hotels are all after people like you."

I smiled, unwilling to show Mabrouka my desperation, but I knew that, by now, she was familiar enough with my situation to see through my attempts at bravado. I had told her about Roberto Magni's proposal and she'd been outraged on my behalf. "Oh!" she said, "How dare he!" Her expression was so vexed and affronted that I began to laugh. "Don't laugh!" she said, but she started laughing as well until we could no longer contain our hysteria at the idea. Omar's mother had rushed in to find out why we were making such a racket, but neither of us would tell her.

It had become a source of tension between Mabrouka and Omar, the fact that Mabrouka witnessed, daily, the toll that my precarious circumstances took on me. Now that they were accustomed to living together once again, Mabrouka felt able to raise certain topics when they were alone, in their private quarters. "I'll wear him down, Sally," Mabrouka said to me. "You will join our household, you'll see. We women know how to get our way." She blushed at this reference to her married life and looked away.

But then one day Mabrouka stopped talking about trying to change Omar's mind. She just stopped, and the topic was no longer within our range. I wondered what had transpired to make Mabrouka give up on this subject. I felt I could imagine their conversation: late one night, after they had been together, in each other's arms, she spoke up as Omar was about to fall asleep. Her tone was, perhaps, sharper than she had intended. "I'm asking you once again, Omar Abu Halaweh, why won't you invite the mother of your son to live in your father's house?"

Omar was not willing to discuss this subject and made that clear by feigning sleep.

"Omar!" Mabrouka hissed.

He rolled towards her. Neither did he want to make her angry. "This is my decision, Mabrouka. I have my reasons."

"What? What are they? You will have your wife live by herself in the city? What kind of a husband are you?"

"Many women in your position"—he paused to give his words more weight—"would be pleased—no, relieved—by my decision."

"Well, I am not. I see her, and I see how she looks, and I am surprised to find the father of my child possessed of such a cold heart, capable of such cruelty. It compromises my honor as well as hers."

Now he was angry. He sat up.

Mabrouka could see she'd gone too far. "Omar, I—"

"Lady Duff Gordon has decided that Sally Naldrett will not live with my family. If I am to retain my position in her household, I must obey her. There. I've said it. I have no choice."

Mabrouka was shocked. "Father of my child—," she began to apologize, but Omar cut her off.

"Sally's an Englishwoman, Mabrouka, and we are Egyptians. Would you rather I shared her bed and not yours?" He got up and left the room, and went to sleep on a mat next to Abdullah.

And that was the end of that particular conversation.

A FEW DAYS LATER WHEN I ARRIVED FOR MY VISIT, MABROUKA rushed across the courtyard. Omar's inquiry at one of the grandest of the new establishments, the Nile Hotel, had been met with enthusiasm by the head porter the previous day. "An Englishwoman?"

he had said. "Speaks Arabic fluently? Well trained? Send her to us, Mr. Abu Halaweh, please!"

"Sally!" Mabrouka said. "You are to be at the Nile Hotel at ten a.m. tomorrow morning!" She was as excited as though she was to accompany me herself.

And so the next day I dressed in my best attempt at proper English attire—boots and petticoat, stays, gloves, and hat, all repaired and carefully ironed (and stained and frayed)—and made my way through the city and up the grand polished marble staircase of the Nile. In the large foyer, with its potted palms and carpets, I was introduced to Mr. Gillespie, the Scottish manager of the British-owned hotel.

"Speak Arab, do you?" Mr. Gillespie inquired.

"Yes, sir."

"How's that? You look like an ordinary English lass to me."

"I am, sir—English. But I've lived here in Egypt for these past years, in service to Lady Duff Gordon."

"Duff Gordon, you say? And where is the great lady now?"

"She's gone back to England, sir."

"And left you here, on your own?" Mr. Gillespie looked outraged on my behalf and suspicious of me at the same time.

I felt sure he already knew my story but wanted to hear what I had to say for myself. "Yes, I—I wanted to stay. In Cairo. I prefer it here."

"You do? How very peculiar. Let's hear some Arab then."

I hesitated, unsure what to say.

"Come on. Allan Dooley, or whatever it is they say all the time."

"*Alhamdullilah?*"

"That's right. I need someone like you. Let's see your reference."

I pushed my half-truths a little harder. "Lady Duff Gordon forgot to give it to me before she left. Most unfortunate. I've written to her though, and I'm certain it will arrive before too long."

Mr. Gillespie harrumphed into his mustache. "All right. Start tomorrow. There are quarters out back for our European staff; I'll get Mrs. Gillespie—that's my wife, head of housekeeping—she'll show you. There are rules, mind—no drink, and no men, though you look as though you're beyond that now."

I absorbed this comment in silence.

"And bring me that reference as soon as it arrives." He stood up and, without warning, bellowed, "Mrs. G!"

AND SO THE SUMMER PASSED, WITH OMAR IN AND OUT OF HIS EM-ployer, Mr. Smith's, cool house, where every evening before he walked home he laid out the clothes he had prepared for Mr. Smith to wear the following day; me in the Nile Hotel, where my fluency in Arabic quickly made me the primary go-between for the British and Egyptian staff, who, truth be told, seemed to need almost constant mediation; Abdullah at home with Mabrouka and Yasmina. I continued to visit my son every day. Mabrouka wanted to hear all about the new, much grander hotel and my life there with my colleagues. I quickly established the cast of hotel characters and entertained myself at work by collecting anecdotes to relate during my visits. To my surprise, I began to tell stories about my life in service in Esher as well, a life that felt as distant as a dream, and I took pleasure in seeing the growing amazement on Mabrouka's face as I told her about how I used to take the train into London—by myself—to visit the Egyptian antiquities in the British Museum. Mabrouka found it difficult to imagine what it was like to move through the world as I did, unprotected, without security—she had never walked down a street by herself in her entire life—to work and, indeed, live surrounded by men. In return, I got to hear all about Mabrouka's day at home with Abdullah and was happiest when listening to a grand tale about the baby and his extraordinary achievements: "He sat up by himself! He pulled himself up to stand beside the table! He ate all the grapes!"

At night in the room I shared with two other women—a much better room than I had when working for Roberto Magni (who had a tantrum and broke a chair when I told him I was leaving the next day)—I tried to picture myself in Mabrouka's life, an Egyptian wife and daughter, closely observant of the established rituals of daily life, faithful to Allah, secure, kept as remote from the city outside as possible. I had realized, from the day of my first visit to Omar's father's house, that I would, in fact, be happy in Mabrouka's life, that I would trade places with her any day, that I had had enough insecurity to last a lifetime, and all I wanted was peace and quiet for myself and my child. But this was not to be. I had made my bed, and now I had to continue to make it, over and over again.

But I felt truly welcome in the house of the father of Omar, and for that I was grateful. I rarely saw Omar on my own; he had dropped into the Nile Hotel to see how I was getting on, but we both quickly realized from the looks we attracted that this wasn't such a good idea. Our situation was unexplainable—"He's my Egyptian husband, but I don't live with him"; no one would believe me. I couldn't afford to have my reputation compromised again. But the Gillespies were good to me and sometimes I was allowed time off in the evening, and I would make my way to my husband's house.

The first time I spent an evening with the family, I sat opposite Omar and Mabrouka and watched as Mabrouka, making a point in the conversation, placed her hand on Omar's knee briefly. Omar brushed at the cloth of his trousers after Mabrouka removed her hand, as though to smooth some dirt away, and looked at me, his cheeks reddening: so, I thought, I was right, she is his wife once again. And what am I? I lifted Abdullah—who was growing heavier every day—into my lap and, like Omar, attempted to brush the thought away.

I did speak to Omar alone that evening. Mabrouka was putting the children to sleep, and Omar's parents were out of the room, busy elsewhere in the house.

"I saw your sister, Ellen," Omar said. "I never had the chance to tell you."

"You did?"

"It was when Miss Janet came to tell my Lady that she would leave for Europe without her."

"Yes."

"Miss Naldrett had traveled with Miss Janet, of course. I thought you had already left for England."

I nodded. "How was she?"

"She was very angry. On your behalf. I thought she was going to strike me, in fact."

I smiled. "What did she say?"

"She told me I was disgusting. I pretended my English wasn't good enough to understand what she was saying. That made her even angrier."

Now I laughed.

"She told me I'd ruined your life. That you'd lost your position while I had flourished. That I'd made my way by climbing on your shoulders and allowing you to sink. She said you'd end up in a London gutter and that it would be my fault entirely."

I smiled and took a sip of my tea. "It's all true, of course," I said, mildly. "Apart from the London gutter bit."

"But you are all right now," he said. "Aren't you? Things are better for you now."

I looked at him. Did he deserve to be put out of his misery? Who knows? I am not, perhaps, the best judge of that. "I'm all right now," I said to my husband. "I think."

My Lady wrote to Omar once while she was away, and the content of that letter was reported to me by Mabrouka; Omar had paid a scribe to come to the house to read it. The journey to Marseilles, as predicted by Omar, exacted a heavy toll on her health, and although the passage across the Mediterranean took only one week, by the time she arrived she was too unwell to continue onwards to Paris. She telegraphed Sir Alick and he traveled down to meet her, and then the whole family traveled by a variety of routes to Soden and, by the beginning of August, they were ensconced in rented rooms. I imagine it would have taken some time for them to accustom themselves to each other, to how much older they all were. Rainey was six now, and tall with it, but despite looking like an entirely different child from the one my Lady had last seen, she remembered her mother, and my Lady reported to Omar that she was ecstatic to be with her. Maurice was grown now, a young man, and my Lady's mother, Sarah Austin, was very gray, and crippled with gout. This was sad news to me, as I was very fond of Mrs. Austin, who had always been kind to me. It took time also for my Lady to remember her European manners, and she said that her English clothes chafed her skin, but I could picture her relish as she revived her German and showed off her Arabic to whoever was interested.

The holiday was to last one month, one precious month of the family all together. Though my Lady did not report this to Omar, I'm sure that things were not entirely easy between my Lady and Sir Alick, as they had not been easy when he visited Egypt the previous autumn. He would have continued to be annoyed by the fact that she was without a lady's maid, and they must have argued over whether or not she could go back to live in Egypt without finding a new one. He had, in fact, arranged the hire of a new girl without consulting my Lady, and presented the young woman, a Belgian named Marie, to his wife as a fait accompli towards the end of their stay. But my Lady was unable to object by then as she had caught a cold and fallen ill once again, coughing until she spat blood continually. It got so bad, my Lady wrote to Omar, that Sir Alick moved into his own room and left my Lady with a whistle which she was to blow if she needed assistance. Late one night, she did indeed blow the whistle with the last of her strength, and when Sir Alick rushed into the room, he found her lying in a pool of blood, hemorrhaging

The German doctor effected a cure and insisted that his patient must not travel until she was completely recovered, but as usual, my Lady was having none of that. As soon as she had felt the familiar pain creeping into her side as her lungs filled up with fluid, she wanted to be back in Egypt, back in Luxor where she would be able to breathe more freely. If she could return to her Arab self, she wrote to Omar, the dry desert air would clear her chest. Besides, it was time for the children and Sir Alick to depart, to return to jobs and schools in England, and she did not want to be left behind on her own in Germany. The Belgian lady's maid turned out to be a good thing after all, as, with her help, she was able to travel much earlier than the doctor had counseled. She would be arriving back in Egypt in early October.

MR. GILLESPIE KEPT FORGETTING TO ASK TO SEE MY REFERENCE UNTIL it was too late and I had made myself as indispensable to the hotel as I had once been to Lady Duff Gordon. The Nile Hotel was a fine place to work, the best place, perhaps, I reasoned, given the circumstances. I rose through the ranks of housekeepers quickly and achieved a kind of unexpected freedom to do as I pleased; my job gave me a greater amount of power and prestige than I had ever experienced, even back when my Lady and I were ensconced in our busy sociable household at the Gordon Arms in Esher.

And then Omar was gone, back to Luxor with Lady Duff Gordon, and Mabrouka was without him once again. I found it easier not to miss him too badly, knowing Mabrouka was missing him as well.

20

C AIRO, 15 JULY 1869: FOUR YEARS LATER.

I AM THERE, WATCHING.

I keep my distance. In the City of the Dead, I want no one to see me.

But I can see what is taking place. I watch the boatmen lowering her body; she is wrapped in a linen shroud, like a Muslim. The boatmen don't need to strain; illness made her light, and death lighter still. The doctor—the same doctor I saw just days before I gave birth and who did not notice my condition—is speaking but I can hear none of his words. There is an imam present, and a Christian priest. Omar is silent, head bowed. Perhaps he is weeping. When I think of Omar I remember our time together in Luxor after the birth of Abdullah and I feel his tears on my belly: warm salt, quickly cooling.

If my Lady had stayed in England, if we had never traveled to Egypt, she would soon have died; Egypt gave her seven years, seven extra years of life. But at what cost? It was as though she died when she first crossed the Mediterranean and her time in Egypt was a kind of afterlife. She chose Egypt, and she kept death at bay, for a time.

And my Lady won her battle in other ways as well: she drove me away and she drove Omar away from me and she kept Omar by her side, as she keeps him to this day. I have every reason to hate her, even now. But I do not. If it wasn't for her, I wouldn't be here, in Cairo, city of my dreams. I wouldn't have met Omar; I wouldn't have had my baby. But that was not her intention, and it is not her victory: it is mine, and mine only.

My aunt Clara could not, or—I don't know which is more true—did not want to keep Ellen and me when our parents died in that train wreck at Clapham. Strange though it may sound, I did not blame Aunt Clara at the time. Our parents were gone—our previous lives had vanished overnight—and it did not surprise me that there was no one who could shoulder the responsibility of our upbringing. I was only a child and life was what was presented to me, nothing more, nothing less. I knew no better.

But now I do know better, and in light of my Lady's behavior towards me, I look back at Aunt Clara and I do blame her. How could she have seen me off, out of her house, into service, so quickly, so soon after the death of my parents? Me, her only sister's elder child? Why is the world full of people who see fit to dispense with others as soon as it suits them? But I stop myself from having these thoughts, from thinking these things, and I get on with the task at hand. I'm very good at getting on with the task at hand: it's what suits me.

Watching, I am unaware of myself, unaware that I am creeping closer and closer to the grave and the small crowd of mourners standing by it. Someone turns my way, a young Englishwoman, dressed as though she's just stepped off a train from London, still pale despite the sun: our eyes meet. Yet another new lady's maid? I pull my *tarhah* across my face and move away. She turns back to the grave.

I've seen enough. Lady Duff Gordon—my Lady—is dead. And I, Sally Naldrett, I am alive. I will carry on living.

I slip away. Back into Cairo. But as I leave the vast cemetery with the dead in their multitude, I see Omar's father, making his way through the graves. And with him, Abdullah. Before I can call out, my boy sees me. And he runs towards me, his arms open, smiling.

AUTHOR'S NOTE

WHILE LUCIE DUFF GORDON'S STORY IS WELL KNOWN AND MUCH celebrated, primarily through her wonderful book *Letters from Egypt*, which has been in print almost continuously since it was published in 1865, next to nothing is known about the life of her dragoman, Omar Abu Halaweh, and even less about her maid, Sally Naldrett.

I first came across the story of Sally and Omar when I read Katherine Frank's excellent biography, *Lucie Duff Gordon: A Passage to Egypt*, in 1995. Through a mutual friend, I met Katherine Frank, who was generous and supportive towards my efforts to write a novel about Sally Naldrett, answering many of my questions, and lending me her copy of Edward Lane's somewhat notorious *Manners and Customs of the Modern Egyptians*, which I still have and still intend to return. My thanks to her.

This novel has taken me many years to write. In 1998 the Author's Foundation gave me a research grant to travel to Egypt. From 2001 to 2007, the Royal Literary Fund awarded me a series of Fellowships, providing financial support that was indispensable to my survival as a writer. And my agents, Rachel Calder and Anne McDermid, have stuck by me, through times more thin than thick. Thanks also to Simon Mellor and Sue Thomas, and my excellent first readers Aamer Hussein, Marilee Sigal, and Lesley Bryce, and Ruthie Petrie for her good editor's eye. Thanks also to Youssif Omar, who attempted to teach me some Arabic.

The Mistress of Nothing is based on a true story. I've altered the timescale to suit my purposes and have telescoped two years, 1863–65, down to one, and reduced Lucie Duff Gordon's two trips home to one, while Omar Abu Halaweh and his family lived in Alexandria, not Cairo. For the Arabic transliterations, I've used Lucie Duff Gordon's own spellings as well as more standard transliterations. All other untruths, fabrications, and mistakes in this novel are mine as well. The quotes from the letters by Lucie Duff Gordon are from *Letters from Egypt*.

 Touchstone Reading Group Guide

The Mistress of Nothing

Introduction

When Lady Duff Gordon, a member of the English social elite, comes down with a debilitating illness that requires exile to a drier climate, she and her maid, Sally Naldrett, set sail for Egypt. Through Sally's keen and vivid narration, Egypt is painted as a place of wonder—of luxuries and freedoms not afforded to native English women in their home country. But luxury, especially for a maid of a lower station, comes with a price. From a love affair with her faithful dragoman to the biting rejection from the woman to whom she devoted her life, Sally travels a road of little reward, and finds that even in motherhood and unerring service, she is the mistress of nothing at all.

FOR DISCUSSION

1. Why do you feel Lady Duff Gordon cast out Sally so harshly? Was she betrayed? Did she truly have an issue with propriety?

2. Following those lines of thought, why does she not treat Omar similarly? Why is she so certain that Sally "tricked" Omar into impregnating her?

3. Should Omar have stayed as loyal as he did to Lady Duff Gordon? Did he fail to protect Sally and Abdullah in the right way? To whom does he owe more loyalty?

4. Sally performs one more "treatment" on her Lady before she is cast out of the house. Would it have been easy, as she stated, to make the cut too deep? Was there a part of you that wanted her take that sort of action against her sick employer?

5. Discuss the relationships and interactions in Omar's father's house. How did you react to Sally and Mabrouka's growing friendship? What commonalities do you see between them? Should Omar have allowed Sally to live with his Cairo family?

6. By story's end, is Sally still an Englishwoman? Is she an Egyptian? Considering Abdullah and her position at the Nile hotel, is she still a "mistress of nothing"?

7. How did the Egyptian setting affect the mood and urgency of the story? Consider the trip up the Nile, the excursion to

the Valley of Kings, the political uprising and spreading riots against the Pasha's Suez schemes, and the French House elevated above the struggling village of Luxor.

8. Why is Sir Alick put off by his wife's appearance and lifestyle when he finally visits her in Egypt? Is Lady Duff Gordon's family still indeed family?

9. Discuss the various members of and visitors to the Luxor household. Which of them did you enjoy reading about the most? Consider Omar, Ahmed, Mohammed, and Mustafa Agha.

10. Is life on the Nile a new beginning, or some form of afterlife?

A Conversation with Kate Pullinger

In your Author's Note, you mention that this story is inspired by real people and events. How far does the novel deviate from actual happenings? Where did you choose to embellish or change things to suit your authorial needs?
I was inspired to write the story of Sally Naldrett after reading Katherine Frank's wonderful biography, *Lucie Duff Gordon*. The episode with Sally is a tiny part of Lucie's eventful and fascinating life. But Sally struck me as a strong character herself and I knew right away that I wanted to try to tell her side of the story. The novel sticks very close to the established facts up to the moment that Sally leaves Lucie's household; for instance, she really did give birth on the Nile on Christmas Eve, she and Omar did marry subsequently, despite Lucie's objections. However, no further records remain of Sally, apart from the fact that she did return once to ask Lucie for money. So from that point onward I was free to imagine Sally's life; since there is no record of her death in England, I felt I could assume that she stayed in Egypt. And that led me into imagining how it might be possible for a woman like Sally to survive on her own in Cairo. This is a novel though, not a work of nonfiction or biography, and all the detail in the novel about Sally and Omar, their affair, how they spoke and acted with each other—the emotional content and context of Sally's life—is the work of my imagination.

You also indicate that you did a large amount of research in Egypt. What was traveling the Nile like? Is the political unrest still palpable in today's climate?
For me one of the great pleasures of writing this novel was the research on Egypt, and I had a great time reading everything I could

get my hands on about this period, as well as lots of Egyptian fiction in translation. I spent nearly a month traveling in Egypt when I was twenty but while writing the novel I was only able to return to the country once; I went to Luxor for four days. I stayed in the oldest hotel in Luxor, built a few years after Lucie's death, near to where the French House would have been. These days most tourists stay on boats so at night Luxor empties of people and returns to the sleepy village Sally and Lucie knew so well. Despite the fact that I could not travel to 1860s Luxor, these few days and nights in Luxor gave me a strong sense of what the village might have been like—the hills across the Nile remain the same, the sky at night remains the same, the awesome presence of the ancient civilization remains the same.

Egyptian politics are very complex and I worked hard to try to understand the situation both in the 1860s and in the present day. However, despite whatever is going on, both then and now, life continues as it always has done and people go about their business, falling in love, having children, working toward a better life.

DO YOU THINK LADY DUFF GORDON'S TREATMENT OF SALLY IS A PRODUCT OF FEELING BETRAYED, OR BORNE OF SOME SENSE OF PROPRIETY? DID YOU INTEND TO WRITE IT TO SEEM ONE WAY OR THE OTHER?

I felt that Lucie's treatment of Sally—which is all based on fact—must have come from a hugely complicated web of emotions that she herself didn't understand and couldn't control. I did not intend to portray Lucie as monstrous; she must have been very frightened, facing prolonged illness and death, so far from her own family. Her near complete isolation from her own family is hard for us to understand in our world of telephone calls and e-mail. The betrayal of her lady's maid pushed her too far, in a direction she wasn't willing to go, and that was why she acted as she did. At least, that's my theory!

I also think that, at the end of the day, you can't really

underestimate the gulf between classes in Britain at that time; the aristocracy has not survived for as long as it has by being fair-minded!

THOUGH SALLY IS THE PRIMARY NARRATOR, LADY DUFF GORDON IS A CHARISMATIC, ECCENTRIC CHARACTER WHO JUMPS OFF THE PAGE. WHICH DID YOU FEEL MORE COMFORTABLE WRITING? WHICH ARE YOU MORE SIMILAR TO?

I found writing about Lucie very problematic, largely because she was a writer herself, and her own writing is so vivid and compelling. It took me ages to figure out whether or not to use extracts from her letters, whether or not to write about her writing, whether or not to try to replicate her voice. I was more comfortable writing about Sally, and the novel only really began to work once I made the decision to write the whole thing from Sally's point of view. Also, in terms of class and background and my place in the world, I have much more in common with Sally, though I admire hugely Lucie's ability to bring people together, her passion for life, and her intellect. Sally's an outsider, and like many writers, I feel like an outsider myself (something that is reinforced by the fact that I'm a Canadian living in London).

DID SALLY SIMPLY CONTINUE HER SPLIT BETWEEN HOTEL WORK AND VISITING ABDULLAH IN THE FOUR-YEAR JUMP AT THE STORY'S END? ARE WE TO INFER THAT ABDULLAH STILL CONSIDERS HER HIS MOTHER?

Ah, that's for you to imagine! I very much wanted the novel to have a kind of happy ending, and for me that final section confirms that Sally has found a way to survive, and that she has managed to maintain her relationship with Abdullah. It breaks my heart to think of all the different fates she might have met in reality, and I'm rather fond of the idea that she finds a kind of power in her work at the hotel, that she is good at it and valued for it, as she once was in the Duff Gordon household.

In a way, Sally's relationship with Omar is a profound rebellion, even though she does not see it that way herself. It seems
to me that to be able to survive in the post of lady's maid for
as long as she did, leaving England, giving everything up for
Lucie, Sally would have to be a very buttoned-up person in
the first place, someone in complete control at all times. So
the fact that she allows herself to embark on loving Omar in
the first place is hugely significant. For me the moment when
she returns to Lucie's boat in Cairo, defying Omar, and asking
Lucie for money, is also very profound, and she would have had
to go against all her instincts to carry that through. So I really do
view her whole life, from the first time she kisses Omar onward,
as a series of steps toward breaking free of the constraints of class,
race, and servitude that bind her.

So many books! Katherine Frank's biography, of course, and also
Lucie's own *Letters from Egypt*—my copies of these are truly dog-
eared and when I give talks about the book I often get these out
and wave them around in the hope that if you enjoyed my novel
you will read these two books as well. Lucie's book *Letters from
Egypt* has been in print almost continually since it came out in the
1860s and is easy to find online, as is Katherine Frank's biography.
I also read a lot of Egyptian fiction in translation; for me the most
useful of the novels were the Nobel Prize winner Naguib Mahfouz's Cairo Trilogy. Though these novels are set more than forty
years after *The Mistress of Nothing*, I drew a great deal of inspiration
from Mahfouz's detailed descriptions of an Egyptian household
and family, especially in terms of what it might have been like to

be a woman in that society, venturing forth from your father's or husband's house only rarely.

Do you speak Arabic?

During the writing of the novel I spent six months having one-to-one Arabic lessons from an Egyptian tutor. Oh my. What can I say? Arabic is incredibly difficult! When it comes to speaking, there are so many unfamiliar sounds! When it comes to reading and writing, you think you've learned the alphabet then you find out that the letters change shape entirely depending where they are in the word! And the vowels! Vowels get left out for reasons that are beyond me! I'll stop with the exclamation marks, but while I found that hour per week with the tutor completely fascinating, I have retained next to nothing of what I learned. But it was very, very useful at the time!

Now that the novel has been published, do you have any further thoughts on the story?

It's been exciting for me to have the novel out in the world, and to hear from readers about what they think of it. Responses arrive in so many different ways these days, from tweets to blogs to reviews on the sites of online retailers. Recently, I had a great shock when I opened my e-mail inbox to discover a note from a woman named Helen who is a descendant of Sally Naldrett. Helen's family traces their family tree straight back to Ellen, Sally's sister. Corresponding with Helen was strange and thrilling, almost like corresponding with one of my own characters. Luckily for me—though not for Sally—the Naldrett family has not been able to trace their great-great-great aunt; she does seem to have disappeared into Egypt. But Ellen—well, that's a very interesting story, but I'll keep that to myself for the time being!

ARE YOU WORKING ON ANOTHER NOVEL? IF SO, WILL EGYPT PLAY A PART?

I'm only at the very beginning of thinking about my next book. At the moment, I don't think Egypt will play a part in it, but Islam will—one of the main characters is from Pakistan. With *The Mistress of Nothing* I really enjoyed learning about Islam through quizzing my Muslim friends and reading. One of my ongoing interests is in the perception of Islam and Muslims in the West, and I feel that The *Mistress of Nothing* participates in this discussion, and that my next novel will continue to explore this theme.

Enhance Your Book Club

1. Visit (on your own, if you're like Sally) a local museum that contains Egyptian artifacts and exhibitions. Do any of the offerings evoke scenes or characters from *The Mistress of Nothing*?

2. Mimic a meal from the parlor at the Luxor house. Try sitting on the floor, eating pastries, and reclining after your meal.

3. A number of books have been written about the complicated relationship between an English servant and his/her employer. Read a comparable title like *Remains of the Day* and compare how masters and servants interact, how employees deal with their oppression, and how far removed the Lady or Sir is from their employee.

4. Read Kate Pullinger's *My Life as a Girl in a Men's Prison*. How do the themes and characters compare? Are there any similarities in tone between one of these short stories and the longer narrative in *The Mistress of Nothing*? Consider art, propriety, gender roles, passion, and crime.

5. If you have the means, brave the Egyptian heat and see how the locales in the novel look and operate in modernity.